A TICKET TO DIE FOR

Also by David J. Walker

Fixed in His Folly
Half the Truth
Applaud the Hollow Ghost

A TICKET TO DIE FOR

David J. Walker

ST. MARTIN'S PRESS ✹ NEW YORK

Library of Congress Cataloging-in-Publication Data

Walker, David J.
    A ticket to die for / David J. Walker — 1st ed.
        p.   cm.
    ISBN 0-312-19345-9
    I. Title.
PS3573.A4253313T53   1998
813'.54—dc21   98-24427
                                                CIP

First Edition: November 1998

10 9 8 7 6 5 4 3 2 1

To Ellen, *sine qua non*

ACKNOWLEDGMENTS

Chi-ca-go *(shi-kaw-go)* n., a city in northeast Illinois, on the shore of Lake Michigan; the name is believed to be derived from the Native American *chicah goo*, literally "stink root" or, perhaps more elegantly, "wild onion."

The above etymological note is pretty accurate, they tell me, but the rest of this book is entirely made up. On the other hand, like all fiction, it is founded on things I've heard and seen, even if I can't remember just where.

What I can't forget, though, is the thanks I owe to my agent, Jane Jordan Browne, for her unflagging zeal and support; to my editor, Kelley Ragland, for her judgment and insight; to Michele Mellett, M.D., for more about blood and stuff; to Judy Duhl, proprietor of Scotland Yard Books and friend of mystery writers and readers alike; and finally to Paul Duggan, C.P.A., who doesn't do laundry but understands it better than I.

A TICKET TO DIE FOR

ONE

A deal's a deal, darling. Like it or not."

That surprised Dugan. The *darling* part. She'd never called him that before. Did she think it sounded like—what was her name? Jennifer?—on those old "Hart to Hart" reruns? At any rate, *darling* sounded out-of-date, somehow.

". . . and don't give me any of that lawyer stuff, either," Kirsten was saying. "Mutual breach or anticipatory mistake or some—"

"You've got 'em backward," he interrupted. "But beyond that, I don't know any more about contract defenses than you do. Haven't seen one since the bar exam." He shifted his bulky frame around. The Celica was her car, and the bucket seats seemed to shrink a little more every time he rode in it. "Actually," he said, "what I should plead is insanity."

"Oh no. You were in your right mind, all right. You wanted things your way, so we made a deal. Now you're trying to weasel out of it."

A gust of wind sent rain slashing across the windows and slamming down on the roof of the car, but she didn't seem to mind the weather. He knew she was enjoying herself—kidding him along to pass the time. He watched her reach across the top of the steering wheel and wipe condensation from the windshield with the back of her hand. Together they peered out across the parking lot. A couple of construction workers in heavy boots and parkas, bundled up against the cold November rain, slouched toward Cousin Freddy's.

"I think it'll be kind of interesting, actually," Kirsten said.

"Interesting, huh? You know, your dad told me once he always thought you should have been a boy—scraped knees, broken bones, always getting into trouble you should have stayed out of. 'A typical boy,' were your dad's words."

"And a typically male comment," she said. "My father was a sweet, kind man and I loved him. But he was an old-fashioned chauvinist, a sexist, and—"

"—and a tough, smart homicide investigator. And he told me to be careful, because you were way too much like him."

"That's something else I hate about men: always talking to each other behind your back."

"Anyway, to get back to the topic at hand, the deal wasn't that we'd be partners or something. The deal was . . . " Actually, he wasn't sure *what* the deal was.

"The deal was," she said, "I wouldn't take that great opportunity out west. Instead, I'd stay in the city and open my own agency."

Out west meant near Aurora, forty miles west of Chicago's Loop. *That great opportunity* had been a chance to be director of campus security at some community college Dugan had never heard of before, but that was growing like crazy, gobbling up the corn and soybean fields that surrounded it. He'd been against her taking the job. She was too damn conscientious, and she'd have been out there night and day.

"So I passed up the job," she was saying, "and—"

"Wait a second. You didn't even *want* that job!"

She reached over and patted his knee. "But you didn't *know* that when we made the deal, darling. What you knew was, I couldn't stand chasing shoplifters around the Magnificent Mile any longer. So we made a deal. I'd open my own agency. You'd spend less than your usual thirteen hours or whatever at your office, and take some time to help me out once in a while."

"I still don't remember the 'helping out' part."

"That's what you said. So . . . here you are, darling, helping me out. A deal's a deal."

"What's with this *darling* stuff?"

"I don't know. It just sounds . . . appropriate somehow." He watched her open the purse in her lap and pull out a little notebook. "The woman's name is Lynne Bulasik. She's a witness to a conversation between your friend Larry Candle and his client. I need to get her signed statement. And in a place like this, I just feel more . . . comfortable with you along. It won't take twenty minutes." She stuffed the notebook back into her purse and snapped it closed.

"My God, Kirsten," he said, staring at her.

"What?"

"There's a gun in your purse."

"Oh, that. It's the same Colt .380 I've had for years. I'm licensed, Dugan, you know that. Actually, you could be, too, since you're my employee."

Another surprise. "Your employee?"

"Just a technicality. I don't expect you to actually *work* for me. Anyway, I don't like to leave the gun in the car. It might get stolen or something." She patted his knee again.

The rain eased up and he rolled down his window to stare out at the Hi-Hope Shopping Center. It was a desolate little strip mall, on Ridgeview Road southwest of the city. A tiny copy shop with a big sign that said LOST OUR LEASE, Ray-Ann's Beauty Salon, three more vacant stores, and finally, at the end in an unattached building, Cousin Freddy's. It was just eight-thirty in the morning and the only other car in the lot had already been there when they arrived. The two customers they'd seen go inside must have arrived on foot, or else they came from a cement truck that was parked just short of the parking lot on the shoulder of Ridgeview.

It was an unincorporated, mostly undeveloped area. Ridgeview was four lanes there, and the traffic was heavy in both directions—school buses, commuters, delivery trucks, all hurrying back and forth through the gray morning, spraying out flat, wide sheets of dirty rainwater from the pavement.

Kirsten pulled the rearview mirror her way and ran some lipstick over her lips. She pursed them out, then in, then darted the tip of her tongue around, as though testing the flavor. It was one of a thousand things he'd seen her do a thousand times, and he never got tired of watching her.

She gave a last little dart of the tongue—not unconsciously, he thought—and pushed the mirror back into position. "I was hoping there wouldn't be any customers this early in the morning," she said. "But we might as well go in while the rain's eased up." Just then, the two construction workers came out of the store. "Oh good," Kirsten added.

One of the men had a brown paper package tucked under his arm. Both their heads turned in surprise as Dugan and Kirsten simultaneously opened the two doors of the Celica. The one with the package, a tall, heavyset man, hesitated, then turned his face aside. Dugan didn't blame him. He wasn't thrilled to be seen at a place like Cousin Freddy's either, even by strangers. The man's companion, another linebacker type, tugged at his arm and they hustled off.

Kirsten and Dugan picked their way carefully across the lot, seeking out high spots in the two-inch-deep river of rainwater that streamed over the asphalt.

"Incidentally," he said, "Larry Candle is not my friend. From all accounts, he's an ambulance chaser, and a low-life schlock who wouldn't know the courthouse from a cathouse. He's—"

"Well, he said you gave him my number, and he's my client. And as for ambulance chasing, what about your own little team?"

"That's different. And it's not a *team*. Those are cops that were mostly friends of my dad's. They'd been sending him accident cases long before I took over the firm and . . . well . . ."

But by then they'd reached the store. The plate glass window was painted over, dark blue, with red, squared-off letters:

The glass door was also dark blue, except for a section where the paint had been scraped off, and a sign taped to the inside of the glass announced:

LADIES ALWAYS WELCOME
See Our New Selection of Feminine Erotica

"See?" Dugan said, pulling open the door and following Kirsten through. "You didn't need me along at all."

To their left were the videotape, CD-ROM, and "novelty" sections, and in the rear wall was a wide doorway, draped with red velvet and holding a set of swinging doors. A sign beside the doors said FANTASY SALONS. To their right were several rows of book display shelves, surrounded by hundreds of magazines spread out on racks around three walls in carefully organized groupings for nearly every imaginable sexual proclivity. What was spread out on the magazine covers, Dugan thought, made *Hustler* and *Penthouse* look . . . well . . . middle-American or something.

Straight ahead, about fifteen feet back from the door, was a raised platform and a counter where the cashier could sit and keep an eye on the store. A sign fixed to the front of the counter faced the door and demanded a nonrefundable five-dollar deposit from everyone who entered, "to be credited against any purchase in excess of that amount."

The cashier had to be Lynne Bulasik, and Dugan guessed her to be maybe thirty years old. She was ordinary-looking, a little overweight, with straight brown hair pulled back like the farmer's wife's in *American Gothic*. She sat slouched in a swivel chair behind the counter, wearing a light blue dress. She was very pale-skinned, with no makeup, and rimless round eyeglasses clung precariously to the tip of her nose.

Her head was cocked at an angle. It was an odd, painful-looking, quizzical tilt, and one she couldn't have held very long—except that someone had broken her neck.

TWO

Dugan and Kirsten spent most of the next six hours in a succession of interrogation rooms. All the rooms had heavy, scarred tables and chairs, and they all smelled faintly of what Dugan thought at first was disinfectant, but finally decided was bug spray.

It was almost three o'clock before they were finished telling everything they knew, over and over, to an assortment of Cook County Sheriff's detectives, to an assistant state's attorney, and finally to a pair of sleek, jaded-looking Chicago Police violent crimes investigators who—for reasons they never bothered to explain—seemed to have taken charge of the case.

Afterward, they headed downtown and had a late lunch upstairs at the Italian Village, on Madison Street. Actually, it was more an early supper, and short on food. For Dugan, just enough bread and salad to keep the alcohol down. For Kirsten, less than that. There wasn't much conversation, either.

"Why Chicago?" Dugan finally wondered aloud.

"What?" Kirsten had been staring into space, somewhere off to the left of his head.

"Those police investigators . . . Chicago cops. But it didn't . . . I mean, we weren't in Chicago."

"Oh. Well, I asked, but they wouldn't tell me," she said. "I think they sometimes assist in that sort of killing, even in the suburbs."

"*That* sort of killing?"

"I mean, anything that's . . . you know . . . Mob-related."

A mouthful of Chianti turned around on its way down his throat. "Mob-related?" he gargled. "It was a robbery. The register was emptied. Why drag the Mob into it?"

"Well, people who rob stores usually just grab the money and run. I mean, they might shoot the cashier if something goes wrong or if they're crazy enough. But this was different, and so . . . *professional,* I suppose is the best . . . "

He'd been concentrating on refilling his wine glass, but when her voice faded away he looked up.

He'd met Kirsten when they were both in training at the Chicago Police Academy. He quit before he got sworn in as a cop, and ended up a lawyer. She'd come from the opposite direction, quitting law school when the chance to join the department came up. She made so many arrests that stuck and scored so high on all the tests that she didn't even need the nepotism that had been rampant for years, or the new affirmative-action decrees everybody hated, and in only a few years she made investigator. She didn't stay long after that. Kirsten never said so, but Dugan knew she had a hard time accepting senseless violence and mangled bodies as part of the routine of everyday urban life. He was convinced Kirsten left the department only because she realized how cynical and hardened she'd have to become, simply to protect her own psyche. And he was forever grateful for that.

Just now her face was pale, and he knew she was fighting to keep the tears in the corners of her eyes from running down her cheeks. He didn't blame her. He'd pulled his feelings inside, too. You couldn't call it grief, actually. More like shock, a mix of disgust and bewilderment—and fear, too.

"I can't help thinking about the tilt of her head," she said, her voice tight and strained. "I guess there are some things I'll *never* get used to."

He didn't try to answer. His mind kept thinking *Mafia . . . Outfit.*

They poked forks at their plates a while longer, finished up the wine, and headed for the door. At Clark Street he started toward

8

the parking garage and the Celica, but Kirsten pulled his arm in the opposite direction. The tears were gone from her eyes, replaced by a determination that he wasn't all that happy to see.

"Larry Candle," she said. "Let's see if he's heard about it."

It was a five-minute walk and then a ride up to the twelfth floor. On the wall by the locked door was a handsome brass plaque that said LARRY CANDLE, ATTORNEY-AT-LAW. THE LAWYER FOR THE LITTLE GUY. There was a button on the wall below the sign.

Larry answered the buzzer himself. He had a round body topped by a round face surrounded by lots of curly black hair, permed and probably dyed. He was fifty years old and had an awful lot of worry lines for a man with so much fat in his face. He'd been out most of the day and he hadn't heard about Lynne Bulasik's death.

Dugan had spoken to Larry only once before in his life—the day Larry called out of the blue, said he'd heard about Kirsten's new agency, and asked for her number. But he knew Larry by reputation, and Larry took the news about as Dugan would have expected.

"Jesus Christ," he whined, "why do these things have to happen to *me?*" He stood up, then threw his pen back down onto his cluttered desk. "Why can't anything *good* happen to me, for God's sake. Am I—"

"Shut up, Larry! Just shut up!" Kirsten was on her feet, too, and nearly shouting.

Dugan thought she might slug her own client. "Let's get outta here," he said, taking Kirsten's arm.

"No. Wait." Larry moved between them and the door of his office, holding his palms up in a gesture of apology. "Wait. I'm sorry. I feel bad about the Bulasik woman, too, you know? It's a terrible thing, sure. But she must have been mixed up with the big bambinos."

" 'Big bambinos'?"

"You know, the Mob. I mean, don't they control all those porno stores? Or at least take a cut or something? Maybe Lynne was holding out on 'em. She and her father."

"Her father?" Kirsten asked.

9

"Hell, yes. He runs that sleaze shop. And there's a cousin involved, too."

Kirsten had a suspicious look on her face. "Larry," she said, "you don't think this has anything to do with your case, do you?"

"My case? What would a goddamn killing have to do with *my* fuckin'—" He stopped. "Excuse the language, huh? But my case couldn't possibly have anything to do with her getting killed. She and her boyfriend just happened to be there in Walloon's when I was talking to Rita Ranchero about her money."

"*Rita Ranchero?*" Dugan said, not able to keep his mouth shut any longer.

"A client of Larry's. It's probably a stage name," Kirsten said. She gave Dugan a look that asked him—again—to stay out of it.

Larry was still complaining. "Jesus, now what am I gonna do? Lynne Bulasik was my independent witness. Now she's dead and they'll pull my ticket for sure, if it's just my word against my client's."

"There's still Lynne's boyfriend," Kirsten said. "And maybe Rita will change her story. Maybe she'll tell the truth."

"You *gotta* be kidding." The despair on Larry's face might have meant he knew Rita wouldn't tell the truth, but Dugan figured it meant the truth was the last thing Larry wanted. "I don't even know who the boyfriend is. I don't think anyone said what his name was. If they did I don't remember. That damn lawyer at the Attorney Disciplinary Commission says she hasn't found him, either. But what do they care? The only one he can help is me, and all they want is to pull my ticket, for chrissake, get me disbarred."

"I'll find him," Kirsten said. "And Rita, too. Don't worry about that."

"Yeah, well, I *am* worried." Larry sat back down behind his desk and rummaged around in the debris until he found his pen. Then he dropped it back into the pile. "The thing is, I need you to find him before the commission does. And I don't want you taking his statement until I talk to him first. I want to . . . well . . . find out whether he's gonna be helpful."

Five minutes later, they'd left Larry Candle's office and were waiting for an elevator. It was after five o'clock, and they let one packed car come and go.

"You have to get out of this," Dugan said.

"I just don't like the idea of dropping something I've started." She pressed closely against him, but kept staring straight ahead.

"Yeah, but the Mafia—or the Outfit—or whatever they call it these days? And looking for the boyfriend of a clerk in a porno shop who's just been murdered, and used to hang around with someone calling herself Rita Ranchero? Uh, what sort of stage does she perform on, anyway?"

"I don't know, but we're both guessing the same thing, I'm sure. Right now, she's apparently unemployed. Anyway, that's not the point. The point is that Larry Candle's my client. Walking away just because things get a little complicated could ruin my reputation as an investigator."

"You hardly even have a reputation—not yet anyway."

"Right," she said. "That's what I mean." A subdued gong announced the coming of another elevator. "Besides, Larry's right. Lynne Bulasik's death couldn't possibly be connected with his case."

They squeezed into an elevator jammed with support staff fleeing the law offices that filled the building. Riding down, Dugan thought that if he'd been able to look into her eyes, maybe he'd know whether Kirsten really believed what she was saying, or was just trying to encourage him—or encourage herself.

They followed the flow through the lobby and out the revolving door into more cold November rain.

"Let's take a cab," Kirsten said. "I don't feel like fighting rush hour. I'll pick up the car in the morning."

It was a twenty-minute ride from downtown to the near-north loft building where they owned the top floor. As their cab darted through traffic, Dugan tried again to picture the two men at Cousin Freddy's. One black, one white. He hadn't been paying much attention and he just couldn't paint their portraits in his mind, as hard as he tried.

"Most people would think at least *one* of us would have gotten a good enough look at those two to be able to identify them," he said.

"I know. Let's just hope they don't think we were lying."

"Yeah. Problem is, cops are suspicious by nature."

"Forget the cops," she said. "I'm hoping those two goons are convinced."

"The goons?" He stared at her. "I don't understand."

"My guess is, it won't take them long to find out what we told the cops. And despite what we said, well . . . " She paused and gazed out the taxi's window a moment, then added, "You're lucky, actually."

He didn't like the sound of that. "What do you mean?"

"Just that I think you were telling the truth. You couldn't pick those two guys out of a lineup of three."

"Of *course* I was telling the truth. And . . . you mean you—"

"I mean it's my job to pay attention to things," she said. "I'll never forget those two faces as long as I live—and I think maybe the homicide dicks know it."

"But, if they really *were* Mob—what?—hit men?—and if they thought you could identify them, they . . . "

"Right," she said.

He paid off the cabbie and they hustled across the wet sidewalk and into the brick-walled foyer of their building. "Anyway," he said, "if they can't take a chance on one of us, they can't take a chance on either. So . . . what's so lucky about being the one that doesn't even know who to look out for?"

THREE

T hrough their whole morning routine—quick showers, gulps of coffee and toast, then paging through separate newspapers on the cab ride downtown—Kirsten noticed they were both strangely silent about the entire affair. She wondered how long that would last.

Dugan's office was the first stop, though, and as the driver pulled to the curb they both folded their papers and turned toward each other as though on cue.

She let Dugan speak first. "What the hell are we gonna do?" he asked.

"Not much we *can* do, for now. At least our names still haven't surfaced." She rummaged around in her purse and finally came up with the ticket from the parking garage. "I'll get the Celica this afternoon and pick you up. We can talk about it at dinner."

He got out and the cab took her on to Wabash and Washington in the old jewelry district. Her tiny, two-room office suite was on the tenth floor, on the Washington Street side of the building, nestled in between Mark Well Diamond Company, Inc., and Brumstein & Brumstein Wholesale Jewelry, Inc.

Mark Brumstein owned both of Kirsten's corporate neighbors. "Along with my son, also Mark," he always put it. "Also Mark" wasn't around much, being mostly occupied with Hebrew school and junior high soccer at the time. There were separate entrances for the two businesses, although they shared one large C-shaped area.

Kirsten's suite filled the space in the C. She had a plate glass door with a chrome handle and painted letters that said:

WILD ONION, LTD.
Confidential Inquiries
Security Services

The reception area was done in pastels, and was just large enough for a couple of chairs and a chrome and glass table with an art deco lamp and one copy of *Architectural Digest.* The walls held large framed prints that might have been fantasies of flowers or drifting clouds—or maybe soft-edged amoebas—all in faded shades of peach and orange and green. She didn't much like the prints, or anything else about the decor. But Mark Brumstein's wife, Andrea, who was a very expensive interior decorator and who picked everything out, had assured her it was all very *du jour* or something.

Kirsten's first case had been for Andrea, and had to do with Spanish tapestries and Turkish etchings and, of course, diamonds. Andrea was more than grateful—mostly because Kirsten didn't say much to Mark about it. Kirsten got paid well, and as a bonus, got a great deal on this little suite that Andrea insisted Mark carve out of his space. The deal was so good Kirsten could put up with an amoeba or two.

But she'd stood by her choice for her agency's name, over Andrea's objections. In about third grade she'd read somewhere that *"Chi-ca-go"* could be translated as "stink root" or "wild onion." She told Andrea any client who was turned off by the name "Wild Onion, Ltd.," was a client she didn't want anyway.

She picked up the pile of mail that sat on the floor outside her door and went through the reception room into her office. The November mail-order blitz was on. She sat down at her desk and started throwing away catalogs.

The phone rang. It was Grace, Mark Brumstein's receptionist.

Calls were forwarded to one of his lines if Kirsten didn't pick up on two rings, and Grace had taken a call for Kirsten that morning.

"A Martin Hoffmeier," Grace said. "Kind of a pushy guy."

Hoffmeier and his partner, Frank LaMotta, were the Chicago violent crimes investigators they'd dealt with the day before. Kirsten paged through a catalog full of expensive garden tools and wondered if she'd ever have a house with a yard. She didn't feel like talking to Hoffmeier just yet.

FOUR

Dugan sat at his desk and stared at the stack of messages from the previous day. It would have been downright depressing, except that phone calls were his livelihood, and not a bad livelihood at that.

Dugan's dad had built the law practice, handling personal injury cases only. "No divorce, no criminal defense, and none of that commercial litigation bullshit," he used to tell Dugan. "Strictly P.I., that's where the money is, kid." He was as tough and blunt—and as honest, in his own way—as an old Chicago brick.

But even bricks break, and this one had a congenital heart condition. The day it took him down was a tropically hot and humid August afternoon. He'd been hustling up a ramp at Wrigley Field with four cups of beer in the top half of the third.

At the moment his dad fell dead in a puddle of Old Style, Dugan had been an assistant Cook County state's attorney for twenty-three months, one week, three and a half days, and was thinking about going back to school to study forestry or eastern religions or something—anything. He'd been offered the prosecutor's job because his dad made all the right campaign contributions and had lots of clout. Taking it was stupid, though. If he'd wanted to lock people up he could have gone ahead and been a cop.

Of course, he didn't really want his dad's law practice either. But it was a way out. Besides, Peter and Fred had asked him to take over—begged him, in fact. Two lawyers in their late fifties, they'd been with his dad twenty-five years or something.

They collared Dugan at the wake, ten feet from the open casket, at the end of the line of family members: Dugan's mother who'd defied her Greek father to marry an outsider, his sister the pediatric oncologist, his older brother the Orientology professor, and his little brother the tennis and ski bum out in Steamboat whom everyone envied but who was even more disenchanted with his career choice—or nonchoice—than Dugan was.

"You gotta come on board," Fred Schustein said, grabbing Dugan's hand as he came through the line of mourners.

"Yeah, join the team." That was Peter Rienzo, shoulder-to-shoulder with Fred.

"Thank you so much for coming," Dugan said, "but you're mixing your metaphors, guys. Anyway, can't this wait?"

The line of well-wishers was endless. They had the biggest parlor at O'Flaherty's and still had people spilling out all over. There was lots of laughter and lively conversation, and anyone interested enough could always find the booze. A great wake. Even the old monsignor, who said a few words in place of the Rosary, had joked about how his dad died on a "mission of mercy"—bringing cold beer to his friends. The old man would have been proud. Dugan himself couldn't quite get into it.

"Can't this wait," he repeated, "at least until after he's buried?"

Fred and Peter lowered their heads in tandem, then looked up and glowered at each other accusingly, each blaming the other for his indelicacy. Dugan figured his dad would have gotten a kick out of this part, too.

Fred answered first. "Uh . . . sure, Dugan. Sorry. We just—"

"Yeah, sorry," Peter agreed. "Maybe we're jumping the gun a little." Then he couldn't stop himself. "We just want you to know the situation. We're . . . well . . . we're kinda desperate, you know? Me and Fred, all we know is working the comp cases. That's it. The common law side? Nothing. Getting clients, signing 'em up? Nothing. The business side? Nothing. Paying the—"

"Fine," Dugan interrupted. "But look . . ." He nodded to his left, where the bulge building up in the stream of mourners was ready to rupture, right there in front of the casket. His mother glared at him over the shoulder of whoever it was that was embracing her.

"Oh jeez, Dugan, sorry."

"Yeah, sorry." They'd both honestly forgotten again where they were. "Uh, we'll talk about it later."

They did. And a month after that he'd moved into the suite on the seventh floor of the old Tomkins Building, a block from the Daley Center in the Loop.

So that's where he was sitting the day after Lynne Bulasik had her neck broken, in his corner office with views of the sides of tall buildings in every direction, paging through his phone messages. He arranged the little pink slips neatly on his desk and stared down at them, wondering which caller would answer the phone with: *I hope you really don't know nothin', pal, or it's curtains—for you and the good-lookin' broad both.*

Silly, of course. He knew better. The unfamiliar names were new clients, certainly . . . probably. But—

"Yoo-hoo, wake up!"

He jumped. It was Molly Wavers, the secretary he'd inherited along with his dad's office.

"I brought your coffee," she said. "And a few more messages—from this morning already." She waved one of the pink slips. "This one here's from a Martin Hoffmeier. Sounded like a policeman to me. I could tell by his voice . . . and his attitude, even without the background noise. Is he sending in a case, you think? I'll have to add him to the—"

"No, Molly. It's . . . something else."

"Anyway, first he says there's no rush. Then right away he says call him by ten this morning. Sounded sort of smart-alecky to me."

"Thanks for the coffee, Molly. And listen, have Denise return these calls, will you?" Except for the one from Hoffmeier, he handed the entire stack of messages back to Molly. "Have her tell them I'll call back. Tell them I'm . . . uh . . . I'm in court. But Molly, make sure she asks what they want. Okay?"

She gave him a strange look. But all she said was, "Fine." Then,

"But you're gonna get behind, and you know how you feel when you get behind."

They both knew she was right. But he couldn't get over how worried he was about returning those phone calls. Worst of all, it felt like one of those worries that doesn't just grow old and die out. It was a worry he'd have to *do* something about.

"Molly!" he called. She was already out the office door, but came back in. "How many letters from lawyers looking for jobs did we get in the last, say, three weeks?"

"Probably four or five. There's one or two every week. They all get the usual letter. Poor things." Molly was everybody's mother.

"Right. Listen. Dig out the last ten résumés and pick five that look good. See if they still want an interview."

"But—"

"Oh, and one of those messages in that stack is from that Winslow woman who twisted her ankle getting off a C.T.A. bus. Case won't be worth the aggravation. Send her the letter that says we're sorry, et cetera. Give her Pierce's name. He might be hungry enough to take her case."

"Of course. But—"

"And I'm not taking any fee on the Rivera case. With no wife and two kids he's gonna need every penny."

"But that's the third pro bono case this . . ." She sighed. "Anyway, about these interviews. When do you—"

"I'm going to Kirsten's. Call and tell her, would you?" He eased past her and got away before she could remind him how often he'd sworn there'd be no more lawyers in the office.

On the way out, he passed Fred Schustein's empty office. Fred would be with Peter by now, going over their "call"—the where and when of that day's cases. They worked all the firm's "comp cases," employees whose job-injury claims were handled according to the arcane terms of the Workers' Compensation Act.

After all these years, Peter and Fred were damn good at what they did, and ran pretty much on automatic pilot. Dugan never bothered them except to object whenever they started to bullshit about those mystical, long-gone days "when practicing law was *fun,* by God." They both got identical decent salaries and year-end bonuses. In exchange, they worked like crazy, but not often more than eight hours a day, five days a week. It was a great deal for them, and they knew it. And a great deal for Dugan, too, which they also knew.

He waved as he hurried past Peter's office.

"Hey, Dugan!" It was Fred.

Dugan stopped and backpedaled. "What's up?" But he knew.

"What's up is us—up to our asses again, so . . . "

"Got it," he said. "I'll take care of it."

That was their understanding. When they had too many cases they told him. He'd bite the bullet and send new workers' comp clients elsewhere for a time. Not an easy thing to do, not for any lawyer. But he didn't want one of them dropping dead on him, either.

Other than comp cases, Dugan handled everything in the office—automobile accidents, and other injury cases. Just he and the office staff. No other lawyer. He didn't bother with marginal cases. The "good" cases he turned over to his crew and the computer that spat out form letters and attorney's liens and requests for medical records. His goal was to settle every case without filing suit. That's how he spent his days—on the phone with clients and insurance adjusters.

But he never sold a client short. Things he couldn't settle before suit—which included most of the big cases, like brain damage or paralysis—he referred out to a litigation firm. He took back part of the attorney's fee: a third to him on the small cases, a fifty-fifty split on the big ones.

Early on, before he wised up, he'd found himself doing jury trials. Exciting sometimes, but like all warfare it was mostly drudgery and meticulous attention, night and day, often for weeks at a time. He gave that up in a hurry.

Actually, by now Dugan wasn't much more familiar with day-to-day work in the courtrooms than . . . well . . . Larry Candle. But the similarity ended right there. Oh . . . and, of course, they both had expenses for "case acquisition." That is, Dugan figured Larry also paid people to refer injured clients. But otherwise . . .

Riding down the elevator, Dugan wrote himself a note about sending new comp cases somewhere else for a couple of weeks.

When the elevator doors slid open onto the building lobby, he nearly collided with two people—two very large people. His breath stopped and his muscles locked up, freezing him in his tracks. Finally, the two decided he wasn't getting off, and they stepped inside with him. It took that long for his brain to register that they were both women. Big women, yes, but not linebacker size. He slid between them and fled as the elevator doors closed behind him.

Ten minutes later he walked into Kirsten's office and sat down across from her.

"Molly called," she said. "Couldn't wait till tonight to talk, huh?"

"Exactly. I mean, I'm sitting over there in my office, scared to return my calls—as though a hit man's gonna phone in and leave a number, for God's sake. Then two people come toward me in broad daylight and I go into cardiac arrest."

She reached back and dropped a catalog in the wastebasket behind her desk. She looked far more calm than he felt. "I agree," she said. "The problem is—"

"—what to do."

"Right. Did you get a call from Hoffmeier this morning, too?"

"Yes. But I didn't call him back."

"So . . . that's as good a place to start as any, I guess." She lifted the phone and tapped out the number.

Hoffmeier must have picked up on the first ring. Once she identified herself, Kirsten's end of the conversation was mostly silence, punctuated by monosyllables.

"Yes . . . good . . . no . . . " She scowled down at her desktop during a few more yeses. Suddenly, her eyes widened. "Oh no!" There was a long pause while she stared at Dugan and said nothing. Finally, she said, "No, he's right here with me now. . . . Right, no need to. I'll tell him. And, uh, thanks . . . I guess."

She hung up. Very carefully, Dugan thought.

21

"Well?" he asked

She shook her head as though to clear her mind. "Well, first, they found an abandoned cement truck. It had been stolen from a construction site about ten miles from Cousin Freddy's. They're going over it for fingerprints and any physical evidence that might tie it to Lynne's murder. But Hoffmeier says they don't expect—"

"Kirsten."

"Yes?"

"Enough about the cement truck. That was *first*, you said. So what was second?"

"Second? Well, second, this morning they found something else, too. They found . . . uh . . . my Celica—or at least what's left of my Celica."

FIVE

t blew away the fire wall and tore the hell out of the front seat and the engine compartment. Bomb and Arson called it a "carefully contained explosive device." Even if there had been other cars in the parking slots nearby—which there hadn't been at five A.M.—they'd have been untouched.

Dugan listened to Kirsten's recitation without really grasping the meaning. "But the really significant thing," she concluded, "is that the detonator was timed."

He was out of his chair by that time and pacing her office. "I guess I don't know what you mean."

"It could have been set to blow when the engine started, but it wasn't."

He turned to look out the windows, but there weren't any windows, so he went to the coffeemaker in the corner. It was something to do besides think. He came back to her desk with two full mugs.

"Don't you *get* it?" she asked.

Maybe it was true what he'd read somewhere: that men all marry their mothers. She sure sounded like his mother always had whenever one of her children was being especially dense. He ordinarily wasn't stupid, not even slow-thinking. But he'd never had a car of his blown up before.

"It was *your* car, though, actually," he finally blurted out, realizing that he'd forgotten what it was she'd asked. He looked at her helplessly.

"A warning, Dugan. That's what it was." He could tell she was losing her patience with him. "They could have fixed it to blow when one of us started the car. But they didn't. They must know we told the police we couldn't identify them. The bomb wasn't to kill us, just scare us, let us know what they can do."

"Why don't I find that very consoling?"

"Well, being scared beats being dead."

She had him there. "I know what we should do," he said.

"Oh?"

"Yes. We should take a cab to the health club. Swim a few laps. Then sit in the whirlpool and figure out where to go away for a while. You're always talking about a cruise. Or maybe that trek your brother took across New Zealand. It's the beginning of summer down there now, I think."

But they didn't go for a swim.

Instead, they went to meet Hoffmeier and LaMotta at the police auto pound and stare at the remains of the Celica for a while.

Hoffmeier said he hoped they weren't leaving town any time soon. "The evidence techs haven't finished with your vehicle yet, and—"

"We weren't thinking of driving," Dugan said. "We were thinking of a cruise."

Hoffmeier's eyes were pale blue and his skin was fair and he obviously didn't like dumb jokes. "Uh-huh," he said. "Well, when the techs are finished we may need to talk to you. And we're gonna want to hold on to the vehicle for a while after that, too. Damn thing's totaled anyway, so you've got no objection."

"Of course not," Kirsten said quickly, not giving Dugan a chance to open his mouth. "Do you need us now for anything else?"

"I'm just wondering," Hoffmeier said, "whether you told anyone about your finding Lynne Bulasik's body. I mean, we can't keep it secret forever, but we haven't made a public statement about it yet."

"We told only my client," Kirsten said, "Larry Candle. He certainly couldn't have had anything to do with this."

"No? Well, who knows. . . . " Hoffmeier's voice trailed off.

"Anyway," LaMotta spoke up, "like we said, stick around. We'll be in touch. Oh, incidentally, you'll get the bill in the mail."

"The bill?"

"From the city," LaMotta said, "for towing your vehicle."

Dugan spent the afternoon back in his office, on the phone. Mostly clients and insurance adjusters. No hit men—as far as he could tell.

By five o'clock Molly had set up interviews with five job applicants for later that week. With some seventy thousand lawyers in the state, over half of them bumping elbows in Chicago alone, getting interviewees was easy.

Late in the afternoon, Kirsten called. She'd rented a beat-up Ford Tempo from Fender Benders, and at seven o'clock they drove to a hole-in-the-wall Thai restaurant a friend of hers kept raving about, up around Wilson and Broadway. They ordered her friend's recommendations, mostly things with two stars on the grease-stained, photocopied menu. The stars meant "hot, hot," but the waiter promised, "Not too hot, not too hot." Dugan ordered a large Pepsi to put out any fires, and a second one as backup.

"Thing is," he was saying, "do I hire some kid too naive to figure out where some of my cases come from, or someone who'll catch on but be smart enough not to ask?"

"I'm surprised you want to hire another lawyer at all."

"I don't *want* to hire another lawyer. But I was falling behind even before we started having cars blown up, and I need someone in the office when I can't be there."

"Can't Molly and Denise and the rest of them handle things?"

"Sure they can. But sometimes people insist on talking to a lawyer, even if the lawyer has to turn around and ask Molly what to do."

"Well, why don't you just have Molly tell people she's a lawyer?"

"Can't do that. It's unethical."

"Oh . . . unethical." She speared a little maroon pepper. Just thinking about her biting into it made Dugan reach for his Pepsi. "If ethics is a concern," she said, the pepper halfway to her mouth, "why pay ambulance chasers to send you cases?"

"They aren't *chasers*. They're police officers. When they come across people who require legal services, they refer them to me."

"You *pay* them, Dugan. They're chasers. It's against the rules. Period. And you do it." She bit into the pepper, and he swore her eyes brightened. But, after a long drink of Thai beer, she continued. "You're as honest as they come. But you need business. And, rules or not, that way of getting clients is no worse than some two-bit creep in a plaid suit hawking himself on cable TV, or for that matter some high-priced creep in pinstripes sweet-talking clients over lunch at his club. It's all the same, whatever the rules say." She drank some beer and set the bottle down with finality. "It's not immoral, and it's not wrong. It's just against the rules."

All this ethics talk was making Dugan uncomfortable. "You're very eloquent tonight," he said. "Must be those maroon things. But excuses aside, I pay those cops for cases because that's the system I inherited from my old man—and it works. I get lots of clients, and the clients make me lots of money."

"And that's despite cutting your fees so often and doing pro bono stuff. Of course, you *do* work twelve, fourteen hours a day."

"And weekends. But . . . one of these days I might get caught. Then I'll have lots of time off. I'll have the Disciplinary Commission on my back, just like Larry Candle."

"Maybe. But his problem's much different."

"What *is* his problem, anyway?" Dugan asked.

"In a nutshell? They think he's as crooked as a welterweight's nose."

"And probably not without reason. But I mean, what's the specific thing the commission's after him for right now?"

"He settled a personal injury case for this Rita Ranchero person.

Then he took some of the money and spent it. He can't deny it, the bank records are clear. But he says she gave him her permission to invest it for her. Rita says she didn't. Larry says Lynne Bulasik and her boyfriend were there when he talked to Rita about it."

"The boyfriend. You got a line on him?"

"Not even a name," she said. He noticed she was sorting carefully through the food on her plate now, taking tiny, tentative bites. "With Lynne dead, Rita Ranchero's my best bet, but she's dropped out of sight. I've left messages at Cousin Freddy's for Lynne's father, and her cousin, too. Not that I expect to hear from them, not till after her funeral, anyway." She finished what was left of her beer, then grabbed Dugan's backup Pepsi. "Wow," she gasped. "I've hardly eaten anything and I'm burning up already. How about you?"

"All I've done is pick the peanuts out of this chicken stuff. By the way, did I ever tell you how cute you look with little beads of sweat popping out along your hairline?"

They apologized to the waiter, paid the bill, and found a place called Bob's Grill a few blocks away. Dugan waited in a booth while Kirsten went to call in for her phone messages. She was gone so long that he ordered for both of them.

"You have your choice," he told her when she finally joined him, "a steak sandwich or a BLT."

"The BLT," she said, then laughed. "Aren't we a couple of urban sophisticates!"

He loved the little crinkles that showed up at the corners of her eyes when she laughed. But she thought of them as crow's-feet, so all he said was, "Any calls?"

"Two. One was from Hoffmeier. I called him back. You won't believe what he told me."

He reached for the stainless steel cream pot as the waitress set their coffees down. "I have an idea I won't like it, either."

"Seems a few weeks ago an adult bookstore in Uptown burned to the ground. Arson. No suspects. No known motive. A week later the cops started getting reports of threats to other porno stores, first in the city and now the suburbs, too—Cook County, Lake County, clear up to the state line."

"Threats?"

"Sent in the mail. Each one got a photocopy of a *Sun-Times* article about the torched store, and a typed note. Always the same message." She took her notebook from her purse and read, " 'Sticks and stones break women's bones, but pornography rapes and kills us. We won't be victims any longer. Shut down, or pay the price.' "

"Pay the price?"

"Hoffmeier says they're trying to keep a lid on it. But he and LaMotta decided they should tell us. Sort of a professional courtesy, I guess. A lot of cops knew me when I was on the force, and . . . Anyway, that's why they got involved in Lynne's death in the first place." She slid her coffee mug around in circles on the smooth tabletop. "Maybe the Outfit wasn't behind the thugs we saw at Cousin Freddy's after all."

"The thugs *you* saw. I wasn't paying attention, remember?"

"Of course, darling." She picked up her mug in two hands and stared over the top of it at him. "Very interesting, though, isn't it?"

He recalled her saying the same thing sitting in the car outside Cousin Freddy's. A lifetime of competing with four brothers had given her an unusual idea of *interesting*.

The waitress arrived with their sandwiches. When she'd left, Dugan said, "I looked it up this afternoon. It's spring right now in New Zealand. We should go. I really mean it." And he did.

Kirsten smiled. A different smile, this one, not the kind that put crinkles beside her eyes. "You know, Dugan, I'm scared, too. It's instinct. But there's nowhere to hide from something like this. We don't know who it is we'd be hiding from. And if we did, and if there were somewhere to go, how long would we have to hide? And how would we know when it was safe again? Do we just spend the rest of our lives wondering what—"

"Okay, okay. I get the point." He squeezed the red plastic bottle and drew a figure eight with ketchup on his French fries. "Anyway, what was the other call?"

"A woman. Her name's Fredrica Kalter. I talked to her, too. She's—"

He groaned. "Her name was really Fredrica?"

"You got it," Kirsten said. "Cousin Freddy. We're meeting her in an hour."

SIX

Dugan wasn't surprised he'd never heard of Palestrina's. It was just another of what seemed like a dozen new restaurants popping up monthly within walking distance of their apartment. He and Kirsten found a lot of good ones—fresh food, creatively prepared and enthusiastically served. It didn't seem to matter, though. Inevitably, a few months later they'd go back again, only to find the place gone bankrupt and replaced by a sports bar.

The sign in Palestrina's window said CUISINE FROM THE ISLE OF CORSICA. Inside, the dark man in the tux greeted them with a smile as warm and Mediterranean as the polyphony floating out from the wall speakers. "Ah, welcome, my friends. I am Paolo." He glanced down at his watch. "I shall persuade my chef to remain open a bit longer . . . especially for you. Come. The hostess will be with you shortly."

Paolo seemed a little pretentious to Dugan. But then, maybe he knew what his customers liked.

"We've already had dinner," Kirsten said, "twice. We're here to see Fredrica Kalter. She's expecting us."

Dugan saw disappointment flit through Paolo's eyes, but the warm smile never wavered. "Ah, Fredrica. She is the hostess." He gestured expansively. "She comes this way."

A young woman glided up to them in a flowing, floor-length gown. In the soft light her skin was pale and smooth, framed by long, dark hair that fell to her shoulders. She wore no jewelry and no makeup, and did just fine without either one.

Dugan swallowed hard. "You mean . . . you're Freddy?"

She nodded apologetically. "That . . . that was my father's nickname for me, right from the day I was born."

She looked to be in her early twenties, and though her smile was warm, to Dugan she sounded uncertain, maybe naive. She was definitely attractive.

"I'll do the talking," Kirsten said, a little too loudly, showing Dugan a smile neither warm nor naive. She handed Freddy one of her cards.

Paolo stepped forward. "Why don't you take your guests to the bar, Fredrica? I am closing now."

Paolo seemed more Greek than Italian, but likable enough. Dugan hoped when the time came he found an honorable bankruptcy lawyer.

The tiny bar near the kitchen was deserted. Freddy poured white wine for Kirsten and Dugan, and popped open a can of diet ginger ale for herself. She sat on a stool, facing them across the bar. To Dugan, she seemed awfully young—and far too innocent—to be mixed up with the dirty-book-and-dildo industry.

"Well," she finally said, once they'd all tasted their drinks and the silence forced her to speak, "the police told me you're the ones who found Lynne. Then my uncle said you called, and told him you're a private investigator, Miss—"

"Please, call me Kirsten. And this is Dugan. He's . . . he's helping me."

"Well anyway, I wasn't going to call you back at first. But I have to talk to *someone*. Everything's so awful. Paolo said I didn't have to come to work, but I couldn't stand sitting in my apartment alone. I asked that policeman, Detective Hoffmeier, and he said he thought you were honest, but he didn't think you'd be much help."

When Freddy paused, Dugan couldn't keep quiet. "You know, I just can't believe someone named a porno store after you."

She lowered her head, as though he'd just slapped her and all she could do was accept it. "Unfortunately, it's me all right. And not just

31

the name. There's a set of trusts and documents that I don't quite understand, but I own the place. That is, it's *half* mine. Half of everything, the building, the property it's on, and the, uh, inventory."

He still found it hard to figure. "How in God's—"

Kirsten cut him off. "I suppose you inherited your share of the store. Possibly from your father?"

"Well . . . sort of. My father's not dead. He's disabled. But a few years ago, long before he was hurt, he had a lawyer put all his property in a trust." She drank some of her ginger ale. "My mother died, you see, when I was very young."

"That's a shame," Dugan said. "I'm sorry."

"Thank you. It . . . was a long time a—"

"You mentioned your father was . . . *hurt?*" Kirsten asked.

"He was mugged. Leaving the store to go to the bank. He went out the back door and . . . They took the money and he was terribly beaten—mostly in the head and face—with an iron pipe. He's been in a nursing home ever since, over a year now. One whole side of his body is paralyzed. His mind is . . . well, sometimes I think he understands who I am and what I'm saying, and other times he seems totally oblivious. Anyway, he can't speak at all and he can barely swallow. The doctor says it's injury to his brain. He's . . . he's not going to get any better."

"And he owned half the bookstore at the time of the beating?" Kirsten asked.

"Actually, no. Turns out I'd been the sole beneficiary of the trust—at least on paper—all along, even though I didn't know it. My trust already owned half, Uncle Anton had a quarter, and Lynne had a quarter. Now, I guess Uncle Anton has half."

"If I were you," Dugan blurted, "I'd sell the place, or at least put in a different business. Who wants—"

"I know." She studied the ginger ale can for a moment. "But neither my uncle nor I can sell without the other. The store makes quite a bit of money, and hardly any other businesses have survived in that area. The store, and that deserted little shopping center beside it, are surrounded by a huge garbage landfill. There's some sort of leakage or something, and no one can build anything on it. So the area can't be developed and that makes the property worth hardly anything."

"If the store makes so much money," Kirsten said, "why are you working nights in a restaurant?"

"Oh, this is just temporary. Actually, I'm an actress." She paused, and Dugan could see she was savoring the idea. "And all the money I get from the store goes for my father's care. He has no money of his own, so public aid would pay if I applied. But I have him in this wonderful nursing home that doesn't take public aid patients and I couldn't bear to move him. His doctor says he's susceptible to all kinds of infections that might . . . might kill him. Or . . . he might live a long time. So, until I'm making enough money as an actress to take care of him, I have to depend on the store—much as I hate the idea." She drank some more ginger ale, then looked at Kirsten. "You said you had something important to ask me?"

"Yes," Kirsten said. "I have a client who says your cousin Lynne was present during a conversation between him and a woman named Rita Ranchero. What was said in that conversation is crucial to my client. I hate to bother you at a time like this, but—"

"Oh, that's okay. This whole thing is very disturbing and . . . frightening, actually. But as for Lynne, well, I feel bad about what happened, of course. But she was nearly ten years older than I and we were never close. I never even knew I had a cousin until Lynne and my uncle Anton, my mother's brother, moved here from Cleveland a few years ago and he and my father opened the store. Anyway, I certainly wouldn't know about any conversation Lynne had with your client."

"Probably not," Kirsten said. "But there was a man there, too. Lynne's boyfriend. I thought maybe you'd know—"

"Boyfriend? Lynne? I mean, we weren't close, but I'm sure she didn't have a boyfriend. Lynne was . . . well, she . . . "

"She was gay?" Dugan asked.

"Yes. At least . . . I mean, that's what she . . . Anyway, I never met any of her friends. My uncle says there won't be any funeral. Just a cremation. I don't think he and Lynne got along very well. I know she hated working in that store." Freddy put her hands palms-down on the bar and looked sadly at Kirsten. "Not much help, am I?"

Dugan stood up. "Don't worry about it," he said. "You've got enough—"

"Wait a minute, Dugan." Kirsten's hand on his arm dropped him back onto the barstool. "There's something else. The business, Freddy," she said, "how much do you know about it?"

"Well, I know the types of things they—I mean we—sell. The books and . . . the other things. I've only been there a few times, actually. It's not the kind of place I like to go into, even if I'm an owner."

"What I mean is," Kirsten said, "do you know the daily or weekly income, the expenses, the overhead? Do you know who the suppliers are?" Dugan watched Freddy's eyes take on an empty look that made the answers obvious, but Kirsten pressed on. ". . . how many employees there are? Who they are? What they're paid?"

"I don't know any of that. It's all handled by my uncle. He manages the store and sends his reports to a lawyer, and I get my check from the lawyer each month."

Dugan was amazed. "For God's sake, Freddy," he said, "what lawyer? And how do you know you're getting what you're supposed to get?"

Her eyes suddenly flooded with tears. "You think I'm stupid, don't you? And naive. Maybe I am. But my Uncle Anton picked out the lawyer. I met him once. I didn't like him very much, but I guess he's all right. He told me he's an expert in this sort of work, a business-law and real estate specialist. The checks are usually almost enough to pay for my dad's care, and . . . I do intend to look into it more carefully . . . sometime."

"If I were you," Dugan said, "I'd—"

"That's all right, Freddy," Kirsten said, her fingernails raking across the back of Dugan's hand. "You can look into it when you're ready. I only asked because I thought maybe you could help us figure out who killed Lynne."

Suddenly Dugan forgot the stinging scratches on his hand and turned to Kirsten. "Hey, wait a minute. Help *us* figure out who killed Lynne? The police are supposed to do that. We're just looking for the damn boyfriend! Or *you* are, anyway."

"But we ought to offer whatever help we can. Besides," she added, "we were there. They might *think* we saw them, even though we didn't."

He could see that her message was meant for Freddy, so he kept quiet.

Kirsten turned back to Freddy. "So, any ideas?"

"None at all. The police asked that, too. All I know is, it frightens me. I called the lawyer who sends me the checks, and he said it might be mobsters or something. 'The big bambinos' is the way he put it."

Dugan groaned. *The big bambinos.* That phrase rang a bell he wasn't happy to hear.

SEVEN

business-law and real estate specialist? Are you kidding? I never said any such thing." Larry Candle yanked hard on the belt of his robe, a white terry-cloth affair, but his indignation was withering in the chill of Kirsten's glare. "Honest to God I didn't," he added lamely.

By the time they'd dropped Freddy at her place it was past midnight, but Kirsten had harassed and threatened the security guard at Larry's building until he got Larry on the intercom. Now they were barely inside his apartment door and Kirsten was after him. Dugan knew she wanted to strangle the plump little lawyer, or at least bounce him around the walls for a while. Dugan did, too, and would have chosen the wall of windows looking out over Lincoln Park and Lake Michigan from forty-one floors up.

"You held out on me, Larry." Kirsten had her finger in the man's face. "You lied."

"Wait a minute. Wait a minute. C'mon inside. Sit down. Have a drink or something, for chrissake."

"We're inside already," Dugan pointed out. "But where do we sit down?"

Larry's huge living room was two steps down from the entrance and had gray shag carpeting and white walls and nothing in it but a couple of puffy cushions tossed in one corner and a plastic folding chair next to a huge telescope on a tripod by the windows.

"This way, this way," he said, leading them past the telescope into a dining room that had its own floor-to-ceiling windows. An elegant brass and crystal chandelier hung directly over a cheap card table and the three other plastic folding chairs from Larry's matched set. In the corner, a portable TV sat on top of the carton it had been delivered in. Larry cleared the chairs, dumping newspapers onto the floor. "Sorry about the mess. I'm gonna get some furniture one of these days. I only been here about—I don't know—a year now, I guess. Since me and my wife split up. Shoot, she thought I'd go right down the toilet. Surprised the hell out of her when I leased a classy place like this. Course, I haven't had, uh, time yet to really decorate it like—"

"Larry!" Kirsten lashed out with her cop's voice and stopped him cold.

"What?" He barely managed a whisper, and Dugan actually felt a little sorry for him.

"Stop babbling. Dugan and I want coffee—and you're gonna need some, too."

Larry hustled through the doorway into the kitchen, obviously happy to escape her wrath for a few moments.

With Larry out of sight, Kirsten sat stone-faced and Dugan couldn't tell whether she was really as angry as she seemed, or just doing her job. They sat at the card table and listened to Larry run water and bang pots around in the kitchen.

He came back with three glasses clamped in the fingers of one pudgy hand and a bottle of Scotch in the other. "Water's on for coffee. Instant's all I have. Uh . . . how about something to start with?"

"Well—" Dugan began.

"Just coffee for us," Kirsten said. "And an explanation."

Larry sat down and carefully poured himself a glass of Scotch. "First off, I didn't lie. Maybe I should have told you I represented Lynne Bulasik and her uncle—and Freddy, too, I guess. But what difference does it make? Lynne's killing has nothing to do with what I hired you for." He downed some of the Scotch. "All I want you to do is find Lynne's boyfriend."

"Oh? And when did I ever promise I'd stick to just what *you* want?" Kirsten asked. "But besides that, I need all the facts if I'm going to find this guy. For one thing, Lynne didn't *have* any boyfriend."

"What are you talking about? I met the guy. At Walloon's. That's a bar where I was finally able to catch up with Rita, to talk to her. I didn't like talking in front of him and Lynne, but Rita said it was okay. I mean, I didn't actually *meet* the guy, like get his name or anything. But he was sitting there."

"Maybe there was a man there," Kirsten said, "but according to Freddy, Lynne wasn't the type to have *boy*friends at all."

Larry looked genuinely surprised. "I wouldn't know anything about that. She said *friend*. I thought she meant *boy*friend. Plus, maybe Freddy's wrong. I mean . . ." He took another slug of the Scotch. "Anyway, we still gotta find the guy, whoever he is. Jeez, I wish I could remember what he looked like. Big guy. Brown hair, or black maybe. Didn't say a word. Just sat there looking mean, or—I don't know—like he thought he was important or—"

"What do you know about Cousin Freddy's, Larry?" Kirsten leaned toward him across the table. "I mean, the business side of it?"

Larry looked blank for a moment. Dugan was surprised, too, at her sudden change in direction.

"The day-to-day business?" Larry said. "Hardly anything. What I know is, every month Anton Bulasik sends me a report of income and expenses, and a check for Freddy. All I—"

"And a check for you, too, right?" Dugan interrupted.

"Yeah, well, of course. I'm on retainer. I review the report and then send it to Freddy with her check. That's all I do. I don't keep any records or anything."

"And they *pay* you for that?" Kirsten asked.

"Well . . . not much, actually. But why complain? They wanna pay me a little bit for hardly any work, that's okay with me. I really don't know much about the business."

"So why was your first thought that the Mob must be behind Lynne's death?" Kirsten asked. "Do they have a piece of the business?"

"That was just talk, you know? I should learn to keep my mouth shut. If the Outfit has a piece of that business, it sure isn't written down anywhere. I read the trust documents once. The store's owned by a corporation. That corporation is owned by another corporation. The second corporation is the beneficiary of a trust that owns all the stock in a third corporation. After that it gets complicated, but if you trace it all the way back you get to B-K Enterprises, and Anton, Lynne, and Freddy own all the stock in B-K Enterprises. Or Anton and Freddy now, I guess. So—"

"Hold it," Dugan broke in again. "I mean, it's late, and maybe I missed something. But what you just said doesn't make sense, Larry."

"Huh? Well, what's the difference? It's something tricky like that, anyway."

"And you set it up?" Kirsten asked.

"Are you kidding? I wasn't even involved back then. Some hot shot at Eames and Barnhill put the papers together. Freddy's father wanted someone from a high-class law firm, and he'd heard about Eames because Bruce Hardison's there. So he called Hardison, and Hardison handed it over to some partner in the firm's trust department."

"Who's Bruce Hardison?" Kirsten asked.

"A top rainmaker for Eames and Barnhill," Dugan said, "and an expert in constitutional law. Handles First Amendment cases all over the country—defends everyone from newspaper reporters to neo-Nazi skinheads to antiwar nuns."

"Right," Larry added. "But he's defended plenty of sleazeball porno shops and strip joints, too. Every creep in the filth business—especially anyone with the megabucks fees he asks for—has heard of Bruce Hardison. How he keeps his spotless reputation beats me."

"Maybe he's honest," Dugan said. "That helps a little."

"Bullshit," Larry snorted. "He's got money, and that helps a lot."

"So," Kirsten asked, "where do you fit in?"

Larry drained his glass, looked longingly at the bottle, then apparently thought better of it. "I handled a personal injury case for

Anton Bulasik and he liked the result. The trust requires a lawyer's review, and after Freddy's father got hurt, Anton didn't wanna keep paying the rates Hardison's partner at Eames and Barnhill charged, so he hired me. I never told that spacey girl Freddy I was a business and real estate specialist. I'm just a lawyer. I wouldn't say I *fit in*' at all. Personally, I think the store is disgusting. You should see the—Well, I guess you did see."

"Yes," Kirsten said, "we saw too much."

"That wasn't my—" Larry jumped a foot as a high-pitched whistle pierced the air. "That's the water for the coffee. Lemme get it." He fled into the kitchen again.

Dugan listened to the rattle of cups and spoons for what seemed like an awfully long time just for instant coffee.

But Larry finally stuck his head through the door. "Anyone want—" He stopped, interrupted by a soft, but clear, tapping from somewhere behind Larry in the kitchen, like a key on a metal door. "Who the hell . . . ?" Larry started to say, then disappeared back into the kitchen.

Dugan heard a door open, and then a loud, harsh sob, like the word "How," but inhaled.

"Larry?" Kirsten yelled, rising from her chair. "What is it?"

But even as she called out, there was a muffled explosion—together with breaking glass and then what sounded like the clatter of a cup hitting the kitchen floor.

"Larry!" This time Kirsten screamed.

Dugan jumped up, but she was ahead of him into the kitchen. Larry was crumpled back against the countertop, his head hanging down, as though staring at the backs of his hands—pink, hairy hands, held crossed over his white-robed chest like some chubby angel on a holy card.

An open door led from the kitchen into the carpeted hallway. Kirsten was already at the door, calling back to Dugan. "My purse! Get my purse!"

"Purse?" he yelled back, confused.

"The gun, dammit!" She was in the hall by then. "The gun!"

Of course. The gun. He ran back and grabbed her purse from the table.

Back in the kitchen, Larry had slid down to the floor, his back against the counter front. Dugan leaped over his outstretched legs and raced out into the corridor. No other doors in either direction were open.

Far to his left, Kirsten was at the stairway exit, her ear pressed to the closed door. When he got there she put a finger to her lips, then grabbed the gun from the purse he'd forgotten by then he was holding in his hand. Waving him back, she depressed the lever-handle and slowly pushed open the heavy fire door.

Dugan peered over her shoulder. The concrete landing was empty, stairs leading up and down. Somewhere far below, a door slammed shut.

"God knows what floor he's on. And he'll probably take an elevator to the parking garage," Kirsten said. She sighed. "Let's go see about Larry."

Dugan really didn't want to *see about Larry,* but he followed.

Larry was still in the same sitting position on the kitchen floor, legs outstretched. His head was up, though, and tilted back. He was staring—bug-eyed and slack-jawed—at the doorway, his face drained as pale as the kitchen countertops.

As they entered, Larry's mouth closed, then opened again. "Jesus," he said finally, "I coulda been hurt."

EIGHT

S on of a bitch had a gun a foot long," Larry said, as Dugan hauled him to his feet. "Everything happened at once. Kirsten yells my name. He jumps a foot and I duck sideways." He swiveled his head. "Bullet musta gone through that cabinet door. Jesus, glass all over the place."

Kirsten closed the door to the hallway. Crouching to the floor, she picked up a coffee mug with a broken handle and an envelope and put them on the counter. "Just one man?" she asked.

"Yeah. Big guy. Piece of paper in his hand. Then he pulled the gun. Except for a red ski mask, I couldn't even tell you what he was wearing."

"Piece of paper?" Dugan asked.

Kirsten took the envelope from the counter, holding it by its edges. "May I?" Without waiting for an answer, she carefully removed a single sheet of paper. Holding it by one corner, she shook it unfolded, glanced at it, then showed it to Dugan.

It was ordinary white copy paper, with a typed message. Dugan read it out loud: *"Pornography is terrorism. And we won't be victims anymore."*

Larry headed for the dining room. "I need a drink."

Dugan followed him, as Kirsten turned the heat back on under the teakettle. Larry had barely time to knock down a gulp of Scotch before the kettle started whistling again, and in a moment Kirsten joined them at the card table. Dugan took one of the two steaming mugs she brought with her.

"Better stick to this," Kirsten said, putting the second mug of coffee in front of Larry, and pulling the Scotch away. "We need to think," she added.

"Actually," Dugan said, "we need to call the police."

"In a minute," she answered. "But first—Larry, isn't it strange that no one on this floor seems to have heard anything. The gun had a silencer, of course, but still—"

"I don't know," he said. "There's just four apartments on each floor, and the soundproofing is great. Besides, you never see anyone around here. A lot of these apartments are second homes for people from the suburbs, or owned by companies that need places near downtown."

"Another thing," Kirsten said. "Why in the world would you open your door at this time of night without first checking through the peephole?"

"Me? I didn't open the door. Damn guy opened it himself. Musta picked the lock. Then he sees me and pulls a gun. Jesus, what a day. First the supreme court, and now—"

Dugan stood up. "I'm calling 911."

"Fine," Kirsten said, but she didn't seem much interested.

He made the call from the phone on the wall just inside the kitchen and sat back down. "They'll be here in a few minutes."

"What the hell is this about?" Larry asked. "Where's that note?"

"It's in the kitchen," Kirsten said. "But we shouldn't touch it." She stood up and looked out the windows into the night. "Messages like that are going to porn shops all over the metropolitan area."

"I don't own any porn shop, for God's sake."

Kirsten turned her back to the windows and faced Larry. "You're connected with one, though. Question is, how would most people know about that connection? You said you just review some records and send Freddy her checks."

"Yeah. Well, there *is* one other thing."

"Of course," Kirsten said.

"I'm also their attorney in a suit brought against Cousin Freddy's and another adult bookstore. The plaintiffs want the places shut down."

"On what basis?" Dugan asked.

"Some mope who raped a bunch of women says he reads a lot of that crap. Says he buys it at Cousin Freddy's and the other place. The plaintiffs raise all kinds of constitutional issues, sex discrimination—a lot of stuff. I filed an appearance on behalf of Cousin Freddy's."

"Why you?" Dugan said. "You wouldn't know a constitutional issue from a traffic ticket, for chrissake."

Larry's face turned red. "I don't have to take—"

"Dugan's not insulting you, Larry," Kirsten broke in. "He's just saying you don't know any more about that kind of case than he does."

"Well . . ." Dugan said.

But Larry's anger was defused. "Anyway, I don't *have* to know anything. They started out suing just one store and that one retained Bruce Hardison. Then they added Cousin Freddy's. Hardison can't represent both because there's potential conflicts of interest down the line if we can't get the case dismissed before trial. No sense paying two expensive lawyers. So I got Cousin Freddy's. Hardison does all the work—research and briefs and stuff. I just show up. If there's a trial sometime, I'll have something to do. Thing is, I'm of record in the case and my name's been in the paper a couple of times." He looked longingly at the Scotch, then took a sip of coffee. "But I'm out of the case, anyway, after today."

"I'd get out, too," Dugan said. "The note alone would do it for me—even without a bullet hole in my kitchen cabinet."

"Hell, I was out before that. The supreme court—"

The phone rang. Larry jumped up and answered it. He listened for a few seconds, then said, "All right. No, no big deal." He came back and sat down. "That was the guard. Cops are on their way up," he said.

"That's the second time you started to say something about the supreme court," Kirsten said.

44

Larry's round face sagged. "Is it? Well . . . they pulled my ticket today. My law license. Suspended. Because Rita says I took her money. Not even a hearing."

"Can they do that?" Kirsten said. "I mean, without any hearing?"

"They sure did it to me," he said. "You think lawyers got any rights? No way! Criminals, punks, thugs—they got rights. Knock down some old lady, kick the crap out of her, grab her purse . . . the next day you're out on the street again, practicing your profession, looking for another old lady. Not lawyers, though. They—"

"Okay, okay, we get the point," Dugan said. "Anyway, Kirsten, it's called an 'interim suspension.' Supposedly used only when there's evidence of ongoing danger to the public from a lawyer continuing to practice."

"Not even a goddamn hearing," Larry growled. "But at least it gets me out of that Cousin Freddy's case. Tell you what, though. With all that's going on, it's gonna be awful hard for Anton Bulasik to find another lawyer."

There was a loud knock on the door and Kirsten stood up. "Oh, I wouldn't worry," she said. "We know a lawyer who's ready to jump right in." She paused at the living room door and smiled back at Dugan. "Don't we, darling?"

NINE

Driving home, Kirsten was keyed up, her mind careening from one thing to another. She was exhausted, but knew she wouldn't be able to sleep.

It had taken an hour of confusion and radio calls, but the police investigators finally decided the shooting at Larry Candle's should be handed over to Hoffmeier and LaMotta. Those two would review the paperwork and contact everyone the next day. When she and Dugan left, one of the lab men was still digging the slug out of the back wall of Larry's kitchen cabinet.

Maybe she'd made up her mind too quickly about their getting more deeply involved. But she wasn't going to waste time going back and forth about it. They were already too far into this thing to get out, and they might as well be where they could learn as much as possible. She'd always trusted her instincts, and she would this time, too.

She figured Dugan was mentally practicing his arguments on their short, silent ride home. He should have known it was hopeless, of course, but after she parked the car and they were headed for their front door, she let him give it his best shot.

"... make a fool of myself," he was saying. "I don't know the first thing about constitutional law. I'll have to write briefs and argue case law and—"

"Nonsense. Just do what Larry's been doing. Follow Bruce Hardison's lead. And besides, suppose you lose the case. What happens? They shut down that crummy store. Think of it—the *worst* that can happen is you *win* the case."

By then they were in the elevator. "Right," he said. "And meanwhile we get threatening notes and bullet holes in our kitchen cabinets, or maybe our foreheads—which I guess I'd prefer to a broken neck."

"But what's the difference? Why not place ourselves where we can learn as much as possible. We're involved, like it or not. We already got a good look at the two men that must have killed Lynne Bulasik. We've already had our car blown to bits."

"*You* got a good look," he said. "And for that matter, *your* car, too."

"What's mine is yours, you know—or was." They stepped off the elevator and Kirsten turned the key that de-activated the apartment's alarm system. "It'll be a team project. I'll provide the confidential inquiries and security services, like it says on my office door. All you have to do is fake the legal work."

"I don't remember hiring on for any team project," he said, but she could see he'd given up.

She knew Dugan enjoyed his self-crafted image as a slightly tarnished, run-of-the-mill lawyer who exhausted his store of courage by sparring with insurance adjusters on the telephone. A comfortable image, and maybe he was tempted to believe in it. But the fact was that Dugan never backed off from any real challenge. At the police academy he'd been near the top in everything—pistol range, martial arts—not to mention number one in the classroom stuff. Dugan was, well, she'd never actually say it to his face, of course—and love might have *something* to do with it—but she thought Dugan was just about perfect.

"You could be on a worse team," she said, taking his hand and pulling him gently into the apartment. "Besides, think of the fringe benefits."

"Fringe benefits?"

"Oh, you'll think of *something*," she said. "And if you don't . . . " Slipping her hand from his, she let her fingertips glide ever-so-lightly across his palm and whispered, "I will."

She felt a familiar shiver run through his hand.

The old fingertips-across-the-palm routine. Works every time. Maybe she'd get some sleep, after all.

TEN

Dugan waited alone on a comfortable couch in the elegant thirty-sixth-floor reception room of Eames & Barnhill. He'd been angry at first when he woke up to find Kirsten already gone—but he wasn't really surprised. She followed her own agenda.

Laid out carefully on the teak and glass table in front of him were that day's *Wall Street Journal,* that week's *Business Week,* and several copies of the law firm's PR brochure. Judging by the booklet's embossed cover and full-color photography, the cost of design and printing might have paid a couple of months of Dugan's office overhead. Like Kirsten said, attracting clients costs money. These guys paid a marketing firm; Dugan paid police officers. He liked his way better.

The brochure was full of rhetoric and buzzwords. Among other glamour clients, the firm represented numerous big-name companies in labor disputes, and boasted one of the city's premier labor law departments. Dugan read the introduction to that section of the brochure:

> Faithful to the ideals of its founding partners some six decades ago, Eames & Barnhill continues its solid commitment to the innovative and aggressive representation of commerce and industry, in the face of those organizational challenges which perennially threaten

the growth and prosperity so basic to a free and flour-
ishing economic environment.

He'd have to show that one to Peter and Fred. They'd love it. Translated, it meant Eames & Barnhill was like that drum-banging
bunny on TV—union-busting for sixty years . . . and still going.

A woman bustled across the waiting room toward him. Gray-
haired and smiling, she looked out of place, somehow—like a Sunday school teacher lost in the halls of Mammon. "Mr. Hardison will
see you now," she said.

Dugan had an eleven-o'clock appointment and it was eleven on
the dot. Not your ordinary lawyer, this Hardison. Folding the
brochure and shoving it in his hip pocket, he followed the secretary
down a labyrinth of hallways.

Hardison's office was the size of a handball court with windows,
and despite scores of books and files, was very orderly. The great
man himself was talking on the phone. His desk was nearly empty.
The closest thing to clutter was the array of papers and casebooks
scattered across a mahogany library table at the opposite end of the
room.

As his secretary steered Dugan toward a leather client's chair,
Hardison set the phone down and rose to his feet. "Bruce Hardison," he said. "Nice to meet you. Thank you, Eleanor."

Eleanor disappeared.

Hardison was close to sixty, tall and fit, with sand-colored hair
receding from his forehead. Although he was pleasant enough, it
was clear that "nice to meet you" was about it for small talk.

"Have a seat," he said. "Larry Candle called this morning. Said
you'd be substituting for him. Too bad about his problems. But . . .
life goes on."

"Yes," Dugan said. "Let's hope so, anyway."

Hardison nodded. "You've heard about the threats, then. Do
they bother you?"

"They don't *bother* me. They scare the hell outta me."

"I think they're ludicrous," Hardison said.

"You didn't see the strange twist to Lynne Bulasik's head."

"Oh, that's right. It was you and your wife that found her, wasn't it. But I'm not convinced her death was related to these threats. That was a professional killing, possibly Mob-related, for motives I wouldn't presume to speculate about. On the other hand, these sophomoric threats to dozens of perfectly legitimate businesses seem absurd. My own clients have taken some security measures, of course, but they don't intend to be intimidated by the rantings of some harmless lunatic."

Dugan wasn't sure he believed in such things as *harmless* lunatics, but he let that go and asked, "How much did Larry Candle tell you?"

"I didn't speak with him. He left a message. Said his law license was suspended, gave your name, and said I'd be contacted by you as new counsel for Cousin Freddy's."

"That's it?" Dugan asked. "Nothing more?"

"Not a thing." Hardison stared at him. "Should there have been more?"

"Last night someone broke into Larry's apartment and took a shot at him." Hardison's jaw dropped, but before he could say anything Dugan continued. "Larry wasn't hurt, but I'd say he's delighted to be out of the Cousin Freddy's case."

"So he thinks the shooting is connected to the case?"

"The shooter left a note. 'Pornography is terrorism,' it said. 'And we won't be victims anymore.' At the very least, I'd say someone's pretty upset about smut."

" 'Pornography is terrorism.' " Hardison repeated the words slowly. "That was the wording?"

" 'And we won't be victims anymore.' That was it—verbatim. Why?"

"I often get strong objections, even threats, when I represent unpopular clients. They never amount to anything. This time, though, I've received no threats. Not yet, anyway." He paused and looked at his watch. "I have a lunch meeting, but first let me tell you a little about this pornography litigation. The wording of that note might be quite significant."

Hardison explained that the suit sought an injunction shutting down the stores. "Of the three plaintiffs, two are women who were brutally raped and sodomized by a man who claims he bought pornography at the defendants' stores. The third plaintiff is a feminist organization called WARP that—"

"Hold on," Dugan interrupted. "Did you say 'WARP'?"

"Women Against Rape and Pornography," Hardison explained. "WARP is the real force behind the case. Their lawyers are a couple of women, militant feminists. Problem is, they don't just *represent* the organization. They're two of its founding members. They say they chose the name WARP to emphasize that women's truth looks warped through the eyes of a male-dominated culture."

"There's some truth to that, when you think about it," Dugan said.

"I find the entire concept ridiculous. Rhetoric, pure and simple. Anyway, WARP's lawyers are something out of a bad dream. Bright, but very hostile. One of them especially, a Debra Morelli, is mean, sarcastic, and utterly untrustworthy. Litigating with those two is like walking barefoot through a vacant lot in Uptown."

"Sounds awful," Dugan said.

"It *is* awful," Hardison answered. "And frankly, I love every minute of it. What many people don't know is that, with a few exceptions, these free-speech cases bring in some very large fees. The troublesome thing about them is that so many of the clients themselves are so repulsive—skinheads and Nazis, Klan members, pornographers, sleazy gossip columnists. I have to keep reminding myself it's the Constitution I'm really defending, and not my dishonorable clients. This time, though, the people on the other side—at least WARP and its lawyers—are almost as despicable as my clients, and I'm having a ball."

"I'm happy for you," Dugan said. "But what does all this have to do with the wording on the note left with Larry Candle?"

"WARP's position in the case is one that's popular with some feminists in their so-called war on pornography around the country. Sexually explicit literature has long been held to be protected by the First Amendment. But WARP argues that pornography isn't entitled to constitutional free-speech protection at all, because it's not really the expression of ideas. They say commerce in pornography is an *activity*, a discriminatory action. They compare it to cross-burning. Torching a cross in the front yard of the first black family in an all-white neighborhood is far more than just an expression of one's belief that African Americans are inferior."

"And it's not constitutionally protected," Dugan said.

"Exactly. Burning a flag is the expression of political dissent. But burning a cross is different. It's an act—"

"I got it," Dugan said. "An act of terrorism."

Hardison stood and walked to the table at the other end of his office. He picked up a four-inch-wide expandable folder. "I've had copies made for you of the pleadings filed in the Cousin Freddy's case. I doubt Larry Candle ever read them."

"You've been carrying the ball so far," Dugan said, cringing as he took the heavy stack of papers, "and I don't expect that to change."

"Fine. But I do suggest you read at least the plaintiffs' brief in opposition to our motion for summary judgment. They continually hammer away on one theme. 'Pornography is terrorism,' they say. 'And the victims are women.' Very similar language to the note you found, isn't it?"

"Are you suggesting some anti-smut group sent a hit man to kill Larry Candle?"

"I'm merely—"

"And how about Lynne Bulasik? You think maybe it wasn't the Mob after all? Do you think it was these WARP people?" Dugan couldn't get himself to speak in anything but questions.

"In my opinion, it's too bizarre to be true—that a feminist group like WARP would send someone to kill a clerk in an adult book-store, or the store's lawyer. But still, the similarity between WARP's statements and the note left at Larry Candle's is undeniable, and I intend to notify the police." Hardison grabbed his suit coat from the back of a chair. "I have to run. Meanwhile, there's certainly nothing you or I can do—or *should* do—about that part of this affair."

"I know. I just wish I could convince my wife of that."

"Oh?" Hardison said, slipping into his coat. "What's she—"

"Larry Candle hired her to find some witnesses, and Lynne Bulasik was one of them. We go to talk to Lynne, and find she's been killed almost before our eyes. Then someone shoots at Larry while we're with him. Kirsten feels, well, personally involved. She was a great investigator with the Chicago Police Department. Now that she's on her own, she's as effective as ever, mostly because she can't *stand* losing. She's not only determined to find the other witnesses Larry needs, but she seems obsessed with figuring out the whole . . . Well, that's not your problem."

"Thank God it isn't," Hardison said. "Let's go. I'll walk you to the elevator."

ELEVEN

K irsten sat down at a table by the window of Dunkin' Donuts to wait. She glanced at her watch. Dugan was probably still talking to Bruce Hardison. Meanwhile, she was waiting for Parker Gillson, and he was late. She'd met Park back when he was on the radio, driving around the city phoning in on-the-scene reports of tenement fires and other urban excitement. Before that, he'd been a rising star, a black man out of the south side's Ida B. Wells housing project who turned into a bright, tenacious reporter for the *Sun-Times.* He'd been on his way to a daily column—if he could only have stayed sober.

But that all fell apart, and he was doing radio and Kirsten was working security on the Magnificent Mile when a bomb scare brought them together. Not just a scare, either, as it turned out. An actual bomb was discovered in the Concordia Building—then three more. They'd spent a frantic, frightening six hours together, having to trust each other first with their lives, and later with their promises never to tell the whole of what had actually happened. In the end, three of the four bombs were disarmed, Park got his story, and Kirsten got the promotion to supervisor and the drudgery of management that soon drove her right out of the security firm she worked for. As for the bad guys, they all got away, except the Syrian with the long hair who'd been smothering the fourth bomb when it blew his torso in one direction and his legs in two others.

It was just how that happened that they'd promised to keep to themselves.

Six months later, the booze swept in again and washed Park off the radio, just as it had at the *Sun-Times*. Kirsten hadn't known about that, until someone remarked at a party one night "what a shame it was" about Parker Gillson. Seems nobody knew where he was.

She'd had time on her hands and no paying clients, so . . .

She found him in a walk-up near Lawrence and Broadway, lying alone on his face on a grease-stained mattress on the floor.

Well, not entirely alone. Flicking on the ceiling light, she'd interrupted a couple of water bugs frantically copulating on the back of his outstretched hand. Roaches were cleaning out the empty bottles of apricot brandy and scavenging the fetid remains of old Big Macs and chicken-leg dinners. She found tiny, round black beetles in his jacket pocket—and she didn't even want to look too closely at the bits of white oozing around on the gaping sore on his ankle.

He smelled like vomit and urine and something worse—maybe death. She rolled him over, and when he was able to focus his eyes, he recognized her. Slurring his words, he called her a "stuck-up little tight-ass liberal honky bitch"—for openers—and told her to get the fuck out of there and leave him be.

She'd gotten him first to Illinois Masonic Medical Center. From there he went to Lutheran General for rehab, then finally to a place called Serenity Lodge in South Dakota. He'd had other friends, too, some of them pretty big names, people he'd been fair with as a reporter—more fair to some people than they deserved. Among that group was at least one justice of the Illinois Supreme Court. Maybe that helped and maybe it didn't, but eventually Park landed a job as an investigator—finding witnesses, taking statements, that sort of thing—for the supreme court's Attorney Registration and Disciplinary Commission.

"Not bad, either," he'd told her on the phone that morning when she called. "Doesn't pay much, but hey . . . what's new about that?

It's clean, it's safe, and I got plenty of time and energy left at the end of the day for AA meetings."

So she waited for Park Gillson and drank coffee and stared out the window of Dunkin' Donuts, watching the amazing array of people on Broadway and wondering why in the world she was going to all this trouble for a guy like Larry Candle. Except, deep down, she knew her determination to find the witnesses he needed really had less to do with Larry than it had to do with her own stubbornness, her lifelong refusal to—

"You look great." It was Park, sliding into the seat across the table from her.

"Thanks." She watched him pour half-and-half into his coffee and bite into the first of two French crullers he'd brought with him. "You're putting on weight, Park. Better watch it."

"Good God, woman, you never change, do you?" He grinned and she noticed he'd had his teeth capped. Nothing like a steady job, with dental benefits. "Always meddlin' in other folks' business," Park said.

"Sorry, but—"

"But it's true, right?" He drank some coffee. "You know, I was thinking as I drove up here. This place is just a few blocks from that rat hole you dragged me out of."

"Oh . . . well," she said, shifting her gaze modestly away from his face, "that's, uh, old news, Park." What she didn't say was that she'd picked this spot for that very reason. She wanted all the leverage she could get out of his gratitude. It was deceitful, but—

"Yeah, just a few blocks," he repeated. "I was thinking maybe you needed a favor, and maybe you picked this spot just to remind me how much I owe you."

"My, what a devious mind you have. I mean, you're the one who told me you'd be on the north side serving subpoenas this morning."

"Right. I said Rogers Park. *West* Rogers Park. That's five miles from here."

She sipped some coffee. "Well, anyway, here we are."

"Uh-huh."

"I need an address."

"S'pose you already tried the phone book."

"If she's there, she's under a different name. What I have may be a stage name. Rita Ranchero."

She saw recognition come and go in his eyes. "Does sound like a stage name," he said. "But how would I know anything about this Miss Ranchero? Unless it was private information I learned in the course of my employment. In which case, of course, you surely wouldn't ask me to reveal it. Because that would be contrary to the duty of confidentiality incumbent on me as a trusted employee of an arm of the Illinois supreme court. In other words," he added, "they'd fire my ass in a minute."

"But only if they knew." She broke Park's second cruller in half and bit into her half. "And how would they?"

He licked some pastry from his fingers and washed it down with coffee. "You really think I'm putting on weight?"

"It's obvious."

"Damn. Maybe I oughta find a gym . . . start workin' out again." He picked up what was left of the second cruller, then set it down and looked out the window. "Used to be this little work-out gym . . . around Diversey and Ashland? First floor of a two-story brick building, next door to a cleaners. Drove by there the other day and the place was gone—the gym I mean, not the building. Cleaners is still there, too. But there's this gift store or something now in place of the gym. Funny name it has, the Cubic Globe Gallery. They say the new owner is this chick that used to dance—at least they *call* it dancing—in one of those glass booths at a second-floor club on Clark Street. Came into some money and bought the building on Diversey. Moved out the gym and put in this Cubic Globe. Don't know what happened to the gym." When he finally turned away from the window, it was to look down toward his stomach. "Guess I better find *some* damn place to work out if my weight's that obvious."

"Well," Kirsten said, "maybe not *that* obvious."

"Really?" He finished off the cruller. "Gotta keep up my strength."

They talked for a few minutes about what was going on in their lives.

Park was on his way to subpoena two witnesses to the signing of a woman's will. "Eighty-eight years old, and she leaves a ton of money to her landlady. Then she dies and the landlady turns out to be the longtime lady friend of the lawyer who drew up her will. So now we're investigating the lawyer."

"Sounds suspicious to me," Kirsten said.

"Course it does. Thing is, I talked to the lawyer, and the lady friend. They say they took care of the old woman. The lawyer swears he begged her to get a different lawyer to write her will, and she just wouldn't do it. I mean, the man's telling the truth. I know he is. Now he's in a bunch of trouble, just 'cause he was too lazy— or too dumb—to get some different lawyer to talk to the old broad." He looked at his watch, then stood up. "But then, that's life, right? People all the time gettin' themselves into trouble they could just as easy avoid." He leaned toward her, his palms flat on the tabletop. "You know what I mean, Kirsten?"

She looked up at him. "I know what you mean, Park. Thanks."

TWELVE

F orty-five minutes later, Kirsten left the Tempo a block south of
Diversey. The signs said you couldn't park there without a special resident's sticker, but she figured Rita Ranchero wouldn't
spend much time with her anyway.

The sun was bright and the air was clear and autumn-crisp, but
mild for November. The blue wool dress was plenty warm, so she
left her raincoat in the car.

It was a narrow street with cars parked along both sides. Most
of the leaves had fallen from the trees that lined the block, giving
a clear view of recently rehabbed two- and three-story residential
buildings standing shoulder to shoulder behind tall, mostly
wrought iron fences. The gates all had locks with security buzzers
and intercoms, belying what was otherwise a scene of tranquil gen-
trification. When she got to the corner, she turned left on Diversey.

The Cubic Globe Gallery was definitely striving for the upscale
look. The window boasted of "Items of Classic Beauty from Every
Corner of the Earth." There was a stylized drawing of the planet,
its continents outlined, not on a sphere, but on a square block floating in space. Below that was written: "R. Randall, Prop." and "Open
Tues–Sat, 11:00 to 4:00." Better hours than some club on Clark
Street, for sure.

It was past eleven and the sign on the ledge in the window said OPEN, but the door was locked. With one hand still on the handle, Kirsten leaned against the glass and peered through. As she did, there was a buzz and a click from the lock and she fell forward when the door swung open.

When she'd regained her balance she looked up and saw a man talking into a telephone at a desk in a corner near the back of the store. He nodded solemnly at Kirsten and swept one white-shirted arm out in a formal gesture that invited her to browse.

The store was one large, high-ceilinged room, the floor a light-colored natural wood, highly polished. Scattered throughout were dozens of white cubes, each cube about two feet to a side, on and around which art works and handicraft items were tastefully arranged. Some of the cubes stood alone, while others were stacked atop each other at odd angles, creating geometrically interesting display shelving. The art and artifacts seemed to be mostly from the Far East and Africa, but there were examples of Native American pottery and weaving as well. A few prayer rugs and other fabric hangings lined the walls, as well as several large photographs, strange Asian-looking landscapes in stark black and white— empty, soulless landscapes.

Other than the white cubes, there were no tables, counters, or display cases. A couch and a couple of comfortable-looking chairs were gathered around the desk where the man sat, but there was no other furniture.

Nor were there any customers.

Kirsten roamed the room. None of the pieces had a price tag, but they all looked expensive and she wondered whether sales warranted the investment in inventory. She decided an operation like this wouldn't hope to make it by selling to people coming in off the street. Most sales would be to designers and decorators. And then there were all those other reasons for going into the upscale import business—smuggling, fencing, and money laundering were a few that came to mind.

Her attention was captured by a foot-high bronze Buddha, sitting alone cross-legged on a single white cube. It looked so . . . solid. She wondered for no reason at all how much it weighed. She reached toward it.

"Beautiful workmanship."

The voice beside her—not two feet from her ear—was deep and soft, but it might have been a banshee shriek, the way she jumped and snatched her hand back.

He seemed not to notice. She had no idea how he'd made it from the desk to where she stood. "That Buddha looks very . . . heavy," she said. He was tall, broad-shouldered, and *hard*-looking, somehow. She had to tilt her head back awkwardly to look up at him.

He smiled, and actually also bowed slightly, holding his huge hands clasped in front of him, chest high. He wore baggy black pants and his white dress shirt was buttoned up to the top, with no necktie. His complexion was dark, still showing the remnants of some very bad acne ten or twenty years ago. His long, dark hair was pulled back into a ponytail. "I was referring to your earrings," he said. "Beautiful workmanship."

"Oh." She didn't like the idea, but knew she was probably blushing. She took a step backward. "They're . . . uh . . . just something my husband gave me."

"I see. Well, is there something you're particularly interested in? The Buddha, maybe? Or perhaps one of those Tibetan landscapes. I'm particularly fond of them."

"No, actually, I . . ." It was hard to gather her thoughts, with the man's eyes boring into her as though looking right through to her mind. "I suppose you're . . . Mr. Randall," she said finally, thrusting her hand out.

He didn't shake her hand, just continued to stare at her. "Mr. Randall . . . " He paused. "Mr. Randall is not here. Mr. Randall is dead."

"Oh. I'm so—"

"You needn't be sorry. No one else is." He didn't say it as though it were a joke.

Kirsten didn't like the way the conversation was going. She decided on a direct approach. "I'm looking for someone," she said. "Rita Ranchero. I thought I might find her here."

His eyes were as empty and bleak as the Tibetan landscapes. "You are mistaken." His voice was flat. "There is no Rita Ranchero connected with the Cubic Globe. Now, perhaps you'll excuse me." He took her left arm just above her elbow.

Although he didn't squeeze tightly, his hand still felt like a steel clamp, and she was surprised at how easily she let herself be escorted out. When the door clicked shut behind her, she took a few steps, then stopped and looked in through the store window.

He was back on the phone already. But his eyes were looking out through the window, right back at her.

THIRTEEN

L ate that same afternoon, although his mind was mostly on why he hadn't heard yet from Kirsten, Dugan had just made his proposal to his staff. The idea wasn't well received.

"What the hell you talkin' about, for chrissake?" Fred Schustein stared at Dugan and threw his arms wide in indignation.

Peter Rienzo jumped away to avoid Fred's swinging Pepsi can. "Yeah, Dugan," Peter said, "it's your decision, not ours."

"I know. I know," Dugan answered. "But sit down a minute, guys, please." He drummed his fingers on his desk while they settled into the clients' chairs across from him. "All you have to do is talk to 'em. The first two are coming in tomorrow." He'd been reading the court papers Bruce Hardison gave him, and he just wasn't up to interviewing potential new associates. "Molly's cut the list to five," he said, "a man and four women. Just give me your best guess."

Fred shook his head. "I don't know—"

"Thing is," Peter said, "whoever you hire won't be working on comp cases, which is all we do. We'll look kinda stupid, they start askin' questions about your side of the office."

"You won't look stupid. You're lawyers, aren't you? Pretending you know what you're talking about is your job. Besides, anyone acts like they know more than you, they're probably a smart-ass and we don't want 'em anyway. So—"

Dugan's phone buzzed and Molly came on the intercom speaker. "It's Kirsten on oh-three."

"Gotta take this call, guys. So, we all set?"

"Yeah, sure. Why not?" Peter said. He and Fred got to their feet and started out of the office.

At the door Fred turned back toward Dugan. "Four outta the five are women, huh?" He put on his best dirty-old-man leer. "Easy. We'll pick the one with the biggest pair o' lungs."

When they were gone, Dugan grabbed the phone. "Been wondering when you'd call," he said.

"You doing anything important?" Kirsten asked.

"Mostly worrying. But I just got Fred and Peter to interview my job applicants. They're looking forward to it."

"You think that's smart? You'll be the one working with the person, you know."

"I know. And I'll be responsible if they screw up, too. But I just can't keep my mind on business, with things going the way they are."

"You mean we should give up the search for Rita Ranchero, don't you? And that other man."

"I wish you wouldn't keep saying 'we.' But what I mean is that these are people who break women's necks, and shoot at lawyers who defend sleazeball porno shops."

"Speaking of which," she said, "what did Bruce Hardison have to say?"

"It's a long story and it's almost five o'clock. I'll leave here about seven and meet you somewhere."

"Make it six-thirty, at Bert's. And, uh, Dugan?" Kirsten paused. "You're not angry are you? I mean . . . you're still with me on this, right?"

He was surprised at her tone, and tried to remember the last time she'd looked for that kind of reassurance from him. He let her dangle a few seconds, then said, "I'm not angry and I'm still with you. I love you and I'll see you at six-thirty. Meanwhile, what are you—"

"Love you, too. See you at Bert's." She hung up.

Kirsten turned away from the phone and walked from the Shell station back to the Tempo. She felt better after talking to Dugan, but was glad she hadn't told him where she was—and what she was thinking of doing.

After she'd left the Cubic Globe Gallery she'd spent an hour driving up and down North Lake Shore Drive, sometimes cutting over to the lakefront and racing back and forth through the parking lots and along the curving parkways from Foster Avenue to Montrose Harbor, then back to the Drive, down to Lincoln Park, and then north again.

When she was finally certain there was no one following her, she left the car near the Farm-in-the-Zoo, then walked to the lakefront and back to kill time.

By four o'clock she was back in the Tempo, parked near Diversey and Ashland, across the street and half a block away from the Cubic Globe. At four-twenty, she saw someone turn the sign around in the window so it said CLOSED. It was nearly five, though, by the time the man with the ponytail came out of the store, tried the door behind him, then went to the curb and hailed a taxi.

That was when she'd called Dugan.

Now she was back in the Tempo again, and waiting. By five-thirty it was as dark as it was going to get on that busy street. She wished her raincoat were a darker color, but she couldn't do without it. It was colder now, and she'd be even more conspicuous not wearing any coat. She got out of the car, put some money in the meter to carry it to six o'clock, and crossed the street at the corner.

The darkened second-floor windows over the Cubic Globe seemed to absorb rather than reflect the street lighting, and she realized they were painted over. Through the store window, dim security lights revealed that most of the merchandise had been put away somewhere. High up in the two back corners, tiny red eyes blinked relentlessly as TV cameras silently scanned the premises.

Kirsten walked to the corner and then south to the alley that ran parallel to Diversey, behind the Cubic Globe. To her left along the alley were the fenced backyards and garages of homes that fronted on the street south of Diversey. On her right was the massive, three-story apartment building whose first-floor stores faced Diversey starting at the corner. Three sets of stairs crisscrossed up the alley side of the building. Vertical wooden slats marched side-by-side diagonally back and forth up the stairways, across second-floor porches past the back doors of apartments, then cut diagonally back and forth again up to the third floor and across those porches. A familiar urban pattern, and somehow comforting in its geometric precision.

Just past the apartment building was the back of the two-story brick building that held the Cubic Globe Gallery. It had its own wooden stairs up to a porch that ran along the back of the second floor. There was one second-floor door, closed and windowless. But faint light came from two windows to the right of the door.

Maybe it was where they stored merchandise from the store. Maybe it was an apartment and Rita Ranchero lived there. Maybe it was rented out and had nothing to do with the Cubic Globe. Maybe Rita had nothing to do with the Cubic Globe. And maybe Kirsten had only imagined that the man with the ponytail lied.

That final "maybe" was impossible. She wanted to look in those second-floor windows.

But this was the only building of those facing Diversey that had a fenced backyard—not a yard, actually, but a parking area with a small loading dock for deliveries. The fence was chain-link, about seven-feet high—and looked brand-new. Not that difficult a climb, but other than having changed into running shoes she wasn't dressed for obstacle courses. Nor was this a particularly smart time of the day for breaking and entering—if there *were* a smart time.

There must have been thirty apartments in the corner building, and it seemed a safe bet most of the occupants didn't really know each other. Kirsten went up the stairs of the porch closest to the back of the Cubic Globe. Leaning out from the end of the second-floor porch, she could stretch across the narrow gangway and almost touch the smaller building. But she couldn't get across to the other porch. The high second floor of the Cubic Globe building fell about halfway between the second and third floors of the apartment building.

She climbed to the third floor. The end apartment was dark. There was a garbage can beside the door—white plastic with a hinged top, like the one in her kitchen—and a push broom leaning against the wall beside it. Walking briskly, as though she belonged there, she went to the end of the porch and leaned across. Again, she could almost touch the bricks, but would have had to leap across and down to get to the other porch. The lighted window couldn't have been more than two feet in from the corner of the building. But looking down from above, and at a very narrow angle, she couldn't see much, just that there was a thin curtain over the bottom half of the window. A strip of foil tape ran around the perimeter of each large pane of glass, signaling the presence of a security system.

As she stared, she suddenly saw something else. Although they were not easily visible, there were bars across the window. Not all that unusual for a city apartment, but these bars were inside—behind even the curtain.

She suddenly caught herself leaning so far over the railing that she almost lost her balance. Frustrated, she turned abruptly and started back toward the stairs. And as she did, she walked right into the garbage can, knocking it over. It was hard plastic and bounced noisily when it fell. Worse yet, it hit the push broom, whose handle flipped out from the wall and banged down on the wooden floor of the porch.

She stood perfectly still, listening to her own breath and to the ceaseless background noise of cars and buses on Diversey Avenue, muffled on this side of the massive building, sounding far away.

"Hey! Everything all right up there?" A man's voice came from two floors down.

"Oh yeah," she called back, her own voice twice as loud as it needed to be. "Everything's fine. Just . . . clumsy, that's all."

"Okay," he answered, and she heard a car door slam.

By the time the car had backed out and disappeared down the alley, she'd gotten her breath back. She picked up the garbage can, then the broom. She stopped and stared at the broom. If there were such a thing as a professional janitor's broom, this was it. It was heavy and solid, with metal braces securing the "T" of the broomhead to the long handle. She carried it back to the end of the porch and dangled it over the railing.

Grasping the very end of the handle with her left hand, she stretched out and down over the railing as far as she dared. She swung the broom out like a pendulum and let its weight carry it back, aiming one end of the broom head toward the barred window.

The first time she missed. The broom banged into the bricks and the impact nearly jarred it from her hand.

But she firmed up her hold and the second try was perfect, ending in a lovely crash of broken glass.

Again, she almost lost her grip on the handle when the broom head got snagged somehow inside the broken window. But she managed to hang on and pull it up, using both hands. She put the broom back against the wall beside the garbage can. Then, as casually as possible, she sauntered back across the porch and down the stairs.

No one was around. No one seemed to have heard a thing.

FOURTEEN

R ita held her breath. She'd heard a noise—like a *thud*—from the rear of the apartment, back by the kitchen. She sat perfectly still in the dark on the couch. Finally she figured it must have been just her stupid imagination.

Then . . . Jesus God! There was this big crash like someone had busted in the kitchen window, and this time she almost peed in her pants. In fact, she *did* pee in her pants, just a little.

Except she wasn't wearing any pants. He'd taken away every last stitch of her clothes. She figured he did that to mess with her mind. And it was working. You could hardly tell night from day if you never put your clothes on and took them off. It was making her jumpy and nervous, which she didn't use to be. She'd always been pretty tough. Maybe scared inside sometimes, but tough all the same.

She ran to the bathroom, bare feet slapping against the wood floor, and finished what fright had started. Then she stood up and stared at herself in the mirror. It was plenty warm in the bathroom, but she was shivering anyway. Some damn wild maniac was trying to break in, for God's sake, and what could she do about it?

Nothing. No phone. Locked in. The Wild Maniac would probably come right in and kill her.

So what difference did that make? She'd be dead pretty soon anyway, once the rest of her money came in. The Really Weird

One—she never thought of him by his real name anymore—kept promising he'd let her go then, but she wasn't dumb enough to believe that. She went out in the hall and felt cool air blowing down from the kitchen. She sat her bare behind down on the cold floor and told herself it didn't matter. Let the Wild Maniac come.

But still . . . she started to cry.

All of a sudden she realized she couldn't hear anything but her own dumb whimpering. Nothing else. No one trying to get in. Besides, she'd be better off if someone *did* get in, for God's sake—even the Wild Maniac, if there *was* one.

She got up and went down the hall. He always left a dim nightlight on in the kitchen, but she couldn't go in because the doorway from the hall was blocked by one of those folding steel gates. Even with the bars, he didn't want her getting close to the windows.

Goose bumps came up all over her naked body from the cold air coming in through the broken window. The floor was covered with glass, but there sure wasn't any sound of somebody trying to break in.

So how could anyone get in anyway? Bars, double locks, burglar alarms . . .

Burglar alarms!

There must be bells or sirens going off, somewhere. So he'd be here again pretty soon. Damn, he'd probably think *she* did it. Except anyone could see the gate was still locked, and the glass was on the inside, anyway, so how could it be her? But he'd still find a way to blame her.

Blame me. Blame me. Her feet slapped the words out as she walked back down the hall. *Blame me.* She went into the bathroom and closed the door. It was warmer in there.

She'd already taken two baths that day, so she just sat back down on the toilet and asked herself, for maybe the fifty-*billionth* time, how all this could be happening. One day she's got the first half of her settlement money and she's on easy street. Big bucks. No problems. She'd even been gonna let that fat little lawyer off the hook.

Course, it really pissed her off when he lost that ten thousand dollars so fast. But then he scraped up some money and paid her back most of it, and she felt sorry for the pitiful little guy. She tried to take back what she'd said at that attorney discipline place—since it wasn't *exactly* true, anyway—but they said they'd subpoena her and *make* her testify against him. So she told them she was leaving town, which wasn't *exactly* a lie, because she *could* have left town. But they said they'd just use her deposition if she did that.

Anyway, one day she's on easy street, and the next day she's mixed up in this Cubic Globe stuff. Of course she shouldn't have trusted the Really Weird One so much, but when Lynne introduced her to the guy, it looked like her big chance to change her life around. Get away from the cage dancing and all that other stuff that would have shamed her mother so bad if she'd still been alive. Rita figured God would probably be happy, her using her money to get herself straight.

Then, when she found out what was really going on, she wanted out. She made threats. She *knew* people, she said.

Big mistake.

So here she was, locked up in this damn apartment. No windows she could get close to. No radio, no TV. Except for the sofa in the living room, the only furniture was in the bedroom, which he locked her out of when he was gone.

The only supplies were bathroom stuff. Lots of tiny little hand towels. Soaps and lotions. And plenty of toothpaste, toilet paper, even douches. Something for every—what'd the Really Weird One say?—orifus?

That's all. Bathroom supplies. And about a zillion dirty magazines and books she wouldn't touch in a million years. Jesus! She was no saint, and God must be mad at her for all the bad stuff she did. But some of those pictures! You hadda wonder about people.

Anyway, she'd be dead already if he didn't need her alive to get the rest of her money, which he wanted for this crazy deal he was trying to do. Plus, he wasn't through messing with her yet. But that wouldn't last forever, either. At least he must not have AIDS or something, or else why did he have her blood tested before he'd even touch her the first time? But now . . . Jesus! She was doing her best, but how many different ways can you—

Her leg fell asleep from sitting on the toilet so long and she got up and brushed her teeth and looked at herself in the mirror and waited for the Really Weird One to come back and blame her for the damn kitchen win—

Hold on! The damn *broken* kitchen window, dummy!

She ran back to the kitchen. Most of the pieces of glass were too far away to reach and too small to be any good, anyway. But there was this one pointed piece, maybe eight inches long, closer to the doorway. She lay on her stomach on the floor and stretched her arm out as far as she could under the steel gate. But it was too far away. No matter how hard she stretched, she couldn't reach it. She gave up and sat on her behind and stared through the gate at that piece of glass. She almost started to cry again, but shook her head to stop herself. Dear God, he'd be here any minute. There had to be some way. . . .

She ran back to the bathroom and got her toothbrush. Again she lay on the floor, with the end of her toothbrush squeezed tight between the tips of her index and middle fingers. She stretched. The bristles of the brush just barely reached the precious piece of glass, but she couldn't get any leverage to drag it toward her. She gave one last stretch, straining her arm—and accidentally pushed the wide end of the glass farther away. Damn! But then she saw that by pushing that end farther away, she'd swung the pointed end around a little closer. With just a little more stretch . . .

She had it!

Back in the bathroom she held it in her palm. It was heavy glass, long and pointed and even curved just a little—like a knife. But no way could you get a strong grip on it because all the edges were too sharp.

She took two deep breaths and tried to think.

The tears started again, and all of a sudden she sneezed—so hard she almost dropped the precious piece of glass. She set it down carefully on the sink, then snatched some toilet paper off the roll to blow her nose. The roll kept spinning around and she stared at the toilet paper unraveling toward the floor. . . .

She unrolled *all* the paper and flattened out the cardboard roll and slid it over the wide end of the piece of glass. Then around that she wrapped layer after layer of toilet paper, until she had sort of a glass knife with a cardboard and toilet paper handle.

Then she put the lid down and sat on the toilet and waited. She never saw anyone but the Really Weird One, but she was pretty sure he had a partner because sometimes he acted like someone was waiting for him downstairs in the car. She hoped to God that this time he'd come alone and not bring along his silent partner.

She stared down at her weapon. Wasn't there some story she remembered, like a fairy tale or something? About a beautiful princess and a glass dagger? No . . . a *crystal* dagger.

Jesus, some princess she was, sitting on the toilet in the dark. And some crystal dagger, too. Piece of broken glass. Probably cut her own stupid fingers off. But what the heck? It was her Crystal Dagger and it was all she had and she'd go after him when he came in. Even if he brought along the Silent Partner. Because it was her only chance. She'd go straight for the throat. . . .

She felt anger boil up in her stomach. Her mother always used to say you weren't supposed to hate people, but she tried to churn up the anger even stronger. She had to be real mad, because she was still scared to death. Then . . . she couldn't help it. She started to cry again.

She was still crying when she heard someone coming up the stairs to the front door of the apartment.

It sounded like just one person.

FIFTEEN

Bert's was one of Dugan's favorite places. More a bar than a restaurant, but great ribs and only a couple blocks from home. Very convenient, especially when he drank too much—which, come to think of it, he used to do with some regularity and couldn't remember doing for a long time now.

But Bert's was still a good choice.

When he paid off the cab driver, it was closer to seven than six-thirty and he had a headache. He stood on the sidewalk and rolled his head around to loosen the stiffness in his neck and shoulders. He hadn't worked out for what . . . four days? five?

God, maybe he was getting old. Kirsten kept talking about her biological clock. Maybe he had his own version, ticking his life inexorably forward toward sleep-filled nights, moderation, a responsible lifestyle—and muscle tension headaches.

Inside Bert's, the noisy crowd around the bar included a few familiar faces, but no one he really knew. As often as he'd been there, Dugan still wasn't sure there really was a Bert. He knew only the ever-present manager, Bridget. She was a good ten years older than he, with short dark hair getting gray here and there, a round pretty face, and an easygoing disposition he marveled at.

Bridget grabbed him by the arm and led him to the room beyond the bar, where there were four tables for four, three little tables for two along the wall, and one uncomfortable booth.

"I saved the booth just for you," Bridget said. "Your wife called. She's on her way."

Dugan slid onto the bench seat. "You ever get headaches, Bridget?" he asked, twisting his head from side to side.

She laughed. "Headaches? Are you kidding?" She leaned closer. "Only every friggin' day, my boy. Only every friggin' day. Doctor calls 'em muscle tension headaches. Myself, I think it's not enough sex." She laughed again and handed him two menus. "You want the ribs, right? And I'll bring you a beer."

When Bridget came back, Kirsten was right behind her. Bridget set two Old Styles on the table, and beside Dugan's beer, a small, flat box of aspirin.

Kirsten ordered a salad, and then gave him a rundown on her day, all the way up to the broken window, and beyond.

"There's an alarm system, so my plan was to see who'd respond," she said. "Eventually a car pulled up—a black Mercedes—and stopped by the fire hydrant in front of the Cubic Globe. I didn't get a good look at the two in the car, but pretty soon the guy with the ponytail got out of the passenger side. He looked in the store window and tried the door. Then he gave a wave, and the car pulled ahead and went around the corner. Meanwhile, the ponytail unlocked the door of the store and went in. I figured I better keep my eye on the Mercedes, so I made a U-turn and went around the corner, too. At the alley, I could see the rear of the Mercedes by the chain-link fence. I drove into the alley and right past the Mercedes. It was empty, so the driver must have gone in the back door. I kept going to the other end of the alley. When they left the alley, they'd have to turn left, because it's a one-way street. So I turned onto the street and waited for them. Maybe ten minutes later, the Mercedes came out of the alley. The ponytail was driving. But he turned *right*, for God's sake." She stopped and stared down at her plate. When she spoke again, it was almost a whisper. "I let them get away, Dugan. My intention was to follow whoever responded to the alarm, but I let them get away."

"Are you *crazy*? I'm glad you did. We had an appointment. I'd have been out of my mind if you didn't show up."

"No," she said. "It wasn't because we had an appointment. They got away because I didn't think he'd go the wrong way on a one-way street." She looked across at him. "I think maybe I was scared, too, and that's why I made that mistake. Anyway, they were gone. Then I called and talked to Bridget, and . . . and I came here."

"I'm glad you did," he repeated. "whatever you think you should have done." His head was aching more than ever now. He was furious at her for having gone to the Cubic Globe in the first place— and scared to death for her, too.

But he knew she didn't want to hear that, so instead he told her—in great detail, to give his feelings a chance to settle down— about his meeting with Bruce Hardison. He even described the huge thirty-sixth-floor reception area and the law firm's PR brochure. Finally, he told her again how he'd asked Fred and Peter to interview his job applicants. "Four women and one man. It's all a guess, anyway."

"Knowing those two, they'll pick one of the women, for sure. Probably the one with the biggest bra size."

"Exactly what they threatened. But I know better. They'll use their heads, and between them and Molly we'll do all right. Anyway, I'll be glad to have someone."

"Well, that's a new tune."

"I know, but it's true. I really need someone to help keep the office going. Especially now, while . . . while we're tied up." Even as he said the words, he felt his headache ratchet up yet another notch. "Because you've been right all along. There's no way we can ignore this thing and hope it goes away—whether you ever find Larry Candle's witness or not." She opened her mouth to respond, but he held up his hand. "I'm in this all the way." He shook four aspirin out of the box Bridget had left. "But promise me one thing. You let me know when you stop being afraid. Okay?"

"Well, I—"

"I'll tell you why." He swallowed the aspirin with a gulp of Old Style. "Because when that happens we're outta here. Both of us. First class, on the next flight to New Zealand."

SIXTEEN

He had locked her in the bedroom when he left, and Rita lay in the bed and thought maybe her luck was changing. Maybe *doing* something—even if it was just making a stupid weapon that was about as likely to get her killed as to get her set free— maybe *doing* something instead of just sitting on her butt and crying about what someone else was gonna do, maybe that was changing her luck.

Because if she'd have gone ahead with her original plan, and not paid attention to what was happening, she'd already be dead now for sure.

She'd been waiting in the bathroom, holding on to her Crystal Dagger, when she heard someone—which turned out to be the Really Weird One—coming up the stairs to the front door of the apartment. She was psyched up, had even started creeping down the hall, when all of a sudden she heard something else. Someone coming in through the kitchen door—real quiet. So quiet that Rita was surprised she even noticed the sound.

But she did, and no way could she handle two of them, so she quick ran back to the bathroom and stood on the toilet seat and laid the piece of glass flat, way up on top of the medicine cabinet where you couldn't see it.

She was curled up in the bathtub, pretending like she was scared to death and crying when the Really Weird One came in. He called out to someone to go back downstairs and wait in the car, because he had found her. Then he made fun of her and called her a pathetic little dumb-ass and stuff like that.

He had a cellular phone and made her call up some glass company to come and fix the window the next day. But when he finally left she was still alive, and she still had her weapon, hidden in the bathroom. And even though she never saw anyone else, she knew for sure now that there really *was* a Silent Partner. And she also knew for sure she was gonna keep on thinking, and paying attention, and figuring out things to do.

Even so, she cried some more. But not as much as she usually did before she fell asleep.

SEVENTEEN

Forget it, lady. I already told the cops everything I—"

"Oh, I'm sure you did." Kirsten smiled. She already didn't like Anton Bulasik, but she smiled anyway. "However, as I said, I'm not a police officer."

"I *know* you're not a police officer. I heard you." There was a harsh, sarcastic tone to his voice that she figured was probably permanent. It fit right in with the narrow, pale face he thrust forward at her, with its pinched nose and pointed chin. He had to be sixty, and probably dyed his thinning, slicked-back hair, because it was as black as the plastic frames of his glasses.

". . . you listening to me?" he was saying. "I said I don't wanna talk about it anymore. To you or nobody else."

Kirsten's mind had wandered. She'd had only a few hours sleep and left home before Dugan was awake so he wouldn't object to her going back to Cousin Freddy's.

"I know this must be a terrible time for you," she said, although the man sure didn't *look* grief-stricken. "And I *don't* want to ask you," she lied, "about your daughter's death. I'm just looking for a friend of hers. I have a client— Well, actually it's Larry Candle, who used to be your lawyer, right? Anyway, he spoke to your daughter in a bar a while back and there was a man with her. So why don't you just give me the names of Lynne's friends?"

"Great lawyer that guy is. He never even talked to me once

about the case. It's that genius Hardison who does all the—" He paused, as though shifting gears. "My daughter didn't have any friends, especially not—" He stopped again. "Anyway, this here's a place of business. So, if you don't wanna buy something, I got work to do." Anton turned his back on her and walked away, toward the store's "Alternative Lifestyles" section.

Kirsten looked around. Buy something? Not hardly. She sure didn't want any magazines or videotapes. Maybe one of those inflatable male members that stood four feet tall on the floor and would pop back upright every time you tried to knock it over. Or a "Ding-A-Donger," a forty-nine-dollar, battery-operated, plastic tubular device that was "guaranteed to ring your chimes with the same tingling sensations as . . . "

She trailed after Anton. There were no customers in the store just then and she might not get a better opportunity. "I'm, uh, surprised you're open today," she said. Anton seemed to be the type who blurted things out without thinking, and she wanted to get him talking.

"Yeah? Well . . . "

But that's all he said, so she tried again. "How did you ever pick the name Cousin Freddy's?"

He turned around. "That was Lynne's idea. Freddy thought she was too good to set foot in this place, so when we found out she owned half of it, Lynne said, let's change the name to Cousin Freddy's." He let out a little snort of a laugh. "Lynne didn't like Freddy very much."

At least she had him talking. Now what? "Lynne . . . I mean, don't you have *any* idea why she was killed?" She surprised even herself when she blurted out the one question she'd decided to stay away from.

Something passed quickly through Anton's eyes. Anger? Fear? Whatever it was, at least he didn't tell her to get out, which she thought he would.

Instead, he turned away from her again and started rearranging magazines on the rack in front of him. "I really didn't like her working here." He spoke in a rapid monotone, as though the words were rehearsed. "Most of our customers are just normal law-abiding guys. But a few of them are pretty strange. It hadda be one of the sickos."

She suspected he was hiding some other opinion, so she pressed him. "I don't know," she said. "There were two of them. Looked professional to me. You haven't been having any trouble with, say, the Outfit? I was thinking maybe they're the ones who beat up Freddy's father."

He spun around, startling her. "How did you— The cops put that down as a robbery, and— Say, why don't you just get the hell outta here?"

"Okay, I'm leaving." She started to turn away, then stopped. "But . . . just one more thing. There's this guy. Tall, strong-looking guy, with ugly eyes and dark hair in a ponytail. Do you know who—"

"No." Anton's head jerked, and another look passed through his eyes. Or maybe it was the same look as before, come back stronger. "I'm just a businessman. I don't know nothin' about some guy with a ponytail, or any so-called Outfit."

"It's just . . . everyone says the Mob wants a cut of—"

"No guy with no ponytail's been asking me to make payoffs to nobody. Now just get the fuck outta here, will ya?"

So she left. And as she drove away, she no longer suspected Anton Bulasik of hiding his real opinion about who was behind Lynne's death. Her suspicions had vanished.

Now she was certain. The man was flat-out lying—and very much afraid of some guy with a ponytail.

EIGHTEEN

Kirsten's next stop was Area One Violent Crimes, but when she left there she was still uncertain.

She'd made arrangements to go in at ten o'clock and give a statement about what happened at Larry Candle's apartment. She'd hoped talking to Hoffmeier and LaMotta again would help her decide whether to tell them about the Cubic Globe and the Mercedes.

But it didn't help.

The bomb in her Celica meant that within hours of their giving statements about finding Lynne Bulasik, someone had learned about Dugan and her. And not only who they were, but probably also that they'd told the police they couldn't make any identification.

She didn't want to believe the leak was Hoffmeier or LaMotta. But it might have been. Or someone higher up, or one of the sheriff's police. Or an assistant state's attorney, for that matter. Or some maintenance person, mopping floors and emptying wastebaskets with wide-open ears. Maybe she was paranoid, but she couldn't afford to take a chance.

Besides, other than confessing that she'd lied to them earlier about not getting a good look at the two men at Cousin Freddy's, what did she have that was new to tell the cops? That she'd gone to the Cubic Globe looking for Rita Ranchero, but couldn't reveal who it was who told her Rita might be there? That while she was there she'd been intimidated by a man with a ponytail? And that as a result she'd gone back later and broken a window in the place?

So what she did was call one of her old cop partners and make up a story about how she was chasing down this witness to a vehicle accident and . . . well, really, she'd put things off and now the case was going to trial and the lawyer that hired her was very, very pissed off and . . .

He'd run the plate number for her.

The black Mercedes was registered to something called Double-M Leasing Company, with a Lake Forest address. Since there wasn't time to drive way up there before she met Dugan for lunch, she headed instead for Diversey Avenue.

It was past eleven, but the sign in the window at the Cubic Globe Gallery still said CLOSED. She parked in the bus stop and ran across the street and back to the gallery. Peering through the glass, she saw that the merchandise hadn't been set out, and the tiny red lights up in the corners were blinking.

She went back to the Tempo and drove around the corner. Approaching the building from the opposite end of the alley than she had the night before, she drove slowly past the chain-link fence. What looked like brown cardboard was stuck up inside the second-floor window, behind pieces of broken glass that were still in the frame. She stopped beside the closed gate. The padlock was in place. But whoever put it there hadn't pressed the lock closed.

She drove ahead and parked in a space reserved for tenants in the corner apartment building, then walked back. When she heard a car pull into the alley behind her, she moved closer to the chain-link fence to let it pass. But it didn't pass at all, just drove slowly behind her. She slipped her hand into her purse, and remembered she'd put the gun in the trunk before going into Area One headquarters.

Just short of the gate she stopped—and heard the car stop behind her.

She whirled around.

It wasn't a car after all, but a dark blue panel truck. Exhaling, she turned again and walked on, past the gate. She heard the truck's door open. Twenty yards farther down, she stopped and looked back. The truck was parked close up against the fence, leaving barely enough room for a car to squeeze by in the alley, and even that space was blocked by the open driver's door. The sign on the door said RUSSO & SONS, CONTRACT GLAZIERS.

A tall, bald man in dark pants and a tan uniform shirt stood at the closed gate. He looked down at the clipboard he held in his left hand, then up toward the broken window. Nodding as though satisfied, he lifted the padlock from the gate latch, hung it on the fence, and went back to the truck. He pushed the driver's door closed, paused, then tossed the clipboard through the open window onto the seat. He went to the rear of the truck, and when he reappeared there were tools hanging from his belt and he was carrying a large pane of glass.

Kirsten watched the glazier go up to the second-floor porch. He laid the new glass on the porch floor, and she hoped he'd have to get inside to fix the window. But he ignored the closed door and went right to work, removing shards of broken glass from the frame.

She walked back to the truck. Beside the driver's door, outside the man's view even if he turned around, she looked through the open window. The clipboard, jammed full of papers, was lying on the seat. The top sheet was labeled "Work Order/Invoice."

Listening to the tapping sounds as the glazier chipped away at glass and old glazing compound, Kirsten stepped up on the truck's running board. She reached through the open window and picked up the clipboard. Back down on the pavement beside the truck, she flipped through the copies of the work order—different colors, marked *Customer, Accounting Department,* and *Miscellaneous.*

Suddenly a car careened around the corner into the alley and came racing straight at her. It screeched to a stop facing the front of the truck, barely ten feet away. It was a bright red Firebird.

"What the hell you think you're doing," a man screamed from the Firebird. His voice was strident, almost hysterical.

"Well," Kirsten said, "I just—"

He hit the horn then, loud and long. "You're blocking the god-damn alley, you stupid fucker!" The man was shaking his fist out his window now, and Kirsten finally realized it wasn't her, but the glazier up on the second-floor porch, that the man was screaming at.

"Whaddaya talking about?" the man above called back. His voice was deep and strong and threatening. "Shut up and learn how to drive your fucking car or I'll come down there and shove your fucking horn up your ass. You got plenty o' room."

"Yeah? Well . . ." The driver sounded intimidated, and he inched the Firebird forward. "Maybe there *would* be room if that goofy broad by your truck would wake up and get outta my way."

"Oh, sorry," Kirsten called. Tossing the clipboard back through the open window, she scurried to the rear of the truck and stepped back out of the way.

The Firebird roared past. When it was gone the glazier called down in a much kinder tone. "Sorry about the language, lady. Couldn't see you down there till just now. Ignorant people like that, you gotta treat 'em back the same way."

She didn't even look up, just waved vaguely in his direction as she hurried toward the Tempo. Backing out, she glanced up and saw that he was back at work.

She was two blocks away before she pulled to the curb and took out the piece of paper she'd jammed into her coat pocket. She laid it on the seat beside her and smoothed out the wrinkles. It was the yellow copy, the one marked *Miscellaneous*.

NINETEEN

D ugan had spent all morning on the phone, trying to settle cases, and he was into his last call.

"Look, Linda," he said, when the insurance claims adjuster came on the line, "let's get rid of this Arthur Watson case. The special damages here are fifty thousand dollars. And two hundred thousand is a very reasonable demand. I mean, this is an unusual case." How often did he use that line every week?

"Where have I heard that before?" Linda asked, but good-naturedly. "What you want is four times your specials of fifty thousand. You got twenty thousand in medical bills, fine. But thirty thousand for lost wages? Your guy just didn't lose that much in six months off the job. If he had, you'd have already sent us his tax returns for the last few years. A bad injury, but no permanent damage. My authority is ninety thousand. That's it. Sorry."

Dugan had probably negotiated a hundred cases with Linda Wagner. She'd have guessed by now, probably accurately, that Watson couldn't prove his income because he wasn't reporting it all to Uncle Sam. "Okay," he said. "Assume I got a problem with the wage loss, which I don't admit. But anyway, chop it in half. So . . . specials of thirty-five. My guy'll take a hundred and forty. Bottom line. Otherwise, I gotta put it into suit."

Two minutes later, Dugan buzzed Molly on the intercom. "I got a hundred and twenty for Arthur Watson. He wants to clear ninety thousand, so tell him I'm cutting my fee. Have him come in next week to sign releases."

"Fine," Molly said. "And . . . ?"

Her tone said she knew he hadn't buzzed her just to tell her to get Arthur Watson in and to cut his one-third fee by ten thousand dollars. He'd have put all that on the dictation tape.

"And," Dugan said, "I'll be out the rest of the day."

"The rest of the day? It's not even noon."

"Oh my," he said, overexaggerating the sarcasm so she'd know he was kidding, "did I forget to ask, 'Mother, may I?' " Molly herself hadn't missed a day since before Dugan took over. She needed a vacation. He'd give her a raise instead. She wouldn't take the time off anyway, and she needed the money.

"You're the chief," she said, "and I guess us Indians can hold down the fort for half a day."

"That's a culturally insensitive mixed metaphor, Molly. Besides, it might be several days."

She probably objected, but by then he'd cut her off by punching the button for an outside line.

After three rings, Mark Brumstein's receptionist came on the line. Kirsten had left word for Dugan to meet her at one for lunch.

He took a cab. The Blue Sunrise Grill was just off Fullerton, a block and a half in from Lincoln Park. The cab took La Salle Street north, then cut through the park. It was a bright fall day and there were plenty of people out, strolling, jogging, just sitting doing nothing. Some of them were men, too. It was Thursday afternoon, for chrissake. Were they all out of work? Or did they know something he didn't?

Dugan was almost never outside during the daytime. Oh, sometimes on weekends. But usually he saw clients on Saturday and took only Sunday off. Then it seemed like half the day was spent in bed, the other half at brunch somewhere.

They drove past the Lincoln Park Conservatory. He'd gone there once with Kirsten, around Easter. He remembered the lilies, mostly, and the fact that inside it was humid and green, like a miniature jungle. Now there were all kinds of people going in and out of the place. Tourists, most likely. Some older, probably retired.

He wondered when he'd retire and guessed he'd be interviewing clients and making phone calls from his seventh-floor office, where you couldn't see the street below or the sky above, six days a week for thirty more years or so. How else could they afford to live close to downtown and go to all those expensive brunch places on Sunday? Maybe there'd be a few Indian summers left at the end when he could shuffle through the fallen leaves in Lincoln Park. If he hadn't had a heart attack or a stroke by then, and if there were still any trees left in—

"Hey, mon! Hey! I say we here!"

Dugan jumped. Cab driver probably thought he'd already had his stroke. He gave the guy a big tip, out of embarrassment more than anything else, and went into the Blue Sunrise.

Kirsten was there already, in one of the booths that lined the windows. As he slid onto the bench across from her, she looked up from a piece of wrinkled yellow paper she was reading. "How would you like a cheeseburger with lettuce and tomato and no fries?"

"I don't know," he answered. "I've been thinking I oughta cut back on fats and greasy foods."

"Right. That's why no fries." As she spoke, the waitress appeared with a salad for Kirsten and a cheeseburger and a mug of coffee for Dugan.

He lifted the top half of the bun. "Lettuce and tomato," he said.

"And American cheese. But here, this'll take your mind off that particular danger." She slid the yellow paper across the smooth table. "Don't drip any grease on it, though. It might be an exhibit some day."

He swallowed a bite of his burger, while he scanned the paper. "Russo and Sons. A work order for replacing a broken window? But . . . Oh, at the Cubic Globe."

"Right."

"I don't think I want to know how you got this, but—"

"I thought it might say who phoned in the order. So I stole it. And you're going to say I shouldn't take chances like that."

He wondered what specific chances this time, but then said, "Not much use in my saying that. Besides, like I told you, I agree we've got to see this through. But there's no name on this, and we still don't know that the Cubic Globe will lead to Rita or the guy who was with her. And then there's Lynne's killing. Maybe we should focus on that, and the suspects we know about—WARP and, well, the Mob, I guess."

"Great. Except how in the world does someone *focus* on the *Mob*? It'd be like focusing on wild animals when you're lost in the jungle."

"Not very specific, I suppose," he admitted.

"Let's start at the beginning," Kirsten said. "We go looking for Lynne as a witness for Larry, and she's killed almost before our eyes. There are only two possibilities. One, she was killed so she couldn't talk about the conversation she overheard between Larry and his client. Or two, she was killed for—"

"For some other out of about a trillion unknown reasons. The second of your 'two possibilities' is a bit open-ended."

"Admitted. But Lynne's killing either *was* or was *not* related to Larry and his problem." Kirsten paused. "My guess is it was *not*, and we just happened to show up at Cousin Freddy's at the wrong time."

"Except that there *is* a connection between Larry Candle and Cousin Freddy's—one that Larry didn't tell us about."

"That's true, also. But why would Larry hire me, or anyone, to poke around, if he knew I might open up a can of worms that included murder? And now this." She tapped her finger on the invoice. "I can't interview Lynne because she's dead, so then I look for Rita. And immediately someone gets in the way. Contrary to what Park told me, the man with the ponytail claims there's no Rita Ranchero connected with the Cubic Globe. We know which one is lying. We don't know why. But that store sure looks like a front for something, the Ponytail looks like he's typecast for a gangster movie, and Lynne's death—"

"—looks like a Mob hit," Dugan said. "Except, don't forget the warnings that track WARP's language, and the note left at Larry Candle's."

"But why no note at Cousin Freddy's? And would WARP choose a *woman* as the first victim in a war on pornography?"

"Um . . . Kirsten?"

"Yes?"

"Are you as confused as I am?"

"At least."

"I think I should eat my cheeseburger."

They ate in silence for a few minutes, until Dugan said, "So, what do we do now?"

"For now, we have to act as though everything *is* related, some-how. Rita Ranchero, Lynne's death, her friend that Larry saw, WARP, the Mob—or someone—shaking Anton Bulasik down, Larry being shot at, someone blowing up our car, that creep in the Cubic Globe Gallery, whoever else was in that Mercedes. Every-thing. Oh, by the way . . ." She told him she'd learned the Mercedes was registered to Double-M Leasing in Lake Forest.

"So we follow up the leads we have," Dugan said, "figuring all the players are connected."

"Right. You take the car and check out Double-M Leasing. See who owns it, what they lease. Meanwhile," tapping her finger again on the work order, "I'll see if anyone at the glass company knows who phoned in this order."

Dugan grinned. "You got it, boss." He snapped a salute at her across the table. "Gimme the car keys and I'm gone."

Outside, he wondered if he should have asked Kirsten for sug-gestions on how to "check out" Double-M Leasing. But on the other hand, he preferred some idea besides breaking windows or stealing documents.

TWENTY

When Dugan was gone, Kirsten sat for a long time staring vacantly down at the work order. She reached out semiconsciously for her coffee, only to find her hand moving through thin air. Then suddenly she had the unmistakable feeling someone was watching her—observing her.

She looked up.

Somehow the table had gotten itself cleared of dishes and wiped clean. And there *was* someone observing her. Hovering over her, in fact, and staring down. It was the waitress, damp powder-blue towel in hand. "Your friend paid the bill, miss. Is there . . . anything else?"

"Ummm . . . another cup of coffee, and a piece of lemon meringue pie."

As the waitress spun around and stalked off with the order, Kirsten saw what was bothering her. Two women, standing together just inside the door with packages in their arms, turned to each other and exchanged exaggerated sighs.

"Sorry 'bout that," Kirsten called to the waitress. "Forget the pie and coffee." Slipping the work order into her purse, she stood up. The two women closed in quickly on the booth, without so much as a thank-you.

Maybe it was all the caffeine, but Kirsten's mind was careening from idea to idea by the time she left the Blue Sunrise. Outside, she was amazed to find the bright blue sky gone, replaced by dark, ominous clouds. She stood on the sidewalk for a moment and pulled the belt of her raincoat tighter. Gusts of cold wind swirled around, carrying just a whisper of thin rain through an eerie, false twilight. She decided to walk to Clark Street for a cab.

Head bent, she hurried along the sidewalk, past the restaurant's windows to her right, and then alongside a brick wall. The sudden cold and rain had her shivering already. But there was something else, too. Maybe it hadn't been just the waitress after all. Because the feeling hadn't gone away—the feeling that someone was watching her.

It had gotten so dark now that the street lights were flickering on. Kirsten walked half a block west of the Blue Sunrise before she noticed that, although both sides of the street were lined with parked cars, there wasn't a soul in sight. No pedestrians, no moving cars—no human beings between her and Clark Street, still a couple of blocks ahead.

She stopped in midstride, digging both hands into her coat pockets as though looking for something she'd just remembered. As she did, she turned casually, her gaze sweeping both sides of the street behind her.

She could go back to the Blue Sunrise and call a cab. But that was silly. There were no people on the street. Nothing threatening. Only the wind and the cold rain, both growing more intense and swallowing up the sounds of distant traffic.

She turned and started walking again, then shuddered involuntarily. It was as though her instinct were warning her—again—of something her senses couldn't perceive. She picked up her pace, and as she did she finally heard something. A car door slammed shut, not far behind her.

She hadn't even been looking for someone sitting in a car.

Glancing quickly back over her shoulder, she caught a glimpse of a man coming around the front of a parked car, maybe twenty yards back. She kept walking, clutching the purse that hung from her shoulder, wishing her gun were inside it. The car hadn't been a Mercedes, she was sure of that, and there was nothing unusual about a man on a city street, was there?

She walked very quickly then, and felt—with no need to look—that the man was hurrying after her. The rain was pouring down now, making it hard to see. But if she ran she could make it to the next corner. Maybe—

Between her and the cross street ahead a man appeared—striding through the sheets of rain toward her on the sidewalk. Where the hell had he come from? His head was bent low, a gloved hand shielding his face from the rain—and from her. She could tell only that he was a tall, wide man, as large as the man behind her, and dressed like a construction worker.

She stopped short, as fear drove deep into her belly and tightened around the muscles of her heart. She felt as though her lungs had seized up, shutting down her ability to breathe. She wanted to scream, to cry out for help . . . but why? No one would hear but her pursuers.

Just ahead of her there was a break in the expanse of brick wall along the sidewalk. An alley led off between the buildings to her right. She had no idea where it would take her, but there was nowhere else to go. She was trapped between the two men closing in on her. Fighting a strange, fatalistic impulse to give up, she forced herself into the alley and then willed her legs—heavy, wooden legs—into a run. And they responded!

Her success in making herself run brought back her confidence, and she was breathing more easily. She'd gone barely ten yards when she dared to look back. The two men were just entering the alley, and also running now. But they would never catch her. She was in great shape, and in her low-heeled shoes she figured she could run longer and faster than most men, especially those two overgrown—

The alley dead-ended less than a half block in front of her.

She kept running anyway, against the driving, swirling rain, pounding recklessly through deep puddles forming on the uneven pavement. As she got closer she could see that it wasn't a true dead-end at all, but a "T" with exits to the right and to the left. She committed herself to the left turn, guessing it was shorter that way to the next street. Negotiating the turn, she slipped and fell to one knee, scraping the palm of her left hand on the rough pavement, ripping away the skin. Then up and running again, hardly losing a stride.

But she'd guessed wrong about which way to turn.

Some fifteen yards in front of her the alley ended—this time for sure—in a brick wall and two overhead garage doors, both closed and blocked by piles of trash heaped on and around a couple of rusting garbage Dumpsters.

She glanced over her shoulder just as the first of the two men rounded the corner. Hopeless, but with no other choice, she scrambled to the top of one of the Dumpsters. The heavy stench of rotting meat made her gag. But she was angry now, as well as afraid, and looking for a way out. Maybe by jumping she could reach the edge of the low roof above the overhead doors.

She struggled to get her footing, sliding and losing her traction on some sort of thick, greasy muck leaking from a torn plastic garbage bag. She righted herself and flexed her knees, looking up, trying to gauge the height. She could do it if she just had a running step or two. But the men were closing in.

One short step, and she leaped up and forward, hands extended high in the air—and came up short, slamming her forearms and palms against the rough brick wall above the doors. She landed on her hands and knees on the slimy metal surface, exhausted, then forced herself to her feet, to try again. This time she'd make it.

And that's when she felt huge hands grab her by the ankles and drag her down off the Dumpster.

She lost track then of up and down, and screamed, finally, with pain and anger, aware that no one would hear her over the wind and rain. Pain flared up to her shoulder as her right elbow crashed hard against the cold steel of the Dumpster. She was swung through the air, felt her arms flailing around at nothing but falling rain, then belly flopped down onto the concrete . . . and felt nothing more at all.

TWENTY-ONE

About eighty percent of Dugan's work was done by phone, and Lake Forest was a thirty-mile drive, so naturally he tried to call first. But there was no listing for Double-M Leasing Company at the address Kirsten had, or anywhere else in the metropolitan area. He took the Kennedy north, and by the time he'd reached the Edens Junction the sun had disappeared and a strong wind was sweeping dark clouds across the sky from the west.

Rain poured down, but not for long, and there was very little traffic. A half hour later he parked the car in Lake Forest and the sun was shining again, with the storm somewhere out over Lake Michigan.

Double-M's address was on the second floor of an old, classy-looking structure in old, classy-looking downtown Lake Forest. School was out for the day, and perfect mothers, looking like Neiman-Marcus models in tan trench coats, hurried along the side-walk towing cute-as-a-button boys in tiny blue blazers and self-confident little girls in plaid skirts. Dugan felt out of place, conspicuously large and male.

The Tudor facade of the building was meticulously restored, with the entrance to the second floor set back a little, slipped in be-tween a travel agency and a custom cabinet shop. The tiny vestibule, though well-maintained, was plain and, well, surpris-ingly *cheap*-looking. Directly ahead was a narrow stairway. The stairs were clean and carpeted, but listing so badly he had to lean to his right to keep his left shoulder from brushing the wall on the way up. The stairs opened onto a short hallway with two doors. Taped to the door to his right was a sign announcing an office suite for rent, and giving a phone number to call. The door was locked.

The other door had no sign, just a security peephole. Two thin wires ran from a push button screwed onto the door frame, up the side of the molding and through a hole drilled in the frame of the transom, which had been painted over, and painted shut, in the same sad green as the hallway walls.

Dugan pushed the button and heard a buzz. After what seemed a long time, there was an answering click and he pushed the door open.

If the name Double-M had a vaguely western twang to it, the place itself had no twang, and in fact, no discernible character at all. A woman stood behind the imitation wood-paneled counter with an inquiring look on her face, as though wondering why in the world anybody would want to come in there.

She was tiny and friendly-looking, with short, soft gray hair. She sure didn't look much like a hired killer, or part of the Mob, or even a member of WARP. But then he remembered that Freddy Kalter didn't look much like part of the pornography industry, either—nor did Lynne Bulasik, for that matter.

"Hi there," he said. He'd rehearsed a dozen clever opening lines, but somehow they all disappeared. "Is this Double-M Leasing?"

"Yes. But I'm afraid we've nothing available just now."

"That's okay. I wasn't thinking of just now, anyway. I'm looking for a place that rents luxury models at reasonable rates, for when I might need one."

"Luxury models?" She seemed confused.

"Say a Rolls, maybe, or a Jag."

She stared at him like he was crazy.

"Or I suppose even a Mercedes would do in a pinch." He *was* crazy, of course, or else he wouldn't have been there. But how did she know?

The woman's hand seemed to drift unconsciously toward a phone sitting nearby, then dropped down to the countertop. "You must be mistaken, sir," she said. "We rent rug-cleaning equipment and floor sanders."

"That's funny. You see . . . What was your name again, ma'am?"

"Alice. Alice McKenzie. But—"

"You see, Miss McKenzie, coupla days ago I was downtown—Chicago, you know?—and two guys get out of this very nice Mercedes. And I'm waiting for the light and one of 'em says, 'Not bad.' And the other guy says, 'Great leasing deal, too. Double-M, up in Lake Forest,' And since I was up this way today I thought I'd stop in here and . . . " He let his voice trail off, hoping she'd say something, because he'd run out of words.

But she didn't say anything.

"Anyway," he started again, "what—"

The phone rang. Thank God.

"Double-M," she said. Then, "Oh, Mr. Morgan . . . yes." There was a pause, while she listened to the phone, nodding her head and staring at Dugan. Then, "No, not really, Mr. Morgan. Just . . . oh nothing, really. I'll just lock up, then."

After she hung up she kept looking at Dugan as though expecting him to say something.

But he was at a loss. "Um . . . must've misunderstood those guys," he said.

"Yes. Well, I have to close up now."

Dugan went back down the stairs, leaning to his left this time. What to do? Follow the woman home and try to talk to her again? She'd think he was a serial killer or something, and call the cops. But he couldn't just give up. Outside, he sauntered to the corner and waited.

A few minutes later she stepped out onto the sidewalk and he followed her, a half block behind. She stopped and looked at her watch, as though making up her mind. Then, nodding once to herself, she marched to the corner, across the street, and into D. K. Chester's, an old-fashioned diner.

At least it was a public place.

She was already seated alone at a table for two along the wall, when he walked over and smiled at her. "Could I talk to you for a minute?"

"Well, I don't—"

He had his wallet open in his hand and he showed her the identification card that lets attorneys enter the Cook County court buildings without having to pass through the metal detectors. The card was worthless, though rather official-looking. It had Dugan's picture on it, and his name superimposed over an outlined sheriff's badge, right above the small words NOT AN EMPLOYEE. There was an expiration date, too, but Dugan held a finger over that. He hadn't needed to enter a courthouse for several years.

He also gave her one of his business cards. "I'm really quite harmless," he said. "Just a lawyer. But special counsel, Consumer Fraud Division. I don't arrest people or anything. Just do spot checks of businesses. Right now I'm doing rental agencies. Sometimes they're licensed to rent one kind of thing and then they rent other types of things." He kept talking as he sat down, so there'd be a conversation in progress before she could get a word in and tell him to go away. "You don't really have any obligation to talk to me, but it sure makes the job a lot easier. Don't have to subpoena people and all that sort of thing."

He was trying to avoid any criminal misrepresentations, although it made no difference because—if it ever came to that—she'd testify to what she thought he was saying and not what he actually said. She laid his card on the table. She'd barely glanced at it and he wished he hadn't given it to her.

"My, that must be an interesting job," she said, when he stopped for a breath. He couldn't believe it. She acted like she was happy to have someone to talk to.

Then the waitress was there. Miss McKenzie ordered the soup and sandwich special with decaf tea, and he ordered coffee.

"Not a full-time job," he said. "Thing is, you've already given me what I need for my report. Nothing out of order at all. But I forgot to verify the name of Double-M's owner." Dugan pulled his appointment book from his coat pocket and opened it as though there were something in it about Double-M. "Let's see. That's *John* Morgan, of Lake Forest, right?"

"John? Oh no, *Charles* Morgan."

"Is that right? Well, maybe John's a brother or something."

"And I don't know if he's the owner. But he's my boss. I've only been there a week and a half. They just started this branch location. Right now, they use one of the rooms in the suite just to lock up a bunch of boxes of papers and things. Not much business yet, but I rent out the few rug-cleaning machines and floor sanders they have here, and take phone messages. I live right in town, and with my husband gone now I took the job mainly to get out of the house. But I'm thinking of quitting. Might as well be home alone as in that office alone all day."

"Well, maybe things'll pick up," Dugan said. "By the way, you don't happen to have Mr. Morgan's phone—"

But a hint of—what? surprise? suspicion?—in the woman's eyes warned Dugan to stop. "Nah, the office has that." He paused. "Boy, tough to work on a nice day like this, wasn't it? But it sure clouded up in a hurry a while ago." He steered the conversation into nothingness.

The waitress returned, and while she set down their orders, Dugan helpfully pushed knives and forks and water glasses around to get them out of the way—and palmed his business card from where it lay on the table.

One sip of coffee later, he looked at his watch. "Wow, I gotta go." He stood up. "By the way, can't swear you to secrecy or anything, but they like me to stay anonymous. Sort of like a restaurant critic. Better if people don't—"

"Oh, I won't say anything, Mr. . . . uh . . . " She paused, eyes searching the table for his card.

" 'Preciate it," he said, and smiled his way out the door.

TWENTY-TWO

I t was really hard to tell time with the bedroom windows boarded up, but Rita knew it had to be at least past noon and the Really Weird One hadn't come back yet. He better hurry up, because she already had to go to the bathroom pretty bad.

At least he hadn't blamed her the night before for the broken window. He was too busy making fun of her and calling her names. She realized then that she did hate him, like she'd never, ever hated anybody before. And she hated his friend, too, the Silent Partner, whoever it was, who had to be as bad as him. It wasn't enough they were gonna take all her money, and then kill her like some kinda insect. In the meantime they had to treat her like she was a piece of dog crap. They were both bad, mean people—crazy people—and she was scared of them. But she hated them, too.

In the morning the Really Weird One had brought her some breakfast from McDonald's, and afterward he locked her in the bedroom again. But while he was there she thought maybe she'd get a chance to go after him with the Crystal Dagger, so she was very, very nice to him. Pretty soon he had his clothes off and she smiled a lot and breathed real loud like he liked, and told him how big he was. What a creep! Him and his dumb ponytail and baggy pants. Always playing big shot and staring at people to scare them. He was scary, all right. But he was a creep.

What she did was, she told him he had got her so excited she had to go to the bathroom, which was her plan for how she was going to get the Crystal Dagger. She had to do it—no sense waiting—even if she was nervous and scared.

But then the creep followed her right into the bathroom and she had to let him watch her take a pee—one of his all-time favorite things, which she thought was really stupid for a grown-up person—and which didn't give her a chance to get her weapon from its hiding place.

Anyway, after that she was still real nice to him even though he made her wanna throw up. Before he left he unlocked the bedroom closet where he kept her clothes. There was a stack of old *People* magazines on the closet floor he said she could read, and then he laughed that really weird laugh like he did sometimes, and told her he had a secret.

She asked what kinda of secret, and her heart started beating real fast.

He said she should be all dressed and ready when he came back that afternoon because they were all going on a trip. He said, "We're *all* going," like someone would be with him. But he wouldn't tell her where or why, and then he locked her in the bedroom again when he left.

She was excited and scared, and she spent the rest of the morning trying on clothes. She didn't have all that much stuff there, but it included panties and pantyhose and bras—and shoes, too. But no coat. There was a full-length mirror on the closet door and she tried everything, in different combinations. She finally decided she'd wear the beige canvas pants that were real bulky, and the blue sweater.

She had long, slim legs—dancer's legs, a gift from God, her mother had told her—and using a couple of pairs of pantyhose, she figured out a way to strap one of the *People* magazines around the front of her thigh. When she put the pants on and looked in the mirror you couldn't really tell anything. The edges of the darn magazine dug into her skin at first when she walked, but she kept adjusting it and trying different ways until she was pretty sure it wasn't going to slip off or anything.

Then she sat on the bed and paged through the other magazines and waited for him . . . waited for *them*.

She'd lost track of how many days she'd been locked up in this goddamn apartment. She didn't think the rest of her settlement money was due yet, but maybe it was. Maybe him and the Silent Partner were gonna take her out to get her money. And then they'd kill her, sure as anything. But she wasn't gonna go down without a fight. No way!

Later in the afternoon he came back, and he was talking to someone else, even though she couldn't hear the other one's voice. They left her in the bedroom while they carried out all those boxes of filthy books and magazines. Then he came in the bedroom and took the *People* magazines, too. She hoped he didn't have them counted or something, but he didn't say anything about one being missing. She still hadn't gone to the bathroom and was almost bursting by then. But she didn't say anything yet because she wanted to wait till the last minute—and she didn't want anyone watching her.

The Really Weird One took the rest of her clothes from the closet and stuffed them in a shopping bag and then went in the bathroom and put everything from in there in another bag.

When he had everything, he said, "Let's go, bitch."

She went down the hall to the kitchen, with the Really Weird One behind her. She noticed that the window was already repaired, and she hadn't heard anything. Then, just at the back door, she stopped and turned around. "Wait," she said. "I gotta go pee."

The Really Weird One looked like he wanted to swat her, except he was carrying shopping bags in both hands. So he just stared at her. "Why didn't you go before this, dumb-ass?"

"I don't know. Too nervous or something. But now I gotta go," jumping up and down for emphasis, "real bad."

"Jesus Christ," he said. "I'll take this shit down." He was looking over her shoulder and Rita realized he was talking now to someone behind her, outside on the porch. "You stay here with her. And lock the door behind you when you come down."

Rita glanced back over her shoulder, and then ran back down the hall and into the bathroom and slammed the door shut. God, now that she'd seen the Silent Partner she was more scared than ever. But at least she'd be alone in the bathroom. The Crystal Dagger was still on top of the medicine cabinet and she got it down. While she sat on the toilet, she tried to slide it into the middle of the magazine strapped to her leg. But with the cardboard and toilet paper wrapped around the wide end of the piece of glass it was too fat, and she had to unwrap it. Plus, she had to pee at the same time, so it wouldn't be too quiet and suspicious. Her hands were shaking, but finally she got the glass slid into place and tied the extra pair of pantyhose around her leg so it couldn't fall out through the bottom. She flushed the toilet, pulled up the beige canvas pants, and asked God to keep the fucking glass from breaking. Then she told God to excuse her bad language—she was trying to do better—and went back out in the hall.

She had to walk kinda stiff on her way down the stairs, and the Really Weird One was watching her from down below. "What are you, limping or something?"

"Just a little stiff," she said. "Plus, you kinda bruised my tushie this morning, you know? Jumping all over me. You're really something, you know? That was really a lotta—"

"Just shut up, and get down here."

Rita had only said what she did because she wanted to get his mind off how she was walking, and she figured he didn't want her talking out loud about her and him doing stuff like he liked to do.

So she went downstairs and got into the back of a van they'd loaded the boxes into. There was hardly any room, and no windows and nothing to sit on but the floor.

The Really Weird One showed her how the door couldn't be opened from the inside, then slammed it shut, and she sat on the cold metal floor and leaned against the wall. At least she was way back by the back door and the two of them were up in the seats in the front, and they couldn't see her with all that crap piled up between them and her.

When the van lurched forward it hit some big bumps in the alley and hurt her back and her behind like hell. Besides that, she was afraid, and she wished she knew where they were taking her. Suddenly she started to shake, and tears poured out of her eyes and ran down her cheeks. But even though she was sobbing like a little kid, she was as quiet as she could be. She reminded herself there'd be another roll of toilet paper wherever they took her. And then she patted her *People* magazine holster under her pants leg— with her Crystal Dagger inside.

TWENTY-THREE

outhbound traffic was light and Dugan was home by six-thirty. Kirsten wasn't there. He called his office, expecting to get his voice mail, since there was usually no one but himself still in the office past six. He was surprised when Molly answered.

But it wasn't a Molly he'd ever heard before. She was crying, incoherent.

Then Fred came on the line. ". . . been trying to find you . . . got a call. Northwestern Hospital, the emergency room. There was an accident . . . or no, not an accident. But . . . some trouble. They said you better—"

"Fred . . . " Dugan couldn't breathe. Maybe he didn't want to breathe. He whispered into the phone. "Fred, tell me. What are you talking about?"

"Well, it's . . . it's her. Some kids found her. You know, it's Kirsten."

Dugan couldn't even remember how he got to the hospital, but was surprised to find Fred and Peter already in the emergency room, talking to a tall, skinny man in khaki pants and a white coat. He had shoulder-length hair but was nearly bald on top, and he had a big Adam's apple that looked like it had been scraped too hastily by too dull a razor.

Dugan walked toward them in a daze. "How did you guys beat

me here?" Knowing there was something far more important to ask. Knowing what it was, too, but not wanting to ask it.

Peter spoke up. "We took a cab. You shoulda seen the way that driver—"

"Shut up about the cab, for chrissake." Fred's voice was too loud. "This is Doctor Walton, Dugan. He was Kirsten's—"

"Was? *Was?* What are you talking about?"

The man in the white coat took Dugan's hand from where it hung at his side and shook it. When he let go, the hand fell back where it came from.

"Was," the doctor said, "because I'm the trauma resident and I'm going home, and she's been admitted and gone for more X rays. Not *was* because she's dead or anything. No." The raw, scratched Adam's apple bounced as the man repeated himself. "No, no, no. Knocked around pretty good. But not dead." He looked at Dugan, then looked down at his watch. "Let's go sit down. C'mon."

Dugan let Peter hold his arm while he stumbled to keep up with the trauma resident's long steps.

TWENTY-FOUR

I t was dark beyond the windows when Kirsten woke up. She was flat on her back, with the head of her hospital bed raised a little. Her neck was stiff and it hurt too much to swivel her head, so she twisted her whole body to look around the room.

What dim light there was came from under the bed itself. There was a small stand with three drawers, a bed table on wheels, and—across the room, by the door—a chair. Dugan was gone now. Some other man sat in the chair.

She guessed the man was Dugan's height, and maybe thirty pounds heavier. He had a Walter Matthau–like face, the same deep creases, but there was something missing. Humor, maybe. His shaggy hair looked gray in the dim light, and a mustache drooped heavily down along both sides of his mouth. He held a Styrofoam cup in his hand, and when he saw she was awake he lifted the cup in her direction.

She went back to sleep.

When she opened her eyes again, morning light was coming in the windows. The same man still sat in the same chair, still had the Styrofoam cup in his hand.

"I'd like coffee, too," Kirsten said.

"Coffee, too?" He stared at her. "Oh, you mean this." Holding up the cup. "This isn't coffee. It's for spittin' into." He reached into his shirt pocket and pulled out a tin of chewing tobacco. He grinned. Not really a pleasant grin. Not a pleasant-looking man.

"You're . . . the bodyguard Dugan said he'd get?" Kirsten asked.

"I don't know what Dugan said. I'm Milo Radovich."

She'd heard of Radovich. An ex-cop who still sent Dugan accident cases sometimes, he was a bully who'd retired after twenty-five years of pushing people around and worked now as a bouncer at a Croatian nightclub on the northwest side.

"Guys call me Cuffs. Knew your old man way back when. We got along okay. Most of those homicide dicks were assholes."

"*Cuffs?*" She'd never heard the nickname.

"Yeah, Cuffs." Another grin. "Had this mope one time locked up in the wagon. Skinny guy. Think he was half-mick, half-spic . . . or maybe half-colored or Arab or something. Don't remember. Anyway, he was mouthing off—you know, like they do—and kept trying to slip his hands outta the cuffs. So I, uh, tightened 'em up a little." He spit noisily into the white cup, then set it on the floor beside him. "I went for some coffee and then I got a call and hadda go handle somethin' else. Kinda forgot about the skinny dumbo in the back. When I got time to check on him, his wrists were, you know, kinda raw." He reached down for the cup again. "Guys started callin' me Cuffs after that. Anyway, how you feelin'?"

"Fine." She closed her eyes again, preferring sleep to conversation with Radovich.

The doctor had given her something to calm her down and she hadn't said much to the cops. Dugan told her he'd asked for police protection and Hoffmeier said muggings are so common even the newspapers don't mention them, and the victims certainly don't get private guard service from the city.

But this was no random mugging.

They'd tossed her purse near the entrance of the alley—with the money removed as though robbery were their purpose. But she knew better. After slamming face-down into the pavement, the next thing she remembered was being on her feet with someone holding her from behind. A cloth—a small, dark pillowcase, she learned later—was pulled over her head like a hood and tied tight around her neck with a thin rope. Muggers don't plan that well.

They'd begun carefully, systematically. One held her from behind, while the other slapped her—twice, back and forth across her face through the cloth—snapping her head from one side to the other, but more humiliating than harmful.

She'd struggled, twisting and kicking. Useless. She was terrified; but besides that, she was ashamed, furious at herself for having been taken so easily. A helpless female at the mercy of a couple of thugs.

Two slaps again, more savage this time.

Then the voice close to her ear. "Just give it up, lady. We just want you to know y'all messin' with the wrong folks." The man holding her spoke in a soft drawl, as though sincerely hoping she'd take his advice. "Big-time folks. Give it up. So you don't get hurt, you hear?"

She was certain he was black, and knew beyond any doubt that these were the two men from Cousin Freddy's.

Then he let go of her.

And when he did, in her frustration and rage she lashed out stupidly at the man in front of her, the one who'd slapped her—swinging wildly, striking nothing but air—except that the tip of one finger glanced harmlessly off what must have been his nose.

The man growled as though he'd been hurt, and drove his body into hers like an angry bull, slamming her back against a solid wall.

"Hey, man, take it easy," the other one said. "Y'all not supposed to kill her or something. Let's go."

"Fuck you. The bitch hit me, asshole. Ain't no fuckin' cunt gonna hit me." And he was punching her, over and over, mostly low and deep into her abdomen. By then she was beyond being able to shout or make any sound at all, just dropped onto the alley pavement and curled into a ball.

She thought they'd go away then, prayed God they would.

But they didn't go.

One of them knelt beside her and pushed her onto her back. He ripped her coat open, then her blouse. She was trembling uncontrollably even before she felt the damp cold air blow across her bare skin. With one huge hand he pinned both her wrists up over her head. The other hand was running clumsily over her, feeling her. His knee pressed into her stomach, and she was going to vomit. He ripped her bra upward, tearing it away from her.

"C'mon, man." This was the other one, the black man, standing above her. "Somebody gonna see us. We gotta go, man."

The man took his hand away from her. "Broad hit me in my nose," he said. She felt his face lean close to hers, smelled the garlic on his breath as he whispered, "I bet you think you're real pretty, don't you, bitch? Well, I got something pretty for *you*, and you're gonna take it."

Through her terror, she felt the weight of his knee shifting on her belly, still pinning her down. With her eyes covered, struggling against the panic that was taking over, she knew exactly what he was doing. Over the sound of her own heartbeat pounding inside her head, she could hear him. Heard him fumble with his belt. Heard the zipper. She *knew*. Heard him exhale, finally, like a happy sigh. She gagged on the bile that rose in her throat.

"Cut that shit out, man," the other one said. "This ain't part of it. She ain't even movin', man."

"Bullshit. She's shaking like crazy. See that, Andrew? Anyway, whadda you care about her?"

"I don't give a fuck about no white bitch. But this ain't right. I'm gone, man." The man named Andrew was moving away. "I'm the driver, I got the car keys," he called back. "And I'm outta here."

Suddenly, she didn't want Andrew to leave her alone with this man. Her breath froze inside her lungs and she waited, aching with fear and humiliation and rage, yet helpless. She waited.

But the man went no further. Instead, he released her arms and stood up, mumbling to himself, "Goddamn chickenshit nigger." Then, louder, "Hold on, dammit. Wait for me." She heard the zipper, the belt buckle. "Not today, pretty lady. But maybe some other time, huh?"

They were gone then and the rain fell even harder, washing over her. She knew she was alone and still she lay there, couldn't scream, was paralyzed. Her mind fell away from her and she was sliding on her back, head first, down a long, dark tunnel. . . .

She woke up a third time, still on her back in the hospital bed, shaking and sobbing and clawing at a cord around her—

"—all right. It's all right. Just a dream. Y'all kin wake up now, honey. It's mornin'." The voice was smooth, soothing. "Here, lemme loosen up this here thing from 'round your neck."

Kirsten opened her eyes to find a large, round-faced woman in a white uniform leaning over her.

"There, that's better." The aide pulled the hospital gown away from Kirsten's neck. "Well, aren't you a pretty sight. And lookit them black eyes! Look sorta like a raccoon!" She laughed, then turned to Radovich. "Would y'all mind leaving the room, sugar? We just be a moment now."

Radovich left and Kirsten tried to sit up, but a wave of nausea pushed her back. She hoped they'd give her something for the pain pounding in her head. Then maybe orange juice and coffee, and a sponge bath if her body wasn't too sore to stand it. But after that, maybe sometime this afternoon, she was outta here. Or at least, first thing tomorrow. She didn't care what the doctor said. She had too many things—

"Might's well git up, honey. Put on them clean clothes in the closet. Doctor say you're discharged, so you gotta be out by eleven anyway. Your husband be here in a little while." She must have seen the surprise in Kirsten's eyes, and shook her head gently. "I know how you feelin', honey. But these days, you don't sit up in no hospital no two, three days just 'cause you hurtin', what with them insurance rules and reform and all."

TWENTY-FIVE

Most of the court calls started at nine-thirty. So at nine-twenty Dugan was part of a river of lawyers pouring past the huge Picasso sculpture on the plaza at Washington and Dearborn, and through the revolving doors of the Richard J. Daley Center. He felt wired, his mind racing from anger to fear to helplessness, and back again to anger. He'd wanted to stay home with Kirsten, but had to get out and do something. He left her with a supply of painkillers, and with Cuffs Radovich watching over her. No one hired Cuffs because he was kindly, or sensitive, or kept any of his prejudices to himself. In fact, there was much about Cuffs that Dugan disliked. But he'd needed someone who was available right away, someone absolutely dependable, and—Dugan hesitated to admit it, even to himself—someone who wouldn't let second thoughts, or conscience, get in the way of protecting Kirsten.

With his ID outdated, he had to stand in line to pass through metal detectors before he could join the crowd waiting for the elevator to the twenty-fourth floor.

Circuit Court of Cook County. Chancery Division. Judge Hanahan. The "motion call" hadn't started yet and the courtroom was jammed. There must have been fifty lawyers, mostly men, of which a mere half dozen were seated at the two counsel tables in the open area in front of the judge's bench, reading documents or rummaging through file folders. The rest stood alone or talking in groups of two or three wherever they could find the space, or sat on smooth dark-oak benches on the spectators' side of the railing that divided the room. Clients seldom attend motion calls and Dugan couldn't spot any. He was the only one in the room without a brief-case.

Even when he used to go to court, Dugan had seldom ventured into the Chancery Division. His clients' cases were all suits for money damages and all filed in the Law Division, to be tried before juries if they weren't settled. In Chancery there were no juries and the judge alone made all the decisions, frequently in the form of injunctions and restraining orders rather than straight monetary damages.

More often than not, of course, there was still a great deal of money at stake. Who'll eat the losses if that shopping mall project is stalled? Who gets custody of this quadriplegic—and control of his trust funds? There was the occasional case less about money and more about emotions—usually identified by the litigants as "matters of principle." Can the owners' association make Unit 310 get rid of that pet cat they've been hiding for years? Must that apple tree be removed, just because of the neighbors' allergies? But most of the cases came down to money, pure and simple.

As Dugan stood just inside the courtroom, the tall door next to the judge's bench opened and a round, black deputy in dark pants and a crisp blue uniform shirt came through, waved his stubby arms aimlessly, and shouted that everyone should *"be seated immediately"*—which was impossible—and *"be silent"*—which everyone then was.

Judge Hanahan entered behind the deputy. She was tall and slim under her black robe, with prematurely graying hair, cut short. She stopped just inside the door and surveyed the room, then turned and struggled up the three steps to the bench, using two metal crutches that were strapped to her forearms. Her clerk held the tall leather swivel chair steady, and Judge Hanahan pivoted carefully and sat down. She removed the crutches and placed them on the floor. Then, hands folded before her on the bench, she smiled and said, "Good morning everyone. I'll take agreed orders first."

A line formed before the bench, and within fifteen minutes half of the crowd was gone, having gotten the judge's signature on orders about which there were no disputes. By that time, Dugan was sitting on one of the benches and had spotted the straight back of Bruce Hardison up at one of the counsel tables.

The judge's clerk began calling cases by name, and the lawyers stepped up to argue disputed motions. Judge Hanahan listened to each side carefully, kept the lawyers from rambling, and ruled on their motions quickly.

"*Anders versus Sexton Enterprises and Cousin Freddy's!*" It was the fifth case called.

Dugan jumped up and started forward. Two women who'd been seated across the aisle from him also rose and followed him. Both thirtyish, with navy blue business suits and white blouses, lugging leather briefcases. One was tall and full-figured, the other very thin and maybe five-foot-two. At the entrance into the open area where Hardison was now standing by his chair, Dugan stopped and held the swinging gate open for the two women.

But they didn't pass through. They simply stopped in the aisle and glared, more at the world in general than at him. By the time Dugan realized they were waiting for him to go first, Judge Hanahan was saying, ". . . this case to the end of the call, if you don't mind, counsel."

Bruce Hardison stayed on his feet. "But your honor, I—"

"You *are* contesting plaintiffs' motions, aren't you, Mr. Hardison?"

"Your honor, these motions are entirely without—"

"So your answer is 'yes' and I'm passing this to the end of the call. Given my previous experience with this case, I'll not keep all these other attorneys waiting while you people argue your motions."

The two women lawyers sat back down, their faces grim. They had the look of some of the women prosecutors Dugan had known in the state's attorney's office, especially some of those in the Sex Crimes Unit. Good lawyers, but good lawyers *on a Mission.* He'd told Kirsten once he thought the *Mission* got in the way of their judgment at times. She reminded him that he was male and was likely to think that way.

She'd been right, too. It's hard to put yourself in somebody else's shoes. Like now, he couldn't entirely buy into WARP's theory about pornography. Still, he was glad Hardison would be doing the talking, because some of WARP's arguments made sense—and it would never do for a trial lawyer to admit that.

Dugan moved forward through the gate and took the empty chair beside Hardison. "Glad I made it on time," he said. "Hadda take my wife home."

"Just getting started," Hardison whispered. "She wasn't hurt badly, then?"

"She's—" But a hiss from the deputy cut him off.

It was nearly an hour before the Cousin Freddy's case was called again, and the droning arguments of lawyers over things he had no interest in had somehow calmed Dugan down. He and Hardison and the two women lawyers stood before the bench and stated their names for the court reporter, the courtroom deserted behind them.

"Your honor," Hardison began, "this matter—"

"Excuse me," the judge said. She turned to Dugan. "You're moving to substitute for Mr. Candle as counsel for defendant Cousin Freddy's?"

"Yes, your honor," Dugan said, handing up his appearance form. "I—"

"Motion granted." The judge peered down at Dugan. "This courtroom's a little far afield for you, isn't it?" But before he could answer, she turned to the women standing to Dugan's left. "It's your motion, counsel. Proceed with argument, please."

And proceed they did.

Forty-five minutes later, the plaintiffs had been given extra time to file further responses to the defendants' motions for summary judgment. Besides that, the judge ordered the defendants to deliver to the plaintiffs' attorneys within fourteen days every conceivable business and financial record the two bookstores had generated over the past three years.

"See what I meant about WARP's attorneys?" Hardison asked. He and Dugan sat in the otherwise empty courtroom waiting while the plaintiffs' lawyers prepared a written version of the rulings to give to the clerk for Judge Hanahan's signature.

"You mean 'hostile, mean, and sarcastic'?" Dugan said. "Morelli, especially. Fincher seemed slightly more reasonable, very slightly."

"Couple of frustrated ladies, both of them. What they need is a good—"

"Anyway, I'm worn out, and all I did was say, 'I agree with Mr. Hardison' a few times." Dugan paused. "But you did a *great* job, Bruce. Handled them, *and* the judge, just right. Far better than I could have."

He watched, with some surprise, as Hardison visibly puffed up under the obvious flattery. Most good lawyers have egos as big as their abilities. But Hardison's reaction was so blatant, it was almost embarrassing to observe.

"Yes. Well, my goal was to educate the judge on our view of the case," Hardison said. "Those ladies are way out of their league and don't even know it. They can have all year to respond to our motions if they want. The longer this bullshit takes, the better." He smiled. "Your client can start gathering documents, but on the fourteenth day I'll present a motion for reconsideration of the judge's decision, and for a protective order. We ought to milk another sixty days out of that." He looked at his watch. "I have to be in another courtroom. Be sure to read that order they're writing up before they give it to the judge. If they haven't chiseled a little, I'll give you fifty bucks."

Hardison headed for the courtroom door. As he passed the tiny conference room where the two women lawyers were at work on the written order, he looked in and waved. "Have a nice day, girls," he called.

Dugan shook his head, imagining the two women's reactions.

But when they handed him the written order for his initialed approval, he saw that Hardison wasn't going to be out his fifty dollars. "What's all this?" he said. Anger rose up again in his throat, as though it were these two who were to blame for what had happened to Kirsten. "What the hell *is* this?" he repeated.

"I'm sure I don't know what you're referring to," the smaller woman answered. That was Cynthia Fincher. Her voice, and the way she cocked her head when she spoke, reminded Dugan of a nervous bird—covering her fear with aggression.

Dugan stood up, still staring at the paper they'd given him. "This business here about the defendants being ordered to sort all the documents into categories, and label them, and stamp numbers on every page, and deliver them to your office no later than noon on— Wait a minute, besides all that, this date is only ten days away. The judge said fourteen days."

"Look, you represent people who promote rape and child abuse and the rest of the sexual violence these stores pander to and encourage, and that's your choice." It was Cynthia Fincher talking, but Dugan's attention was on the larger woman, Debra Morelli. She would have been quite attractive, except that something in her eyes reminded Dugan of Cuffs Radovich, only meaner. ". . . cooperative or as uncooperative as you like." The bird-woman finally stopped talking, long after Dugan had lost track of what she was saying.

"Hey," he said, "let's not argue about this. Maybe we can—"

"I recall clearly," Debra Morelli interrupted, her words slow and deliberate, her eyes boring into Dugan's, "that the judge said ten days." Her forceful certainty was startling, and had him almost questioning his own recollection.

But then the Fincher woman spoke up. "The judge isn't here now. So, what do you suggest we do? Come back after lunch? Just to ask whether she said ten days or fourteen?"

Dugan stared at the two of them in disbelief. "I suggest," he said, struggling to keep his voice level, "that in this order you stick to what the judge said. I suggest that if you want organizing and numbering and the rest of that crap you file another motion. And I suggest that you don't try to chisel me and my client out of four measly extra days. Otherwise, I'll be happy to meet you here at two o'clock. By then I'll have a copy of the transcript of the hearing we just had and you can try out your Bobbsey Twins routine on the judge."

What Dugan didn't say was that his dad had been one of Tricia Hanahan's major backers when she was first elected to the bench. She was honest to a fault and wouldn't bend for anyone. But she wouldn't let Dugan get pushed around, either.

There was a sullen silence in the room for a moment. Finally, Debra Morelli shook her head, as though disgusted with the entire affair. "You mean you'd actually waste everyone's valuable time to come back and argue something so *insignificant?*"

Dugan leaned toward her. "I don't know about you, counsel, but my time's not valuable at all. In fact, I'm on sabbatical. This is my only case—and it's pro bono. So . . . see you here at two."

It wasn't to be, though. Claiming that both his incivility and his objections were "far too petty to bother with," Debra Morelli crossed the extra bullshit out of the order and wrote in the proper date. "I believe you'll regret," she said, "that you ever got mixed up in this case. You don't know the kind of people you're dealing with."

Dugan stared at them, uncertain whether the woman was referring to his own client or to WARP and its lawyers. Fincher dropped her gaze and started fidgeting with the clasps on her briefcase. But Morelli stared right back at him, challenging him for a moment, then turned and walked away, pulling Fincher along with her.

Dugan left the corrected order in chambers with the judge's clerk for signing. He walked out of the Daley Center feeling slightly victorious—and very uneasy.

Pornography is terrorism. And we won't be victims any longer.

It seemed pretty far-fetched that WARP had anything to do with muggings and broken necks and Celicas going up in flames. But their lawyers would sure lie and cheat and push people around when they could. Morelli's aggression bordered on the pathological, and Fincher seemed willing to go right along. Who's to say how far they'd move out on the continuum?

We won't be victims any longer.

TWENTY-SIX

Multiple orgasms, for chrissake."

"What?" Kirsten looked up from the kitchen sink, happy to see Dugan back from court, but at a loss for an answer to his opening remark.

"Multiple orgasms," he repeated. "Your bodyguard's in the living room watching a bunch of mostly overweight women lined up on chairs in front of a live studio audience discussing multiple orgasms on national TV at one o'clock in the afternoon." He opened the bag he'd set on the kitchen table and started pulling out pita bread sandwiches. "I wonder what WARP would say about that."

Kirsten unwrapped the sandwiches and put them on plates and Dugan took a few out to Cuffs Radovich. Kirsten didn't want Cuffs joining them for lunch. After a soak in a warm tub, she'd alternated periods of sleeping and walking around the block all morning. Now she was feeling better than she'd hoped for—at least physically. Inside, though, she was still furious for letting herself be trapped by those two men.

When Dugan came back she handed him a can of Diet Coke, and listened to his recap of his run-in with WARP and its lawyers. "Plus, you should have seen Hardison. No wonder Larry doesn't like him. He enjoys baiting those women as though they were children. To me, their arguments make sense, even if I don't agree that they outweigh the First Amendment issues."

"It sure would be ironic," she said, "if it's WARP that's behind this. On the one hand battling against pornography because it victimizes women, and then sending thugs after me, and . . ." She let her voice trail off, as she popped open her own Diet Coke.

Dugan sat down across from her. "Are you okay now?" he asked, and she could tell how badly he wanted her to say yes.

"They could have killed me. And it was my fault, you know? I should have been more careful. I should—"

"You should cut out the bullshit about it being your fault. Because you know better." He chewed on a bite of sandwich. "But anyway, let's stop and think about this. First, the warning notes that sound like WARP and the arson of that Uptown porno store, were those—"

"Wait," Kirsten broke in, "there was no warning or note at the store that was actually burned down."

"True. But someone torched it, and someone warned the other adult bookstores to shut down or the same thing would happen to them. Was that WARP?"

"It was WARP's message. 'Pornography rapes and kills us.' "

"And 'We won't be victims any longer,' " Dugan continued. "So then somebody sends hit men to kill Lynne Bulasik. Was that WARP? Showing they were serious about their threats? Or was it an Outfit killing, like you—and Larry Candle, too—thought right away?"

"Whoever it was that hired them, those two must be Mob-*connected* somehow. I mean—"

"Agreed. So, it could have been a job done for the Outfit, or for WARP, or for . . . who knows?"

"Someone who'd know how to hire professional killers," Kirsten said.

"Next, they go after Larry, but we get in the way."

"I was thinking," she said. "If they don't try again with Larry, that could be a sign that it *is* WARP, and since Larry's not connected with a porno store anymore, they—"

"They should have switched their attention to me. But they didn't. Instead, the two goons go after you. And whoever sent them, it wasn't to kill you, or that's exactly what they'd have done. And it's a safe bet they weren't supposed to . . . to assault you, either. Just slap you around a little, give you a warning." He paused, "Thing is, we don't even know if it was the same two guys."

The businesslike tone of their discussion was helping Kirsten turn away from her disgust with herself. "I agree with everything you're saying," she said, "except . . . they *were* the same men, I'm sure of it."

"You couldn't even see them."

"Right. But they were big men. And I could tell by their voices that the one who . . . who held me down on the ground . . . was white, and the one who talked him out of it was black. It's just too big a coincidence."

"Maybe. But who sent them? WARP?"

"Like I said, it seems impossible that a group of women so dedicated to protecting other women would—"

"No more impossible than crazies running around, so dedicated to protecting *life* that they shoot down receptionists in abortion clinics. And I've *met* those damn WARP lawyers. They may not be murderers—but they're certainly, well, close to being *obsessed*, for God's sake."

"I don't know. Maybe those two guys came after me on their own. Maybe they changed their minds and thought I could identify them from Cousin Freddy's."

"Nope. Like I said, they'd have killed you. Someone sent them, as another warning."

" 'You're messing with the wrong kind of people. Give it up.' That's what he said. It *was* a warning, for sure. But nothing said about pornography."

"And whoever 'the wrong kind of people' are, they want you— *us*, I guess—to stop poking around where we're poking around."

"But why? Because someone doesn't like us trying to help Larry Candle keep his law license?"

"I sure *hope* that's not the reason," Dugan said, "because there'd be too many suspects. Nobody in town wants Larry to keep his license."

"So let's say it's got nothing to do with Larry, and nothing to do with WARP. Let's say someone doesn't want us looking for Rita Ranchero, or the guy that was with Lynne, for some other reason."

Dugan finished a sandwich. "I've been thinking," he said, and licked mayonnaise from his index finger. "Maybe we oughta give up trying to figure this out. Just go dump it in Hoffmeier's lap."

"We can't," she said, and when Dugan started to object she kept on talking. "We've been through this already. Hoffmeier, or LaMotta, or both of them—or somebody they report to—might be . . . on the other side. We both agreed that someone knew who we were within hours of us leaving Cousin Freddy's. Who we were and what car we drove and—"

"But we have to trust *somebody*. How the hell else are we gonna get out of this mess?"

"Maybe one day we'll find out who we can trust. But meanwhile—"

"Meanwhile, we can't just walk away from the whole thing, because it'll hang over us all our lives. And we can't go to the cops, so . . ."

"Right," Kirsten said. "So . . ."

". . . we're on our own. Just you and—" A howl of laughter came from the living room. "You and me and Cuffs Radovich, I guess."

Kirsten shook her head. She was almost getting used to Cuffs being around, which made her all the more anxious to get rid of him.

She didn't say anything, though, and they ate the rest of their lunch in silence. When they were finished, Dugan asked, "So? You got any ideas?"

"As a matter of fact," she said, "I do."

Three hours later, Dugan rang the bell at Larry Candle's office. The brass plaque on the wall beside the locked door was covered now by a new sign, black letters on white posterboard: LARRY CANDLE. REAL ESTATE AND INVESTMENT ADVICE FOR THE LITTLE GUY.

On the third ring, Larry finally opened the door. "Sorry, pal, but

Mr. Candle isn't—" He stopped. "Oh," he said, "it's you. C'mon in. Didn't recognize you through the peephole."

"You look awful," Dugan said, stepping into Larry's outer office. Packing cartons were piled everywhere. "Where've you been? I left four messages on your voice mail."

"Yeah . . . well . . . I haven't been checking my messages. Too depressing. So, I suppose you're here to tell me your wife doesn't wanna keep looking for Lynne's boyfriend, or whatever the guy was. Right?"

"No. Why do you think that?"

"Because everything's going wrong. My ticket gets yanked. I get shot at. And now the fucking Disciplinary Commission says they don't even want me being here in my office 'cause I'm suspended. I changed my goddamn sign, but they think I'm still practicing law. Suspicious bastards. You know, I oughta— Wait a minute. Did you say 'no'? I mean, is she still looking for the guy?"

"She would be, except that with Lynne dead and Rita missing, there's not much to go on. Are you sure you can't describe him?

"I told her. It was pretty dark in that bar and I wasn't paying much attention to him. He didn't even say anything."

"But you said his hair was brown or black, right?"

"Yeah. I mean I know it wasn't blond, and it wasn't real curly or anything."

"What kind of style was his hair in? I mean, for instance, did he have, well, a ponytail?"

Larry's eyes lit up. "Jesus Christ! I forgot all about that! He *did* have a ponytail, and a little earring in his ear. Or . . . maybe *not* an earring. But a ponytail for sure. I remember now."

"Anything else you remember now?"

"No, really, I can't think of anything." Larry shook his head slowly. "Except . . . like I said before . . . he looked kinda mean. Like a guy you wouldn't wanna meet in an alley or something." He looked around, as though suddenly remembering where he was. "Jesus, what a mess. But hey, you wanna come in the back? We can sit down and talk about how you're gettin' along with the great Bruce Hardison."

"You really don't like him, do you," Dugan said.

"Guy treats me like I'm lower than whale shit. Acts like he's still pissed that Anton'd rather pay me a coupla bucks than one of the partners at his firm, damn money-grubber. He's not so clean, I bet. You defend major porno dealers like he has, you gotta deal with the big bambinos sometimes. 'Lie down with dogs . . . ' they say, y'know? Anyway, I gotta coupla beers in—"

"I have to get moving. If you think of anything more, though—"

"Don't worry. I'll call. And, uh, could you tell your wife to kinda . . . hurry up?"

"Don't push your luck, Larry," Dugan said. "You haven't exactly been helpful. And I just found out today that you haven't even paid her the rest of her fee yet, for chrissake."

Larry shrugged and looked down at the floor. "Yeah. Well, I've been a little short, but I'm working on a few things. If they hadn't pulled my ticket, I—"

"Good-bye, Larry."

On the crowded elevator ride down, Dugan was surprised at himself. While he should have been mad as hell at Larry, he wasn't. In fact, he was feeling a little sorry for the guy, despite all his griping. He shifted his shoulders around, trying to throw off the idea. Next thing you know, for God's sake, he'd be starting to actually *like* Larry Candle.

TWENTY-SEVEN

When Dugan got home after his visit with Larry, Cuffs left, then returned with a duffel bag and a portable TV, and moved into the spare bedroom. Then all three of them went to the health club. Dugan headed for the weight machines where, Kirsten guessed, he'd worry about those pounds he couldn't shed and beat up on himself for not working out more often. As for her, except that she'd be stiff and sore, the doctor said she was fine. So after some lazy warm-ups, she took the long escalator that was the only way up to the track that encircled both the pool and a major portion of the workout area, about a story and a half up from floor level. She ran two miles, pushing herself hard. Then, nearly ready to collapse, she went and sat in the whirlpool.

Meanwhile, ignoring the club rules, Cuffs hadn't changed out of his street clothes. He was never very far away, except when she was at the opposite end of the track and he was by the escalator. Kirsten knew his eyes were on her every minute. She knew, too, that as far as everyone else could tell, all he did was wander around silently intimidating the male fitness instructors and ogling the women on their treadmills.

She hated the very idea of a bodyguard. But she was putting up with Cuffs Radovich hanging around to satisfy Dugan, who was taking longer to get over what had happened to her than she was.

The next morning Cuffs convinced Kirsten he knew what he was doing, and she let him inspect the Tempo for explosives and tracking devices before returning it to the rental agency. He came back with another car, a Pontiac Grand Am, from a different agency and rented in his name. Then, leaving the Grand Am with Dugan, Cuffs drove Kirsten downtown in his Blazer.

At ten A.M. on a Saturday, traffic was light and they easily found a parking spot not far from their destination, at the south end of the Loop. It was an office building from a bygone era, still fighting to maintain a vestige of respectability. Inside, Kirsten pushed the bell for the elevator, then turned to Cuffs. "You wait down here."

"The hell I will." The big man stayed right with her as she stepped inside the elevator and the ancient wrought iron cage struggled upwards. "But I'll stay out of sight."

When they got out on the fifth floor, Cuffs leaned against the corridor wall beside the elevator and pulled a folded *Sports Illustrated* out of his back pocket. "You need any help, little lady, you just holler."

She glared back. "You know, you're really—"

"Just wanted to be sure you were awake," he said, without a hint of a smile. He jerked his head to his left. "Sign says five-oh-four is that way," he added, then buried his face in his *Sports Illustrated*, a well-worn copy of the swimsuit issue.

There was no sense in talking to him. She turned and went down the hall. Most of the suites seemed empty, but the lights were on inside 504, and the sign painted on the old-fashioned frosted glass door said:

MORELLI & FINCHER, LTD.

and below that, in slightly smaller print:

WARP—Women Against Rape and Pornography

Taped to the glass was an index card with the hand-printed words: "Please ring buzzer."

Kirsten opened the frosted glass door and walked in.

The empty waiting room was probably twice the size of her own. Exposed fluorescent lights glared down on four cheap oak-and-plastic chairs and two wood-grained plastic end tables that were stacked with dog-eared magazines of the type you'd expect in a dentist's office. The wall opposite the corridor entrance held a closed wooden door, and next to it, a receptionist's window with a sliding glass panel—closed. Another index card was taped to that glass. It had an arrow pointing diagonally downward, and said: "Please ring buzzer for service."

Kirsten opened the wooden door and walked in.

This room was quite large. Besides the receptionist's desk under the window into the waiting room, there were two other desks, apparently for secretaries. The walls were lined with metal file cabinets. Although files and papers were stacked on just about every available horizontal surface, the room had a distinctly organized, tidy appearance.

To her right, a wide doorway opened onto a hall. Just as Kirsten started in that direction, a small, slim woman in blue jeans and a plaid shirt stepped into the hall from the other end. Kirsten smiled and waved.

The woman stopped, clearly startled, then put her hands on her hips. "Well," she called, her voice just short of shrill, her head tilted to one side, "are you unable to read, or just intentionally rude?"

Kirsten held on to her smile as the woman came down the hall and into the secretaries' room. From Dugan's description, it had to be Cynthia Fincher. "I'm so glad I caught you in," Kirsten said. "You must be Debra Morelli."

The woman ignored Kirsten's outstretched hand. "I'm Ms. Morelli's partner. What do you want?"

Discarding a number of subterfuges she'd been considering, Kirsten simply stated her name and held out one of her business cards. "May I call you Cynthia?" she asked.

Shoving the card in her shirt pocket without looking at it, Cynthia Fincher picked up a manila folder from one of the desks.

"What you want to call me is irrelevant. I've no time to talk. I'm very busy and clients will start coming in at eleven o'clock."

"Clients?" Kirsten couldn't restrain herself any longer. "How do you know *I'm* not a potential client? Which I'm not, by the way. But acting like you are, how could you possibly attract a client? Except maybe someone who can't afford a lawyer who has time for them, or someone so desperate that—"

"Wait," Cynthia Fincher said, and to Kirsten's surprise there was a sudden new tone in her voice—a tired, almost sad tone. She was very pale, with no makeup to camouflage the dark circles around her eyes, and her face—thin, not unattractive—looked as fatigued as she sounded. She half sat on the corner of one of the desks. "Just wait," she repeated, exhaling a sigh. "After all, you're the one who burst in on me, not vice versa. There's a buzzer in the hall and a buzzer inside and you went right by both of them."

"I'm sorry," Kirsten said, softening her own tone. "I was in a hurry."

"I'm in a hurry, too. And very busy, and . . . overtired." Cynthia's eyes seemed focused somewhere beyond Kirsten's left shoulder. "You're right about the clients. All of them are women. Too many women, really, with too little money. And they *are* desperate. They've been beaten up, or tossed out of their apartments, or lost their jobs, or lost their kids, or . . . God knows what. I always thought I was a strong person. But I'm tired."

"It must be difficult work," Kirsten said.

"And then, when we try to work within the system to help them, the system comes down on us and just crushes—" She stopped. "My God, what am I telling *you* this for?"

"I suppose it's because you need to talk to *some*one." Kirsten thought maybe Dugan had misread the two WARP lawyers—or at least this one. "And I'm a great listener." She'd never run into anyone whose need to talk was so obvious.

"I don't know. I . . . I really can't . . ." Cynthia seemed just short of breaking into tears. "I don't even know you."

"Look," Kirsten said, reaching a hand out to the woman, "on the back of that card I gave you is the name of a woman you can call to check my references. If there's something I can—"

"There's nothing *you* can do. I have to dig out of this myself. And my partner just—"

"Out! Outta here, damn you!" Loud, angry shouting—a woman's voice—suddenly broke out from the hallway outside the office. Kirsten turned and looked through the receptionist's window.

A tall woman burst through the waiting room door, still shouting. ". . . away from here!" It had to be Debra Morelli, and she was clearly angry, not afraid. "Cynthia! Call 911!"

Cuffs Radovich pushed through the door before Debra could close it behind her, but he stayed in the reception room while she barged ahead into the secretaries' area. The smirk on Cuffs' face told Kirsten he was enjoying himself.

Cynthia already had her hand on the phone. Her other hand was over her mouth and she was staring at Kirsten as though she'd suddenly realized she might have been talking too much.

"Wait!" Kirsten said. "This man is my— I mean he's with me." She pushed open the door to the reception room. "I thought you were going to wait out of sight, dammit."

"But that broad has—" He stopped. "Hell, maybe she'll enjoy it." Twisting his entire face into an exaggerated wink, he held up his left thumb and forefinger in a circle, and went back out into the hall.

Kirsten turned. "You must be Debra Morelli," she said.

The large woman stared at her, then turned toward Cynthia. "Who *is* this woman? And what is she *doing* here?"

Cynthia cringed, shrinking into herself. "Well, Debra, I—"

"I'm an investigator," Kirsten said, "and I'm looking for a woman . . . " She was digging into her purse for another card, but changed her mind in midsentence and closed the purse. She didn't like Debra Morelli. Didn't like the way she leaned forward, as though on the edge, ready to strike out. Didn't like the way Cynthia retreated so easily before her. "I'm . . . uh . . . looking for a woman's law firm that prefers to use a woman investigator."

"Look, lady," Debra Morelli said, "first of all, I'm not sure I believe you. But second, any woman investigator we hire won't be one that's afraid to go out and look for work without dragging a man along to protect her—especially some pervert with his exploitative magazine." Debra shook her fist, and Kirsten noticed for the first time that she had Cuffs' *Sports Illustrated* in her grip. "Am I right, Cynthia?"

"Exactly," Cynthia said. "She marches in here unannounced, as though we should drop everything." Kirsten was stunned by how Cynthia's demeanor had changed yet again—more brittle and sarcastic—adjusting to Debra's presence. "I was just asking her to leave when you came in. Now I'll call 911."

"Hold it." Kirsten backed toward the door, holding her palms up in a sign of surrender. "I'm leaving."

Out in the hall, Cuffs followed her to the elevator. As they rode down, he chuckled. "Loudmouthed and mean," he said. "My kinda woman."

She didn't answer because she wasn't sure he was kidding. Besides, she was too busy wondering just how the system was crushing Morelli & Fincher . . . and why she had such a strong feeling that she'd met Debra Morelli before somewhere.

TWENTY-EIGHT

The phone rang. It was Anton Bulasik, asking for Kirsten.

"She just left, but you can talk to me," Dugan said, identifying himself.

"Why would I wanna talk to you?"

"Well . . . for one thing, I'm your lawyer."

"I know that. But you aren't gonna do anything in that case but go along with whatever the genius says, right?"

"You mean Bruce Hardison?"

"Yeah, the genius. But look, your wife was asking me some questions, you know? About Lynne, and I, uh, I got a problem. I think your wife and I had the same idea about who it was killed my daughter."

"Oh?"

"But I been talking to—I been thinking maybe we were both wrong. I figured out a few things, and maybe your wife could help me figure out some more. So . . ."

"Why don't you just call the police?"

"Great idea. And why don't I just sign myself into the loony bin? I told you, pal, I needa talk to your wife—in person, not on the phone."

"Then it'll have to be sometime late this afternoon—more likely tomorrow."

"I can't wait that long. This is impor—"

"I'm working on the investigation with her," Dugan said, surprising himself. "It's me or nobody, unless you want to wait."

"I don't— Well, shit. Yeah, come on."

"Also, it'll give me a chance to pick up your records. Remember? I sent word we needed them for the case."

"I remember. But I'm not gonna—I mean, there ain't no records. Me and the lawyer went over that already. Go talk to him about that."

"You mean Larry Candle?"

"Are you kidding? Who'd tell Candle anything? I mean the genius—Hardison. Anyway, I just been talkin' to him and—"

"Hardison? What'd you talk to him for? *I'm* your attorney."

"Yeah, I know that. But he's the *real* lawyer. Anyway, there's some things I think I figured out and they worry me, you know? So I need to talk . . . in a hurry. So, you coming out here or not?"

With a stop for gas and all but one lane closed on the Stevenson Expressway, it was over two hours later when Dugan drove past several cars huddled together around the front of Ray-Ann's Beauty Salon. Down near Cousin Freddy's end of the Hi-Hope Mall there was just one car, a blue El Dorado. He pulled in next to it, thinking he should have left a note for Kirsten about where he was going.

Cousin Freddy's front door was locked.

Anton surely wouldn't have changed his mind that fast. And even if he had, that was no reason to lock up a store that still claimed to be "Open 24 Hours To Serve Sophisticated Tastes." Dugan stooped to peek in around the edges of the "Ladies Always Welcome" sign, where the paint had been scraped off the glass. There were lights on inside, but his range of vision was too limited to see whether anyone was there.

Down at Ray-Ann's, he opened the door and came face-to-face with two hairdressers and four customers in various stages of having strange things done to their heads. "Does anybody know . . ." He stopped and stared back at the six women, suddenly imagining their reactions to an inquiry from some oddball on a Saturday morning about why the local pornographic book and sex-toy shop wasn't open. "I mean . . . did anybody see . . . uh . . . a Doberman pinscher run through the parking lot?"

That didn't chase away the suspicious stares, but it brought out a couple of wary head shakes.

Back at Cousin Freddy's, he tried the locked door again, then went back and sat in the car and thought about going home. A minute later he reluctantly got out and headed for the rear of the building.

The north wall was concrete block, with the only opening way up near the roof, where an exhaust fan was running. The back of the building had no windows either, but there was one sturdy-looking steel door. He knew it would be locked, but he went up and pulled on the metal handle anyway.

The door swung open easily.

"Damn," he said, letting it fall back shut without going in. "Son of a bitch!"

But finally he pulled the door open again and stood in the doorway. The sound of the exhaust fan was louder from the inside, and he smelled something—ashes, or smoke. But there was no smoke to be seen and the odor was faint. If there'd been a fire it was no longer burning.

He stepped inside and let the door close behind him. When he did, there was a change in the sound of the exhaust fan, as though it were laboring harder to draw old air out, now that there was no new air coming in through the back door. Dugan stared down a dimly lit corridor that ran from the rear exit to what had to be the opening into the store. He remembered the red velvet that was draped across the top of the wide doorway, and the swinging doors like a saloon.

Standing there, he became aware of another smell besides smoke. Not gasoline, but some oil-based product. Maybe insect spray?

The fan clattered on, high up and off to his right, but there was no other sound. His neck and shoulder muscles were rigid, and when he tried to relax them and take a deep breath, he found he was too tense to draw in much air. What the hell was he *doing* in here, anyway?

He forced himself to inhale. "Mr. Bulasik!" he finally called out. "Hey! Is there anybody here?"

Motionless, he strained for an answer. But all he could hear was the sound of the struggling fan.

He started forward.

The wall on his right along the hallway was plastic-laminated, imitation-oak paneling. Every six feet or so was a narrow door. All the doors were closed, and each one had a sign that said FANTASY SALON in a sort of Victorian script, and below that was a brass number—the numbers running backward from 6 down to 1 from the rear exit forward. He walked quickly, the mixed smells of smoke and petroleum growing stronger as he went. At the end of the hall he pushed through the swinging doors.

The store was as he remembered it—with just two differences.

One difference was that someone had tried to torch the place—not very successfully. There were a half dozen white plastic charcoal-lighter containers lying around. It appeared that their contents had been sprayed liberally over the rows of magazines and paperback books and in lines around the floor, and then been ignited. The only results were lines of char marks running all over the place, and lots of partially burned magazines and books.

The second difference was behind the raised counter in the center of the store. There was no woman's body sitting stiffly in a chair. This time the body was that of a man, and he was lying flat on his back on the floor with his head turned slightly to one side.

Dugan never doubted for a minute that it was Anton Bulasik—or that he was dead.

There wasn't much blood to be seen, just a tiny border around the edge of the small neat hole in the center of Anton's forehead, and a thin line that ran down from the side of his mouth and had dribbled onto a piece of paper that was folded in three like a letter and was tucked under Anton's head.

Dugan stood for a moment, staring down. He felt suddenly

dizzy, light-headed, as though he might faint. He knew for sure there was writing on that piece of paper, and he even had a pretty good idea what it said. He had no idea, though, why he felt compelled to pick it up and unfold it.

But that's what he did, and he was right about the message:

"Pornography is terrorism, and we won't be victims anymore." He refolded the paper and stood there, creasing the edges and staring down into Anton's empty eyes.

The store had a phone. He should call the police. But his stomach was churning now, and his mind was whirling. He remembered how insistent Kirsten had been that they shouldn't trust anyone, and Anton himself had seemed suspicious of the police.

Dugan needed some time to think.

Suddenly he found himself running, his shirt clinging wet and cold to his back under his jacket. Pushing through the swinging doors, he stumbled into the hallway. He was about to vomit, and it seemed somehow very important that he get outside before he did.

Then, halfway to the exit and just past Fantasy Salon number 3, he heard a door open—right behind him. For a split second he slowed, wondering whether to turn and fight or run for the exit. But then something solid slammed into the back of his neck with a terrible crush of pain. His head whiplashed—first backward, then forward—and he didn't decide anything. He didn't feel much of anything, either—only that he was throwing up already, even before the side of his face slammed into the tile floor.

Dugan didn't know how long it was before he was up on his hands and knees. A minute? Five minutes? He knelt there and stared down at the floor. The pulsating pain in his head was almost overpowering, but he was alert enough to be thankful that he could focus his eyes—even though there was nothing to focus on but the vomit smeared on his hands and coagulating on the cheap linoleum tile.

With the slime on his hands, the smooth wall didn't offer much support, but he managed finally to get to his feet. Once again there was no sound other than the exhaust fan. The door to Fantasy

Salon number 3 was open. He looked in on a tiny, empty booth, with a bench seat built against one wall. The bench faced a glass window on the opposite wall. Feeding quarters into the coin box on the wall beside the window kept the fantasies of a patron's sophisticated taste alive on a screen behind the glass. There was nobody in the booth, and the screen was blank.

Whatever bits of breakfast still remained in his stomach were threatening to evacuate, and Dugan turned and walked unsteadily to the back exit, using his handkerchief to wipe vomit from his hands and chin and then stuffing it absently into his jacket pocket. At the end of the hall he leaned his shoulder into the exit door. It held firm. He twisted the knob and pushed again, but the door had been locked with a keyed dead bolt.

He went back down the hall and through the swinging doors into the store. Passing between the rows of books, he thought he was forgetting something, but hadn't thought of what it might be by the time he got to the front door. That was locked, too, but with a turn bolt that could be thrown from the inside.

He was maybe a quarter mile down Ridgeview Road when two sheriff's police patrol cars swept around a bend up ahead and roared past him in the opposite direction, sirens screaming. He watched in his rearview mirror as the two patrol cars turned into the Hi-Hope Shopping Center.

He took a deep breath and noticed the stench of vomit, then remembered his handkerchief. He dug deep into his jacket pocket—and found something else in there, too.

"Damn," he said. "Son of a bitch."

The words came softly, but out loud, as he pulled his handkerchief from his pocket—and along with it came the bloodstained folded note he couldn't even remember putting in there.

TWENTY-NINE

They had an all-news radio station turned on low in the background, but the second murder at Cousin Freddy's hadn't been reported yet.

"Maybe whoever left you there called the cops, hoping they'd find you and you'd be a suspect." Even as she said it, Kirsten decided it didn't make sense.

"But the note makes it an anti-porn killing," Dugan said. "And I'm not anti-porn. Not that I ever gave it much thought, but . . . how can I be anti-porn if I'm Cousin Freddy's lawyer, for God's sake?"

Kirsten wasn't happy about Dugan having driven home without calling the police. But she was the one who'd warned against trusting anybody, and by the time he'd told her the whole story it was after two o'clock, and it seemed a little late by then to call.

"I could tell them I didn't think of calling till now," Dugan said, "because whoever it was knocked me silly."

"I suppose you could."

"But maybe we should skip it. Like you've said all along, we don't know who to trust, and we're better off if no one knows we're doing anything."

"Yes. I was wondering, though, about . . . fingerprints."

"Damn. You don't really think there'd be—"

"I have a feeling we should think about telling the cops."

"You think about it." Dugan stood up. "I need a hot shower. Then we'll decide."

Kirsten watched him leave the kitchen. Cuffs was taking the afternoon off and she'd planned to stay inside the rest of the day. She stared down at the untouched cup of tea on the table in front of her and dipped the tea bag in and out of the lukewarm liquid. Maybe she should take the advice of the men who tried to scare her off. Maybe she should tell Larry Candle she was giving up looking for his witness, after all. Just go away for a while. Maybe not New Zealand, but somewhere.

She couldn't do that, though. She just couldn't—and she wondered why.

She suddenly remembered seventh grade, and a couple of bullies who'd been relentlessly taunting her about her good grades. Her friends said she should tell the teacher, but the boys warned her not to. She didn't want to give in to them, but she didn't want to be a "tattletale" either. She went to her dad in tears. But he'd been careful not to tell her what to do. "You can't always think your way to the right answer," he said. "Sometimes you just have to feel around for it, go with your gut." The next day she found her bike tires slashed. She'd been scared, but then her fear turned into anger. She didn't tell the teacher, and she didn't back down. Recalling the defeat on those boys' faces when they saw what was left of *their* bikes still made her smile.

And now? She'd like to think what was driving her now was a sense of professional responsibility. But just to save Larry Candle's law license? Not hardly. Larry's precious ticket wasn't something she wanted anyone to die for. The trouble was, she had a nagging suspicion her real motive was neither professional nor responsible, a feeling she might have walked away right at the start—if the bad guys just hadn't blown up her Celica. If all these damn *boys* would just stop trying to scare her off . . .

But this wasn't seventh grade, for God's sake. And she was dragging poor Dugan right along—

The doorbell rang.

She pressed the button, and when Hoffmeier started to identify himself on the intercom, she interrupted him. "Thank goodness," she said. "We were just getting ready to call you."

". . . so why didn't you call us right then, when you couldn't get in?" It was LaMotta's third interruption already and Dugan had barely started. He'd begun with Anton's call, and gotten only as far as his going back a second time and finding Cousin Freddy's front door still locked. "Sorta strange," LaMotta added, "just goin' home like that."

Kirsten sat with Dugan on one side of their dining room table, with LaMotta across from them, scribbling in a notebook. Hoffmeier was standing at the window, his back to all of them.

"I don't guess if I was going to kill Anton Bulasik," Dugan said, "I'd check in with the beauty salon first, to make sure someone could identify me."

"Nobody said you were a homicide suspect," Hoffmeier said, still not turning around. "My partner just wonders why you came home, why you didn't call the police when you had an appointment and then found Cousin Freddy's door locked and—"

"Look," Kirsten said, "when you showed up, we were getting ready to call. And if you'd let Dugan tell what happened, we'll save a lot of time. Because if you think he should have called you guys as soon as he found the door locked . . . you're going to *really* wonder why he came on home after finding the body."

The room was silent.

Hoffmeier's back stiffened visibly before he pivoted slowly and stared at them. His voice was very low when he spoke. Not so much soft, but low, like the rumble in the throat of a guard dog. "Are you telling us that—"

"I'm telling you my husband could hardly talk when he got home, and we were just going to call you, like I said. Now why don't we all keep quiet a few minutes and let him tell his story?"

So they did.

They didn't interrupt much, either, even when Dugan gave them the note with Anton Bulasik's blood on it, but they had a lot of questions when he finished. He answered everything. And if he stressed anything at all, it was his panic and disorientation after he'd been hit from behind, and how it still seemed so unreal, and he wasn't certain he was remembering everything exactly, even now.

And if he left anything out, Kirsten thought, it had to do with his watching the squad cars arrive as he left the scene.

An hour later, as the two investigators were leaving, Hoffmeier stopped just outside the door. "I'm going to tell you both, just this once. Stay away from this thing, far away. It's a homicide investigation, and you both got licenses you don't wanna lose. Understand?" He didn't wait for an answer, but stared straight at Dugan. "As for you, you're damn lucky you poked your face into that beauty parlor. Otherwise, you'd be coming with us." He paused. "Maybe you will be later anyway."

Kirsten stepped in front of Dugan, smiling at Hoffmeier and ever-so-slowly closing the apartment door. "We wouldn't think of interfering," she said. "And if you have anything else you want to ask, Dugan will be happy to answer if he can. Any time. Just call. 'Bye."

And the door was closed.

"Just what I need," Kirsten said softly, "another guy with a warning."

"What?"

"Nothing."

She watched Dugan's shoulders slump with fatigue. "Jesus," he said. "To think I could be sitting at my desk right now, peacefully paging through some client's hospital records."

"It's Saturday afternoon, remember? You think you'd really rather be at your office?"

"I don't know, boredom seems better than being charged with murder, or even conspiring to impede a police investigation."

"Don't be silly. They don't think you killed Bulasik, or committed any crime. That's just Hoffmeier, trying to scare you—or *us*."

"And not a bad try, either," Dugan said.

"Baloney." She figured Dugan wasn't as frightened by Hoffmeier's remarks as he pretended. "Speaking of which, I'm starving. Where should we call for—"

The phone rang.

Dugan started up to answer it, but Kirsten stopped him. "We've had enough for today," she said. "Let the machine take it."

They listened to Dugan's recorded voice announce that they weren't able to take the call.

There was a brief silence, followed by a sort of a cough, and finally a very timid female voice. "Kirsten? This is . . . Freddy. Re-member? Fredrica Kalter? I need to talk to you . . . or . . . to *some-one*. My uncle's been murdered and that . . . that store is all mine now and I don't know what to do and . . . anyway, would you call me? Please?"

There was another silence.

And then, before she hung up, Freddy asked, "Are they going to kill me, too?"

THIRTY

R ita wasn't crying anymore.

She had cried a lot at first, a few days ago, when they stuck her in this new place. It was way worse here than in the apartment over the Cubic Globe. Still no windows to look out, just vents high up by the ceiling for air. But this time just one room. Not very big, either, and half the space was taken up with those darn boxes of dirty magazines and books. And the Really Weird One had changed, too. Acted like he didn't wanna even touch her, which was okay—but different.

Rita was more sure than ever that they were gonna kill her as soon as her money came in, which could be any day now. Anyway, they let her keep her clothes, even if there was nowhere to put what she wasn't wearing except in a plastic bag in a corner of the room. She couldn't wash the few things she had. There wasn't even a place to take a shower, just a little room down the hall with a toilet and a sink.

So she cried like a baby for a day or so, till she couldn't cry anymore. She had thought at first she was going to go crazy. They weren't even around most of the time. One of them would come in once in a while with some food and cans of Diet Pepsi, and to walk her to the bathroom. When she told them she couldn't hold it so long between visits, they just laughed. Then the Really Weird

One came back with this huge plastic 7-Eleven cup for her to pee in when they weren't there.

But it was a few days now, and she didn't go crazy.

It seemed like what changed things was when she got the 7-Eleven cup. For some reason, that made her think of this movie she seen on TV when she was a little kid. About this guy in prison—like Alcatraz or Sing Sing or some place like that. Maybe it was in a foreign country. Anyway, one thing was how the guards were trying to drive the man crazy but they couldn't do it because he wouldn't let them. She didn't remember all that much, but she remembered that all the man had in his cell was this cot with no mattress and this funny-looking little pot in the corner to go to the bathroom in and she remembered how as a kid she'd thought how that would be the worst part of all.

Thing is, she remembered the guy did exercises and stuff . . . and *thought* about different things or whatever . . . and that helped him not to go crazy. And at the end he got out somehow, but she couldn't remember how. She mighta been asleep by the end.

Anyway, she decided she wouldn't go crazy either. She'd pee in her 7-Eleven cup, and do exercises like that man. And she'd try to *think* about stuff, too, as much as she could. But if those two creeps thought she was gonna go crazy . . . well, she'd show them.

One thing Rita had that the guy in the movie didn't have. That was the Crystal Dagger. They didn't find it when she had it on her leg, and then she hid it in her bag of clothes. It had a new cardboard and toilet paper handle, and she thought about it a lot and sometimes she'd even take it out and look at it. At first she thought she'd just go after one of them the next time they came, and hurt them as bad as she could and then let them kill her if they wanted to. She'd draw some blood, too.

But then she thought some more and decided maybe God wanted her to get away, although she didn't know why, since she had done an awful lot of bad things. But who else gave her the Crystal Dagger if it wasn't God? She shouldn't waste it by just using it in some stupid way where she might hurt one of them, but still not get away. Jesus, she might as well let herself go crazy if she did that.

So she wasn't just gonna be dumb and desperate. *No way.* Even if she hated those two creeps, she wasn't gonna get killed just doing something stupid to hurt them.

Uh-uh.

She was gonna get killed trying to get her ass outta there.

THIRTY-ONE

I t was Tuesday morning. The two men who used to work as clerks had quit as soon as they heard what happened to Anton Bulasik, so Cousin Freddy's hadn't reopened yet.

"I talked to both of them on the phone, and I don't think I'd have liked them anyway," Freddy said, as Kirsten pulled into the Hi-Hope Mall and parked in front of the store. Cuffs and Dugan were there already, waiting in the Blazer. "Actually," Freddy added, "*that* man, too . . . Mr. Radovich . . . I don't think I—"

"Cuffs? You don't have to *like* him. I mean, who *would*? That's what makes him so perfect. Since you insist on reopening the store, you need a security guard, and Cuffs'll be great. He'll understand your clientele, that's for sure."

"Maybe. But I wonder if I can afford to pay him."

"Oh, Dugan's already paid him a month in advance for . . . something else. But that's over, and this'll keep him busy."

That part had been Kirsten's idea, actually. She'd caught herself counting on Cuffs being around, and she didn't like that. He'd demanded a nonrefundable month's pay in advance, so she was happy to have an excuse to get rid of him, and still make him work for his money.

They unlocked the front door and the four of them went inside. The day before, Kirsten and Cuffs had cleaned up the fire damage and changed some of the signs, while Dugan and Freddy were going over what little they could find of any accounts and records. The lawyer from Eames & Barnhill who'd originally set up the business had retired, and Dugan had asked Bruce Hardison to get the law firm's file out of storage for him.

None of them knew a good way for a porno shop to recruit decent employees—if that wasn't an oxymoron. So Freddy's plan, for now, was to keep the store open every day but Sunday and Monday from eleven A.M. to eleven P.M. She and Cuffs would work the entire twelve-hour shifts together.

"Are you sure you can do this?" Kirsten asked, watching Freddy switch on the register and fill the cash drawer. "Twelve hours a day?"

"I have to try," she said. "At least until I can decide if I should close up, or sell, and how to do that, or what. Really, it's not the hours I'm worried about. It's being shut up in here with all these pornographic books and these . . . these strange *things.*"

"Just pretend you're selling . . . *ordinary* things," Kirsten said, "vegetables, maybe, like peas and beans and stuff."

"Yeah," Cuffs said, looking around, "or zucchinis or cucum—"

"Skip that," Dugan said. "Kirsten and I have to go. We'll check with you this evening."

Outside, a man slammed the door of a rustling Toyota Corolla and walked past them into Cousin Freddy's. Then as Dugan backed the Grand Am out of its parking slot, another car pulled up.

Kirsten was amazed. "Business is booming already," she said.

"Store's been closed a few days. Maybe there's a lot of pent-up—"

"Let's just get going. Anything anyone says around here has a double meaning."

Once they were out on Ridgeview Road Kirsten asked, "So . . . did Peter and Fred hire a new lawyer for the office?"

"Yeah, they did. Girl who worked for an insurance defense firm but quit. Wants to try the plaintiff's side. Very bright, they said. Very self-confident, too, but not real bitch— I mean, not overly aggressive. They were to call her yesterday and tell her she's hired. She might even start today."

"You didn't say *girl,* did you?" Kirsten asked.

"Sorry. Female person."

"*Young woman* would be just fine. Anyway, I hope she works out." She remembered Fred Schustein's comment and almost asked—jokingly, of course—about bra size, but thought better of it. She certainly didn't want Dugan to think she actually *cared* what the new person he'd be working with all day five or six days a week *looked* like, for God's sake.

"So now where to?" Dugan asked.

"Your office."

"I'm not going to the office. With Cuffs gone, I'm staying with you."

"But you have to train your new associate."

"Molly can do that. Molly trained *me*."

"Well, you ought to go and at least meet her." When he didn't answer, Kirsten said, "Anyway, *I* want to meet her."

Still no answer.

"We can take her to lunch," she said, "or something."

"You'll meet her one of these—" He paused. "Uh-oh, I think I understand."

"Understand what?"

"Why you're so anxious to meet her. You're thinking of Fred's hiring criteria. You're worried she might have . . . big boobs or something."

"Don't be silly. The thought never occurred to me."

At Dugan's office, they found Molly staring at her lunch on the desk in front of her, but talking on the phone and taking notes. She hung up and took a tiny bite of her sandwich. "New client," she said. "Some of us have been *busy* around here."

"Great," Dugan said. "Is our new lawyer in today?"

Molly raised her eyebrows. "You better go talk to our two *old* lawyers about that."

Fred and Peter were busy eating corned beef sandwiches in the firm's law library. They stood up and practically fell over each other greeting Kirsten. They hadn't seen her since the attack in the alley.

"So," Kirsten asked, "when's the new associate start?"

"Well," Peter said, "there's a sort of a problem about—"

"Like hell there's a problem," Fred broke in. "Thing is, Dugan, there *woulda* been a problem, sooner or later. So . . . I fired her."

"You fired her?" Kirsten asked. "Before she even started working?"

"Well, we told all the applicants we needed someone right away. One guy said he couldn't start for a month, so we scratched him on the spot. But all the rest said fine, including her. So I call to tell her she's hired and she starts talkin' about needin' a couple more weeks of relaxation and I figure she shoulda said something about that in the first place and she's kind of jerkin' us around before she even gets started and . . . Well, I got pissed off and I fired her. Sorry."

"Don't be," Dugan said. "I told you to use your best judgment. So, what about one of the others?"

"All losers," Peter said, "except the guy who couldn't start for a month."

"So," Fred cut in, "me and Peter decided if you're gonna be gone a lot, we'll fill in. Maybe learn more about the common law side of the office now, before we get any older."

"Right," Peter said. "With the friggin' legislature always on the edge of being taken over by the business and insurance interests, they'll be screwin' up the whole Workers' Comp system pretty soon. So what the hell . . . "

A few minutes later, Kirsten left Dugan alone to catch up on his mail. Using the phone in the empty office that was awaiting a new associate, she called her own office for messages. There was only one call that interested her, and she returned it on the spot.

"Yes," Cynthia Fincher answered, "I called. I found your card in my pocket and I talked to the woman whose name you'd written on the back of it. Andrea? The one whose husband's a diamond dealer? She told me you— Well, anyway, I'd like to talk to you."

"I'm downtown now. How about two o'clock at your office?"

"I can't. I . . . actually, I'm on my way out of town and . . . well . . . could I see you right away? Maybe for lunch?"

They agreed on a cafeteria down the street from Cynthia's office.

"I'll be there in ten minutes," Kirsten said.

On her way out, she stopped at Molly's desk. "Tell Dugan I'll be back in about an hour." She turned to go, then turned back. "Kinda funny, isn't it, Molly, hiring and firing the new lawyer in one phone call?"

"Probably just as well, though," Molly said. "I really think Fred and Peter had second thoughts and realized maybe she'd sweet-talked her way into the job. Didn't seem better than any of the others to me." She tapped the end of her pen on her desk. "Of course, she *was* awfully good-looking."

"Oh? Really?"

"Yeah. But . . . well, you know the type. Great figure, and dresses so nobody'll miss it."

THIRTY-TWO

They pushed brown plastic trays along the cafeteria rail and paid the cashier. Much of the lunch crowd was still hanging on over dessert and coffee and the only empty booth was in the smoking section.

Kirsten's tray held a small tossed salad with fat-free French dressing, a hard roll, and iced tea in a tall plastic glass. She watched as Cynthia slid carefully onto the bench seat across from her. Cynthia looked even smaller and more unhealthy than Kirsten remembered her. Dark circles around her eyes made the rest of her face appear drawn and pale. She held her thin body in a strangely stiff way, like an asthmatic child in grown-up's clothing. Funny she bothered with a tray at all, since it held nothing but a white ceramic mug filled with very black coffee.

"So that's the secret of your trim figure," Kirsten said, still wondering what this meeting was all about.

"I've had some weight loss, but it's not diet. It's more . . . tension, I guess. And these certainly won't help," Cynthia added, pulling a pack of Virginia Slims from her purse. She lit a cigarette, then shook the match long after it was out before finally dropping it in the ashtray. "Started again just yesterday—after three years."

"You, uh, said something the other day about working too hard?" Kirsten was still feeling her way.

"I don't eat. I don't sleep. Since my marriage fell apart I live alone and work maybe twelve, fourteen hours a day. I just—" Cynthia dragged deeply on the cigarette. Her glance flitted around the room, then came back to Kirsten. "Look, I can't explain why I picked you in particular. I didn't even know your name until I found your card in my shirt pocket yesterday. But you're not a lawyer and you're not a client and it seems like a lifetime since I've talked to someone who wasn't one or the other." She leaned forward across the table. "You seemed, well, sympathetic the other day and I . . . I suddenly realized how far down I've let myself go. I actually called a therapist. But she can't start seeing me until next week, and I need to talk to someone, right now. I need help."

Stunned by the odd mixture of despair and determination in Cynthia's voice, and by her personal tone, Kirsten scarcely moved, afraid even buttering her roll might break the mood. She'd been in similar surprising situations before. People seemed to trust her, for reasons she couldn't understand. She couldn't ignore the fact that she had a job to do. But for the moment, whether Cynthia knew anything about Rita Ranchero, or Cousin Freddy's, or any of the rest of it, suddenly didn't matter much. What mattered was that this woman, who scarcely knew her, seemed to be waging a fierce battle just to get herself to reach out to *some*one. So Kirsten had to help her.

"You don't look well, Cynthia. Are you . . . ill?"

"No. That is, I have an ulcer that kicks up once in a while. And headaches. But what I really am is worn out. There's too much work. And too little money coming in. We've a matter now that I was counting on to bring in a fee." She lifted her cigarette, then reversed herself and jammed the burning end down into the ashtray. "But with my partner acting as she is, that damn case will just drag on forever, like all the rest. Which brings me," she added, staring down at the table, "to something else."

"Something more . . . worrisome."

"Much more. I need . . ." She took a deep breath. "I have to get away from her."

"You mean Debra Morelli."

"We've been partners just over a year. I thought she was a good lawyer, but she's not. And, believe it or not, I *am.* At least when I'm on my game, I'm damn good. It's easy for women lawyers to just buy into the system as it is, but I'd like to make changes. I left a large firm to go on my own, to provide good legal services to women in trouble."

"And Debra?"

"I was looking for a tough feminist lawyer as a partner. I was so excited about the work we could do. I didn't know Debra well, but I saw that she was very aggressive, and I thought . . . But really, she's not a feminist at all. She doesn't give a damn about women's issues. Like the case I mentioned. It's a chance to make some new law in this state, set a precedent for how to close down pornographic book stores. But all she can think of is squeezing the biggest possible fee out of it."

"Sounds like someone you'd find it hard to work with."

"That's putting it mildly. I don't know *what* she cares about, other than wishing she had more money, and venting her incredible hostility and anger. Gradually, I've found myself overwhelmed by her. She's caused some major problems."

"Like the ninety thousand dollars in fees and penalties you owe Investi-Cal Company?" Kirsten asked. "From that sex discrimination case the court threw out?"

Cynthia's eyes widened. "You know about that?"

"I did a computer search for your firm's name in the local media for the last year and turned up that case. False pleadings, failure to obey court orders, withholding and destroying evidence. Frankly, the sanctions against you sounded pretty reasonable."

"Yes. Well, there *was* another side to it. The defendant was represented by a huge law firm that was running us into the ground with motions and discovery requests. Then I found out our own clients hadn't been entirely honest with us. We got desperate and Debra— Well, I can't say I didn't participate. But Debra is so . . . so *strong.* I can't seem to fight her. Especially now, when I'm so stressed out. The Disciplinary Commission even looked into it, and we're lucky we didn't lose our licenses. Investi-Cal's lawyers have made it clear they'll never stop coming after us for the money." She lifted her mug from the table, her hand trembling visibly. "I feel like everything's out of control. I need to get away from Debra. But—"

"I can't help thinking I've met her somewhere, before last Saturday," Kirsten said. She decided she could butter her roll now. "But I can't think where."

"She didn't say she'd ever met you. But she thinks you were lying about why you came to the office. Says you were snooping around. She even accused me of calling you there."

"Oh? Why would she think that? What does she have to hide?"

"I don't know. Maybe nothing. I *do* know she's been away from the office a lot. In the last five days I've only seen her twice—once in court on Friday, and then Saturday morning when you were there. If I question her about it she gets furious. Tells me to shut up and be happy *some*body's working on a way to pay off our debts. My energy level has gotten so low that she intimidates me—and she knows it. That's really what made me call you. If Debra's going to do something illegal, I don't want to be dragged into it. But I find myself simply unable to confront her." She pulled a cigarette halfway from the pack, then pushed it back in. "I hate to admit it. But . . . I'm afraid of her."

"Why don't you just split up the partnership?" Kirsten asked.

"I want to, but I can't. We have clients and an office lease and joint debts and—"

"Look. My husband . . ." Kirsten stopped, suddenly remembering Cynthia wouldn't know who her husband was, and maybe that was better. "My husband knows lots of lawyers. He'll find someone for you who handles partnership breakups."

"I suppose that's a good idea. But I don't have money to pay an attorney."

Kirsten was amazed. This woman, who seemed otherwise so competent, was apparently unable to take ordinary steps on her own behalf. "You can borrow money. Pay it back later. Whatever. Just *do* something."

"But Debra will find—" Cynthia stopped, then suddenly smiled. The very first smile Kirsten had ever seen from her. "Damn," she said, "*listen* to me. I could be one of my own clients. I'm like a battered wife who can't figure out how to open the door and walk away."

"You *can* do it, though. I'll help. And so will your therapist. And Debra needn't know until you're ready to make the break. I'll talk to my husband and call you later this afternoon."

"No, I won't be in. We've closed the office until Monday. My bags are in my car, and when I leave here I'm driving to Midway for a plane to Buffalo, for a conference on representing women prisoners. Debra was to go, too, but she left a message that she had to go to Miami for a few days on a family emergency. Which is odd, because she always claims she has no family. Anyway, I think that's why I had the nerve to call you—because I won't be facing Debra until at least next week."

"It'll be good for you to get away. Where are you staying?"

"A Holiday Inn. Downtown Buffalo somewhere. I've never been there." She smiled a little girl's shy smile. "I haven't been anywhere away from the office in years. When I get in I'll call you and leave a number." She paused. "Would that be all right?"

"Of course."

"It'll be nice to have someone to call and . . . and tell that I arrived safely." Her head down, she was fumbling around in her purse. She pulled out a billfold and set it on the table, then dug out a tissue and blew her nose. "I'm really going to get away." She spoke slowly and softly, then finally looked up. "Thanks."

Kirsten had a sudden inspiration. "Um . . . Cynthia, I hope you parked your car in a safe place. You know, with your bags in it and all."

"Oh, it's my usual lot. You leave your key and the attendant locks up the car."

"That's good." Kirsten smiled. "I'm glad you reached me before you left. Let's talk while I finish my salad. I'd really like to hear more about WARP and that pornography case. And, say, are you *sure* you don't want something to eat?"

"Well," Cynthia smiled back at Kirsten. She lifted her billfold from the table. "Maybe just a piece of chocolate cake."

Not exactly health food, to Kirsten's mind, but certainly a giant step in the right direction—in more ways than one. Because, while Cynthia headed for the dessert counter, Kirsten went through the woman's purse.

THIRTY-THREE

When Dugan finished returning his calls, Molly told him Kirsten went out without him, and he wasn't happy about it. But no way was he ever going to rein Kirsten in, and when she came back she *did* have interesting news about Cynthia Fincher.

"I asked all sorts of questions—in a roundabout way—and I'm convinced she has no idea at all about threats to porno stores, or who killed Lynne and Anton; and she's never heard of Rita Ranchero or the Cubic Globe Gallery. She's the moving force behind WARP. And you're right, Dugan, whether you buy into the whole idea or not, their objections to pornography at least make sense. Cynthia's no fanatical killer. She's a deeply committed person. Badly beaten down right now, but with good intentions."

"I don't know. Both women seemed pretty obnoxious and fanatical to me," he said. "But even if you're right about Cynthia, that doesn't mean Debra Morelli hasn't flipped out and taken WARP's ideas to a crazy extreme."

"Except Cynthia says Debra's not a feminist at all, and not really dedicated to what WARP stands for. If it's *she* who sent hit men after Lynne and Anton, and Larry Candle—and *me*—her use of WARP-type language in those notes must be a subterfuge."

"You mean to hide some other motive? But that's . . . *anyone* could do that."

"True," Kirsten said. "But only someone familiar with WARP's arguments."

"Those are a matter of public record. They're being made in courtrooms all over the country."

"Maybe, but *I* never heard them before. So who do we know who *has*—besides Debra?"

"Cynthia . . . Hardison . . . us . . . Larry Candle . . . Judge Hanahan . . . the cops, maybe." Dugan shook his head. "Freddy? Would Freddy know WARP's theories?"

"I don't know."

"At least Freddy has a motive, when you think of it," Dugan said. "With Anton and Lynne gone, the store is all hers, and she—"

"Anything's possible, I guess. . . . Anyway, we can speculate forever. Just now, there's another thing we can try."

The glazier was way out west on North Avenue, and Dugan's suggestion was, as usual, to use the phone. But Kirsten insisted she'd have a far better chance of getting answers in person, so they drove out there. She went in by herself—also her idea—while Dugan sat in the Grand Am and waited . . . not all that patiently.

The building in front of him did nothing to soothe his worries. A rusting corrugated steel structure in a run-down industrial area, it was a glass company completely devoid of windows, except for one small pane of what looked like bullet-proof Plexiglas in the steel front door. On the building's otherwise unpainted front wall, huge red letters spelled out: RUSSO & SONS, CONTRACT GLAZIERS. Below that was a list of names: SALVATORE RUSSO, ANTONIO RUSSO, ANGELO RUSSO, BENITO RUSSO. Dugan caught himself sounding each name out in his head. Of course, they weren't *necessarily* Mob-connected but . . .

He switched his attention to his law practice. He was actually relieved not to have a new associate just yet. He still wasn't sure how much to tell the person about how some of his clients found him. Paying police officers to refer accident victims had never really bothered his conscience. His cops never pressured the people, and certainly never sent him a phony case. He understood why there were rules against paying people to solicit clients. On the other hand, the supreme court's prohibiting something didn't make it *wrong*. Sometimes you just had to follow your instincts about right and wrong. But if you started trying to keep things secret from your own employees, you were headed for disaster. And maybe it was time he stopped paying those cops anyway. They'd certainly find other . . .

Whatever, he needed another lawyer. He'd have to keep his eyes open, maybe have Fred and Peter start interviewing again. . . .

Kirsten finally came out of Russo & Sons, and he knew by the look on her face that she'd learned something. And it hadn't made her happy. She got into the passenger seat and just sat there silently, staring straight ahead.

"Well?" Dugan asked.

When she didn't answer, he reached for the ignition key.

"Wait," she said, raising her hand in the air between them. "Just sit a minute and let me think. Something's wrong."

He let a minute or two more go by, then asked, "Did they . . . threaten you?"

"What? Oh, you mean the Russos?" She seemed genuinely surprised, and he was glad of that. "They were as nice as they could be. Seems like the whole family works in the business. Wives and sisters, too."

"So what's the problem?"

"On the work sheet, which I told them I found blowing down the alley, it doesn't say who ordered the window repair. Just says 'Cubic Globe, second floor rear.' But according to Francesca Russo, who was on the phones the night the order came in, the caller was a woman. Said her name was Rita Randall."

"And naturally you think Rita Randall was Rita Ranchero."

"Of course. Parker Gillson said Rita Ranchero bought that building and opened the gallery. The sign in the window said R. Randall, which I figured was Rita. But when I asked, the clerk said R. Randall was dead. And then when I mentioned Rita Ranchero he got, well, mean, and pushed me out the door." She paused, then said, "Rita was there all the time. In the building. She was right there on the second floor when I broke the window."

"You have no idea whether she was there," Dugan said. "And besides, if she was, maybe she doesn't like visitors."

"But I believe she *was* there—locked up in there—and still is. I told you, there were bars on the windows."

"C'mon, Kirsten, lots of people in Chicago have bars on—"

"No, not hidden *inside* the glass, they don't. They have them outside, where even the dumbest potential burglar can see them and be encouraged to go somewhere else. And why haven't I been able to find Rita? I tell you, she's locked up in that building." She paused. "We ought to at least go look. What time is it?"

"Almost five o'clock."

"Damn," she said. "This time of day, it could take forty-five minutes to get there."

In fact, it took over an hour. They went north to Diversey and took that east. Dugan had skipped lunch, so they decided to stop for a sandwich at the first place that looked quick and decent and wasn't a franchise. It turned out to be a take-out stand called Lupo's, near Western Avenue. The beef and pepper sandwiches were great, but Dugan wondered why fate kept leading them to Italians.

"It's an omen or something," he said, as they drove away. "We go from Russo's to Lupo's, to find Ranchero. I mean, this city's gotta have a hundred other ethnic—"

"Oh, don't be silly. Ranchero doesn't sound Italian to me. Besides, it's a stage name, for sure. She could be Irish or Puerto Rican or anything. Randall is obviously made up from Ranchero, and . . . Anyway, the middle of the next block is the Cubic Globe Gallery. Better get over in the right lane."

So he did. But when he stopped, there *was* no Cubic Globe Gallery. There was just an empty store with a large sign in the window:

BUILDING FOR SALE

PRIME COMMERCIAL LOCATION WITH APARTMENT ABOVE

"Well," Dugan said, "if Rita was locked away up there last week, she isn't now."

"Maybe. There's a telephone at that gas station across the street. I'll call the realtor."

Dugan made a U-turn and parked.

When Kirsten came back from making the call she said, "Both the store and the apartment are empty and they can show us the place tomorrow at nine in the morning. So you're right. Rita's not there anymore."

"You don't know if she ever was there."

"She was there. I know she was. They took her someplace and we have to find her. We're starting right now."

"She could be anywhere in the world, for God's sake."

"But there's one place we *know* about that has ties to Mr. Pony-tail. So that's the place to start."

THIRTY-FOUR

It was almost eight o'clock when Dugan pulled the Grand Am into the nearly empty parking lot at the Metra Station in Lake Forest, not far from Double-M Leasing's office.

"Look," he said, giving it one last try, "suppose we do find Rita here. So what? What do we do then?"

"We talk to her," Kirsten said. "First we ask her about Larry Candle and whether she gave him permission to use her money. Then we talk to her about Lynne and Mr. Ponytail, and Anton and Cousin Freddy's, and how all these things fit together—if they do."

"And then what?"

"Then, if she's said anything that sounds interesting— Say, where's my purse?" She was fumbling around under the car seat. "Oh good, here it is. Anyway, then we can call Hoffmeier and LaMotta and they can do whatever they want to about it. How's that?"

"That's wonderful," he said, recalling Hoffmeier's warning to keep out of it.

The front door, between the travel agency and the cabinet shop, was locked. The rear entrance was locked as well, and when he saw Kirsten step back and look up toward the second floor, Dugan took her by the arm. "Not this time," he said. "No way."

"What *are* you talking about?"

"We're not breaking any windows."

"Oh, don't be silly," she said. "I didn't really expect the place to be open. But . . . didn't the receptionist tell you she lives in Lake Forest?"

They got Alice McKenzie's address from the phone book. It was a ten-minute drive, the end unit of a row of two-story town homes. A man who looked like he might have played college football a few years ago came to the door. He called out for his mother, and when Alice came down the stairs he retreated through the open dining area to the kitchen and left her with them in a small parlor. The furniture was plain and comfortable, as was the slight odor of hamburger and fried peppers that hung in the air.

"Do you remember me?" Dugan asked.

"Of course." That's all she said, but Dugan detected a touch of humor in her voice, and wondered about it.

The sound of a Bulls telecast leaked through the partially open kitchen door. "My son's visiting me," Alice said.

"I'm glad he is," Dugan said. "I was afraid you'd be alone and wouldn't even let us in the door. I . . . I may have misled you a little the last time we met."

"Well, you certainly left me wondering."

"I did?"

"When you left the coffee shop I thought hard and finally came up with the name on that business card you snatched up. I called the attorney general's office and they never heard of you. They suggested I call the Attorney Registration and Disciplinary Commission. I did, and at first they said you're a licensed attorney and that's all they could tell me. I kept asking questions, though, and they transferred me to one of their investigators. He was a very nice man and—"

"Not a Mr. Gillson, was it?" Dugan asked.

"Yes, as a matter of fact it was. When he said he knew you personally, and your wife as well . . . " She turned to Kirsten. "That's you, I suppose."

"Yes," Kirsten said.

"He told me you were a former police officer. He just couldn't say enough good things about your honesty and integrity and—"

"I'm very happy to hear that," Kirsten said, "but—"

"Anyway," Alice turned back to Dugan, "Mr. Gillson said you *might* be on some special project for the attorney general's office that the person answering phones wouldn't know about, maybe with your wife. He said I needn't worry, and suggested I not mention the operation—that was his word, *operation*—to anyone. He said to call him if I had more concerns. He even gave me his direct number. He didn't actually say so, but I got the distinct impression you could be working on something important and . . . confidential. Actually, I thought I'd never hear any more about it. But," she smiled again, and Dugan suddenly realized she was imagining herself in on some important, clandestine operation, "here you are again."

"Uh . . . right. Here I am."

"It's about Double-M Leasing, isn't it? It all seems very mysterious to—"

"I wouldn't say mysterious, Mrs. McKenzie," Kirsten interrupted. "Here's my card. It's just a search for a witness. Her name is Rita Ranchero."

"Oh, please call me Alice. But . . . Rita Ranchero? Sounds like some kind of singer or something," Alice said.

"A dancer, actually."

"Really? I was on the stage myself, years ago. Legitimate theater, I mean. Some Off-Broadway things, you know, and summer stock. Even did *The Mousetrap*, in London, for nearly a— But forgive me . . . " Her voice trailed away in embarrassment.

"Anyway," Kirsten said, "Rita seems to have disappeared and I thought she might have shown up at your offices."

"*my* . . . ? Oh, you mean at Double-M. Actually, I'm not sure I work there anymore."

"Not sure?"

"I got this rather bizarre phone call from Mr. Morgan when I got home Thursday evening. He said they were reorganizing the business—whatever that means—but he didn't actually fire me. Just said I shouldn't come in Friday, and he'd let me know if they needed me again. Then he came by unannounced later that very same night to pick up the keys. Which I thought was rather rude, as though they were afraid I'd let myself in. But he did give me my paycheck, along with an extra week's pay. That's the last I've heard from him. Can't say I'm that sorry, either."

"Was there someone with him?"

"He came in a panel truck, and I really didn't notice if there was anyone with him or not."

"Why did you say what you said . . . about not being sorry?"

"As I told your husband, the job was very boring, although I *did* get lots of time to write letters to friends. And besides the monotony, I didn't like Mr. Morgan, not one bit. He's just . . . not a very nice person. Years ago, young men with ponytails seemed the gentle and peaceful type. Hippies or something. But this Morgan person isn't like that at all. He just seems . . . oh . . . self-important and rude and—"

"Did you say *pony*tail?" Dugan asked.

"She sure did," Kirsten said. "Mrs. McKenzie, I have to confess there's a little twist to this search for Rita Ranchero. I think maybe she's in trouble. Maybe the man with the ponytail doesn't want her to be found."

"Oh my. I *knew* he wasn't a nice person. Well then, hadn't we better call the police?" Dugan noticed she said *we*.

"I . . . we . . . really can't do that. And, as Mr. Gillson implied, I'm not at liberty to say why." Kirsten closed her eyes and clenched her fists. "I just wish we could look around in . . . " She opened her eyes again. "You turned in the keys, you said?"

"Oh yes. But, well, I was so upset when he came barging in here for the keys that I forgot."

"Forgot what?" Dugan asked.

"I have a bad habit of losing keys, so I had an extra set made for myself." She paused, managing to look embarrassed and proud of herself at the same time. "I'm sure I still have them in a drawer somewhere."

THIRTY-FIVE

Dugan was afraid Alice McKenzie would want to come with them to Double-M. But despite her intrigue at the idea of some confidential operation, she apparently wasn't crazy enough to go that far. She *did* suggest, though, that she could "accidentally drop the keys, out on the sidewalk. And then if you happen to find them, well . . . "

Not a very sophisticated plan, to Dugan's mind. But breaking into Double-M didn't seem a particularly intelligent thing to do in any event.

"We're not *breaking in*," Kirsten insisted. "We *will* have *keys,* after all."

"Right. Keys we found on the street. It's got to be a felony."

"We'll discuss it later," Kirsten said. "Besides, I have a better idea than us finding the keys." She looked at her watch. "And it's still early enough to be plausible. Alice, is it possible you left something important behind at Double-M? I don't know . . . a bracelet or a ring or something? You might give me the keys and ask me to go get it for you, tell me right where it would be if it were there, which I'll find that it isn't?"

Alice sat silently for a minute, her brow furrowed. "Actually, you know," she said, "it *is* there. I just thought of it!"

"*What's* there?" Dugan asked, almost afraid to hear.

"Well," Alice's eyes sparkled, "my *appointment* calendar, of course. A little loose-leaf thing with a place to insert each year's calendar, and a section for all my addresses and phone numbers, with birthdays and anniversaries and everything. I wrote so many letters at work, I just left it there. But since I'm not working, I'm leaving town tomorrow with my son for Spokane, and I'll be gone weeks and weeks and I'll certainly need my calendar."

"And where is it?" Kirsten asked.

"In a drawer under the front counter. Way in the back behind the rental applications and receipts. The drawer closest to the phone."

"Which reminds me," Kirsten said. She used Alice's phone to call Double-M. "Good," she said, hanging up. "No answer. Let's go. If anyone questions us, we'll have them call you."

"Fine," Alice said. But then she turned toward the kitchen. "Eugene," she called, "would you come here a minute, please?"

Her son appeared in the kitchen door.

"Eugene, you remember that leather appointment calendar your father gave me, don't you?"

"Sure I do."

"Well, this is Kirsten and Dugan. They're friends of mine and I just remembered I left that calendar at work, so I'm giving Kirsten the extra keys and she's going to get it for me. Isn't that nice?"

"But Mom, I could take you—"

"Oh no, you're busy, and *I'm* certainly *far* too busy getting ready to leave town. Besides, Kirsten owes me a favor, don't you, dear?"

"Uh . . . yes, of course."

"And Dugan," Alice said, "you go with her, okay?"

"Sure," Dugan said. "That's a great idea."

Looking as though he wondered why his mother had bothered to call him, Eugene disappeared back into the kitchen.

Alice walked them to the front door. "Thought it might be smart to have another witness—in case we get caught." *We* again, Dugan noticed. "Eugene *is* a family member, of course," she continued, "but he's very believable. He's a police officer, you know, in Spokane."

In the car, driving back to downtown Lake Forest, Dugan said, "Am *I* crazy, or is *she?*"

"Don't be ridiculous, darling. No one's crazy. We're just doing our job. And we got such a shining reference from Park that Alice is happy to help us do it."

Dugan drove for a while in silence, but then said, "You used that word again."

"What word?"

"*Darling.* You never call me that, except when—"

"I don't?" Kirsten asked, sounding surprised. "Well, anyway, here we are. Let's just park right out in front."

"The sign says no parking."

"I know. That'll make it look even more like we don't have any reason to hide."

It was nine-thirty. The storefronts along the block were dark, and the street was deserted under the soft glow of colonial-style street lamps.

Alice's ring held three keys. Dugan guessed right about which one would fit the outer door, and they went inside and up the tilted stairs. In the hallway outside the door to Double-M he studied the two remaining keys, but before he could pick one Kirsten stopped him.

"Wait," she said, and pressed the button beside the door frame.

The sound of the buzzer from inside was clear, but there was no response.

"Okay," Kirsten said, "try a key."

He guessed right again, and the door swung open.

They switched on the lights in the reception area and found Alice's appointment calendar where she said it would be, beneath a jumble of blank rental applications in the back of the drawer near the phone. Kirsten shoved the leather booklet into the purse that hung from a strap over her shoulder.

Behind the counter an unlocked door led into a small, carpeted office, holding only an old wooden desk, a swivel chair, and a file cabinet. Kirsten pulled the door closed behind them. Heavy drapes were pulled back from two large windows, and enough light came in from the streetlights to let them determine that the desk drawers and the file cabinet were empty.

The walls to the right and left of the desk each held one door. The third key in the set unlocked the door to their left, and it opened into a small, windowless storage room with a meager assortment of carpet-cleaning machines and floor sanders.

The other door was locked also, and none of the keys fit.

There was something about the way Kirsten stood and stared at the locked door that Dugan didn't like. "So far," he said, "we might get away with this, even if someone walks in on us. But if we start picking locks . . ."

"That's a dead bolt lock and I don't know that I could open it if I took an hour." Her words came slowly, as though her mind were elsewhere. She stood motionless for a moment, the tips of the fingers of her left hand stroking her chin, her right hand thrust deep inside her purse.

"Oh well," she said, her tone that of a person resigned to her circumstances.

Dugan turned to go and then, from the corner of his eye, saw Kirsten's hand come out of her purse.

"Wait," he said, his voice just short of a shout. But she certainly couldn't have heard him.

The wood of the door around the lock burst into splinters, and Dugan imagined he actually heard them landing on the worn carpet in the deep, marvelous silence that followed the explosion from Kirsten's gun.

"I've never done that before," Kirsten said. "It actually works, though, doesn't it? At least with a cheap, lightweight door like this one." She pulled the door open and disappeared into the room.

Dugan stood still, waiting for screaming sirens and shouts from the street below. All he heard was a ringing in his ears that turned out to be the rhythmic clang of a warning bell and then the roar of a diesel-powered late-night commuter train pulling into the Metra station a block away.

The sound of a cardboard carton being torn open finally drew

Dugan through the open door after Kirsten. This, too, was a windowless storage room, twice as large as the other, and about one-third filled with stacks of unmarked boxes. Kirsten was crouched down, tearing open a second carton, a lighted flashlight sitting on the floor beside her.

"What the hell are you doing?" Dugan asked.

In response, she held up a magazine from the box she'd just opened, angling it so he could see the cover in the light of the flashlight. The black-and-white picture was similar to the covers that lined the shelves at Cousin Freddy's, the kind Dugan was getting used to—sort of—by now. Three naked, not-all-that-beautiful people, in somewhat bizarre sexual poses. These three happened to be Asians—not so unusual, as he had come to learn.

But this photo was different—in a way that turned Dugan's stomach. Two of the three people portrayed were almost certainly not yet ten years old.

Mercifully, Kirsten shoved the magazine back in the box almost at once, while Dugan swallowed hard in anger and disgust.

They opened enough boxes to decide that they all contained similar material. Dugan stood for a moment with his eyes closed, while a heavy, dull blanket of depression settled over him. Then he heard Kirsten inhale noisily, twice.

"Are you going to cry?" he asked.

She didn't answer, just sniffed again and looked around the room. "Isn't there an odd smell in here?" she finally asked. "Like . . . perspiration maybe? Or dirty clothing or something?"

"It's just the smell of cheap ink, and maybe the rotting of twisted minds." He took her by the arm. "We have to go, before someone finds us."

"No one seems to have heard the shot," Kirsten said, still staring around the room, "and whoever owns this . . . garbage . . . isn't very likely to call the cops."

"Jesus, cops are the least of our worries." Dugan led her out of the storage room. "I'm more concerned about—"

He stopped, frozen, just inside the office with the empty desk. Punctuating the dull, steady glow of the streetlights through the windows was a staccato flashing of blue and red, coming from down on the unseen street below the windows.

"I think," Kirsten said, pressing close to his side, "the least of our worries has arrived."

Twenty minutes later, dropping off Alice's appointment calendar, they declined her invitation to stay for a while for coffee. They told her they were surprised the police would use their flashing lights just to leave a parking ticket on the Grand Am and then drive away.

"There's so little crime in Lake Forest," Alice said. "I suppose they don't get much chance to use them."

They also told her there'd been no clue to the whereabouts of Rita Ranchero. But they didn't tell her about blowing away the lock on the storage room door, or the cartons of kiddie porn they'd found inside.

Back in the car, Dugan drove aimlessly for a while, then pulled up to an outdoor phone at a gas station. "We should call the police," he said. "We can make it anonymous."

"What good will that do?"

"They'll find that crap in the storage room and they'll arrest the Ponytail, and—"

"Maybe. Maybe not. But will that help us find Rita?" She stopped. "One of my messages today was from Larry Candle. Very important, supposedly. Call him, no matter what time. I didn't call."

" 'Very important.' Wants to know why it's taking you so long to save his ass."

"I suppose. But I should call him anyway."

She got out of the car and went to the telephone. Dugan knew she was stalling. She didn't want to call the police, but didn't know what else to do. So she'd call Larry for something to do while she thought.

He stared at her. She *was* very good at thinking, he had to admit. She tapped out the number by memory, and he could tell that she'd gotten Larry on the line. But when he saw the look that came over her face, he lowered the car window.

". . . hell, Larry," she was saying, "how could you *not* have thought of . . . All right . . . all right. Yeah. Good-bye." She slammed the receiver down and when she got back in the car, she slammed the door, too.

"That was Larry," she said, needlessly, then took a slow, deep breath and let it out in a sigh. "Let's not call the police about that crap just yet. There's something else more *urgent*. I think I know now what I smelled in that storage room. And, if Larry's right, we've got about forty-eight hours to find Rita alive."

THIRTY-SIX

Rita was glad at first when they moved her again after only a few days. But not now. Now things were even worse, and she knew her time was almost up. She'd lost track of how long ago it was that they'd made her call and give a new address for where to send her check, but the check hadda be due by now. She used to wonder at first why they didn't just kill her and forge her name on the check. But she guessed they were scared the forgery would be noticed and they wouldn't get the money. That's why she was still alive, until they had the cash in their hands.

And that stuff about letting her go after that was all bullshit.

Thing is, she knew all about the stupid scheme they wanted to use her money for. They were too dumb to see they'd never get away with it, even if the cops didn't catch them. Everyone knows, you try something with those Syndicate people and you end up in the trunk of some stolen car under a viaduct—and that's if you're lucky.

But these two were so greedy they couldn't think straight. And now that the time was close, it seemed like they were getting dumber than before. They took for granted that she was helpless, like a baby. So she acted more that way, too. They never even searched her or her bag of clothes anymore—or they'd have found the Crystal Dagger.

The Really Weird One still wasn't interested in screwing her, or any of that weird stuff, either. Maybe he was getting his rocks off just thinking about all that money gonna come in. Plus, she'd been watching, and she was thinking maybe him and the Silent Partner . . . Jesus, she didn't even wanna *think* about it. Course, she never saw them *doing* anything . . . but sometimes the way they talked and acted. Wouldn't *that* be gross! Rita had a sister and a couple brothers herself, and they all did a lotta bad things, but never anything like that. Her mother woulda thrown a fit.

What was really awful now, though, was where they kept her locked up. The room was small, almost like a closet. And when they left they tied her up and gagged her. She'd have gone crazy this time for sure, but she kept thinking of that man in Alcatraz or wherever it was. She was still waiting for the right time to use the Crystal Dagger—kinda dumb, but she still called it that—waiting until there was a real chance she could get away. She was thinking more and more that God would tell her the right time to use it, and God would arrange things so she had a chance.

Thing is, so far the chance never came up. Or if it did, she didn't see it. Sometimes she worried God might've already given her the chance and she was too dumb to see it. Especially now, when she was tied up so much and the weapon was out of her reach. But that didn't make sense, for God to give her a chance and then not make her see it. That would make God as dumb as her.

No way. That didn't make sense. Did it?

THIRTY-SEVEN

After her midnight call from Lake Forest to Larry Candle, Kirsten couldn't think of anything to do except go home. So they did.

There was a message on their answering machine from Cynthia, in Buffalo. "Just leaving my number. Call . . . uh . . . if you get a chance?"

Kirsten called. Cynthia sounded awfully sleepy, but the obvious gratitude in her voice made Kirsten glad she'd awakened her, even though it was nearly two A.M. in Buffalo and Kirsten had forgotten to ask Dugan for the name of an attorney to recommend to her.

"The hotel is great," Cynthia said. "I've been to the whirlpool twice already. The only bad thing is . . . I noticed I must have lost my keys out of my purse somewhere."

"Oh, how *awful*. But you won't need them at the conference. You can worry about the keys when you get back to Chicago. Meanwhile, have a great time. And Cynthia, call if you get lonesome, okay?"

"Oh, I will. I can't wait to get back and start therapy and . . . and everything."

The next morning, Kirsten and Dugan made plans over coffee and toast. It was clear Dugan didn't like the idea of working separately, but if she was right, time was running out. And if not? Well . . . she knew she *was* right.

Dugan left after breakfast to follow up on Larry's sudden recollection that Rita Ranchero's settlement payment had been divided into two installments. Larry had no share in the second payment, and Rita was to have informed the insurance company where to send her check—which was due by the day after tomorrow.

When Dugan was gone, Kirsten made some phone calls, waited half an hour, and then left the apartment.

Except to walk through the Loop the previous day, to meet Cynthia for lunch, this was the first time she'd been out on the street alone since the attack. She scanned the block in both directions before locking the street entrance behind her, telling herself she wasn't afraid, just being cautious. Then she told herself that that was a lie and she was afraid and she might as well admit it.

She wanted to take a nice, safe cab, but instead she walked five blocks and then took the Ravenswood El downtown. She did that because it was the more frightening thing to do. *You can't beat fear by running the other way.* Her father used to say that. You have to meet it head on, push through it, and keep on pushing. Eventually the fear vanishes, evaporates. Always.

Until the next time.

But while you pushed through the fear you could still keep your eyes open, which she did—and which she should have done more carefully outside the Blue Sunrise. *Whatever happens, it's a blessing.* This time the words were her mother's. Even a bad experience could be helpful—if only, as now, to remind her of some truth easily forgotten.

So Kirsten walked all the way to the Ravenswood El and rode downtown, along the west side of the Loop, across the south end, then up the east side to Randolph Street. She walked down to street level, east to Michigan Avenue and across, and then two more blocks to the Prudential Building.

She kept her eyes open. No one was following her.

The office of the Attorney Registration and Disciplinary Commission was on the fifteenth floor, but Kirsten walked past the elevators to the east end of the lobby, and into a newly opened sandwich shop that was all chrome and black and white, designed to look like a corner café in Paris.

She ordered decaf at the counter and took it to the last table in the corner to her left. "How about trading seats?" was the first thing she said, looking down at Parker Gillson.

His cup stopped halfway to his lips, and his eyebrows lifted, but he said nothing as he gave her his place, then sat down again facing her—and the wall behind her. He reached over and dragged the little basket with what was left of a chocolate croissant across the shiny black surface to his side of the table.

"Nice to see you, too," he finally said.

"Sorry. A lot's been happening and . . . "

On the phone she'd given him only a list of things and people she wanted to know more about. But now she decided it wasn't fair to keep him in the dark, so she spent some time bringing him up to date. She didn't say *keep this to yourself*, or anything of the sort. She simply trusted him and told him.

When she finished, he stood up and said, "How 'bout a raspberry croissant?"

"Split one with you."

She watched him move across the room to the counter. He *was* getting overweight, no question about it. But with the excess calories coming from food, not alcohol, at least his brain was being spared. Park was probably a certifiable genius. Way overqualified, certainly, for his job with the ARDC. He was a walking encyclopedia, constantly revised, of politics and politicians—city-, county-, and state-wide. In addition, but closely related, he knew who most of the major players were in the local law, business, and real estate worlds, where they came from, and even many of their secrets. And, also closely related, he knew more than most people wanted to know about organized crime—not only the traditional Outfit-style variety that still had a firm, quiet grip on too much of what happened, but also the vicious street gangs that more openly terrorized major portions of the city's neighborhoods.

And what Park didn't know, he was able to find out.

When he returned, he solemnly sliced the raspberry croissant in half with a serrated white plastic knife. He gave her one half and set the other on a napkin in front of him.

"Are you sure this is all right?" Kirsten asked.

"What, raspberry? Almost as good as chocolate."

"You know what I mean. Am I getting you in trouble?"

"No way. None of this stuff comes from any ARDC file, and no one ever told me I couldn't use my computer, or my contacts, to moonlight a little." He took a small spiral notebook from the pocket of his suit coat. "Number one, Cousin Freddy's. If the Outfit doesn't already have it, they want it, or a piece of it. Either way, you can bet they were in touch with Anton."

"And will be with Freddy?"

He nodded. "Maybe not right away, though. Number two, Anton Bulasik. He's got a sheet in Cleveland. Small-time stuff. No convictions. Nothing since his wife died and he moved here with his daughter."

"Lynne."

"Uh-huh. She's number three. Legal name Evelyn. High-school dropout. Couple drug busts. One misdemeanor conviction. Hangs— *Used* to hang around a lotta north-side late-night party places. Gay and lesbian mostly, but not always."

"Anton and Lynne, any Outfit connections?"

"Need more time for that. But they ran that store, so . . . Anyway, number four, Charles Morgan of Double-M Leasing. Zip, so far. Five, a ponytailed gentleman from the Cubic Globe Gallery. Zip, so far."

"Better make that four-A and four-B. It's the same guy. I'm sure of it. And 'so far' means you'll keep checking?"

"Right." He paused to chew on a bite of croissant and flip a page of his notebook. "Number Six— Ah . . . make that five, a large black gentleman named Andrew something who associates with . . .

six, a large white gentleman whose name is unknown." He swallowed some coffee. "Do you know how many large black men named Andrew—if that's his real name—there are within a thirty-mile radius of us, even as we speak?"

"Thousands," she said. "But I have to say I'm grateful to this particular Andrew, since he—"

"Don't overdo the gratitude. He was saving his own behind."

"Maybe," she said. "But still . . ."

"Guy's a punk. Maybe a killer." Park wiped his fingers on the paper napkin, rolled it into a ball, and dropped it in his cup. "Let's see," checking his notebook, "the last three are all lawyers, so I got more on them. But I gotta be careful I don't even appear to be using any confidential—"

"I understand, but—"

"Right. So . . . Mr. Bruce Hardison. Knows everyone; everyone knows him. A top-notch litigator, but not personally well-liked. Partly because of some of his clients; mostly because he likes himself so much. His divorce caused a stir a few years ago when he got the judge to put the file under seal after his wife threatened to drag him and his business affairs through the mud. Seems very wealthy—even for a partner in a silk-stocking firm—and spends like crazy. A quiet rumor once had it he made a bundle investing in a client's porno operation. Supposedly his firm at the time looked into it and found nothing, but he left that firm to join Eames and Barnhill. A lot can be ignored if you bring in enough fee-paying clients."

"Y'know? Larry Candle said much the same thing. Your take on Hardison?"

"I've met him. He's a very bright egomaniac. But only one among many." Park glanced again at his notebook. "Then there's Cynthia Fincher. No bad marks, except that recent fiasco where her firm got socked for fees. Maybe a little too . . . doctrinaire."

"What's that mean?" Kirsten asked. "Too *feminist*?"

"No. Too dogmatic to use good sense. First she leaves a good firm, where she had a great future. Not bad in itself. But then . . . she hooks up with *real* trouble."

"Debra Morelli?"

"Exactly. Morelli's from Detroit. First admitted to the bar in Michigan. Fincher probably wouldn't know this, but Morelli's admission was vigorously opposed. She had a long history of being beaten and sexually abused by her father as a kid, and—"

"A father's abuse is no reason to keep a daughter from being a lawyer."

"No. But this father's head got blown off his shoulders with a shotgun. Not a shred of evidence as to who did it, and no one liked him much. But the list of genuine suspects was short."

"Debra?"

"And maybe a brother of hers who was abused, too. They were young teenagers at the time, and both had plenty of problems after that. But fifteen years later she managed to become a lawyer in Michigan—God knows how . . . or why. Moved here and got admitted to the Illinois bar through reciprocity. Fired by two divorce firms, then joined up with Fincher."

"And nobody was ever charged in her father's murder?"

"Nope. Lack of evidence, and a certain amount of sympathy for the kids. Besides—even apart from the abuse—no one thought the father was any great loss."

"Oh?"

"Manny Morelli was a bum, a bagman. He collected protection money for the Outfit in Detroit." Park looked at his notebook, and then at his watch. "And with that, dear snoopy lady, I gotta go."

There was plenty more Kirsten wanted to ask, but Park got to his feet.

"I do have a *real* job, too," he said.

She smiled. "Thanks, Park. Hey . . . you know? I think you've lost a few pounds, just since—"

"And I think you," he glared down at her, "are a surprisingly unconvincing liar—especially for a white girl."

THIRTY-EIGHT

D ugan sat silently across the desk from Emerson Croft the Third. The twerp had actually said "the Third" when he introduced himself. Said it with a capital letter, too. Dugan would have responded with something smart-assed if he hadn't been looking for help. Croft & Kilgallon was counsel for the insurance company that owed Rita Ranchero the second and final installment of the settlement proceeds Larry Candle had wrung out of them on her behalf.

The first Emerson Croft died long ago. The firm's other founding partner, Jake Kilgallon, was said to appear in the firm's office just twice a year, for partners' meetings when the profits were divvied up. Although they'd usually represented defendants in personal injury cases, they'd been friends of Dugan's dad and both had been more like Fred and Peter than like Emerson Croft the Third.

"I wouldn't even show up for the goddamn partners' meetings," Dugan once heard Jake Kilgallon tell his dad, "if I wasn't afraid some of those bright young A-holes might get together and vote me out of my share." That's exactly how he said the word, *"A-holes."* That's why Dugan remembered it so well.

Jake had only daughters, and they were about ten years too early to feel drawn to law school, so that left the road clear for Emerson

Croft, Jr., to become the firm's managing partner, though rumor had it he was losing interest now, too.

Anyway, Dugan was sitting silently across from Emerson Croft the Third, while this particular bright young A-hole was on the phone, debating with Larry Candle.

"... hate to repeat myself, Mr. Candle," Croft was saying, "but I'm afraid we have it in writing—over your signature, I might add—that you are no longer counsel for Miss Ranchero. She has instructed us where to send the settlement draft—incidentally, it's a draft, not a check—and has not authorized us to reveal her address to anyone. Now I'm afraid I don't have time to—" There was a pause, during which Croft's face grew very red. Finally, he just hung up the phone.

Larry had lost the debate.

"Obscenities and vulgar anatomical threats," Croft said, looking at Dugan as though he thought Dugan might try the same approach. "I'm afraid the ethical rules require that I report such conduct to the ARDC."

The ethical rules, of course, required no such thing, but Dugan kept still about it.

Croft looked across at him. "I'm afraid I must tell you that the publicized dispute between Mr. Candle and Miss Ranchero has raised considerable concern on my client's part about the motives, and the integrity, of both of them. Perhaps that need not concern you. But at any rate, I'm afraid I'm not at liberty to reveal the young lady's address to you either."

Dugan wondered if the man *always* punctuated every other sentence with *"I'm afraid,"* and whether that was a sign that somewhere in his unconscious psyche he *was* afraid—maybe afraid the whole world might discover he was just a garden-variety young A-hole, not especially bright, just lucky enough to be born with the right grandfather.

A fact that the whole world—at least the part that cared—already knew.

"... nothing more to discuss," the man was saying.

"You know what I think?" Dugan said. "I think that you were just lucky enough—" He stopped himself just in time, then started over. "What I think is that Larry Candle is not the issue here. The issue is that I have given you a signed letter, stating that I am counsel for Rita Ranchero. I have told you that a significant component of my computer system has crashed and that I need to contact my client about something important and don't have her address."

"I understand. But unfortunately Miss Ranchero entrusted that information to us, and I'm afraid it's information which is private and confidential."

"Mr. Croft, please. Remember, you can't possibly have a relationship of confidentiality with Miss Ranchero. You're not her lawyer. You *can't* be her lawyer. You're on the other *side*, for God's sake. Pardon the expression."

"But I'm afraid—"

"Wait. You have in your hand a signed statement from a perfectly reputable attorney—me—who identifies himself as counsel for an individual who has a serious, immediate legal need and you are withholding—for what you believe is good cause, of course, don't get me wrong—but you are witholding information the woman has given you which is not, and cannot be, private or privileged."

"Well, I—"

"I respect you, Mr. Croft, and maybe the computer wizards can extract the information from my system in a few weeks. But that will be too late, for reasons which the attorney-client privilege prohibits me from divulging. However, I can tell you that despite your *very* questionable decision, I'm convinced that you are acting in good faith and I personally am *not* about to report your conduct to the ARDC."

Emerson Croft the Third looked stunned at the possibility.

"But my client might do so when she learns what you have done, or not done," Dugan continued, "and I can't stop her. You're familiar with the disciplinary rules and you know that. So . . ." Just how much of what he went on to say was true, and how much wasn't, even Dugan had a hard time sorting out. But Croft was wavering, and Dugan kept on alternately stroking him and raising nagging concerns in his mind.

Ten minutes later, when Dugan stood up to leave, he'd learned that Rita Ranchero's draft was already in the mail, and the address she'd given was nothing but a post office box.

"It's always a pleasure," Dugan said, hiding his disappointment and playing out the game, "to meet a lawyer of obvious integrity."

Emerson Croft the Third beamed as he shook Dugan's hand. "Let me escort you out."

As they stood waiting by the elevators, Croft said, "Oh . . . one final thing. When Mr. Candle advised orally that he claimed no right to any portion of the payment, we requested a release of his attorney's lien. I'm afraid he never sent one. So, to protect itself, the insurance company included him as a payee. As I said, the draft's been mailed to Miss Ranchero. But the transmittal letter states clearly that she can't negotiate the instrument without Mr. Candle's endorsement and, further, that the company won't pay out on the draft unless both endorsement signatures are guaranteed by a federally insured banking institution."

Dugan almost hugged the bright young A-hole.

THIRTY-NINE

hat's right," Kirsten said, feeling like a mother talking on the phone to a child with an attention deficit. "So, if you go out, Larry, be careful. And if your phone rings, don't answer."

"Shoot, with my office closed I got nowhere to go, and I haven't had a friggin' phone call in a week. Except my ex-wife, of course. She—"

"Just leave your answering machine on, and be sure to monitor your messages. Either Dugan or I will be in touch. Oh—and Larry?" she added. "Do what I say and I'm gonna get your . . . your ticket back, you hear me?" She hung up.

"Think he'll obey orders?" Dugan asked. It was noon, and they'd met at Kirsten's office to exchange notes and eat sandwiches.

"If it were just for Rita's sake, I don't know. But to beat the ARDC? Probably."

"You know?" Dugan said. "Maybe we're being too hard on Larry. He's not that bad a guy."

"What? Say that again, please?"

"I know his reputation stinks. And I guess he's a favorite target for the ARDC. But he got a great result for Rita Ranchero, considering he sued a motel after her husband was killed in a robbery in the parking lot and there was a question whether he himself was the robber or was just there to meet a hooker. Besides, despite Larry's reputation, no one's ever actually *proven*—"

Kirsten's phone buzzed. "You mean not *yet*," she said, and picked up the receiver. She started to say her name, but was interrupted.

"This is Radovich. I found something important. Where's Dugan at?"

"What dif—" But it was no use trying to convince Cuffs this late in his life that a woman might be worth reporting to. "He's right here. Hold on." She handed the receiver across the desk.

Dugan identified himself, and Kirsten punched the button for the speakerphone.

"I found 'em." Cuffs' voice rasped through the tiny speaker. "Took a while but they were here, goddamn it, like you said they hadda be. Or . . . maybe it was your wife said that. Anyway, I found 'em under some loose floorboards. I mean, I looked—"

"Cuffs?" Dugan said.

"Yeah?"

"What the hell are we talking about? What did you find?"

"The financial records, ledger books, whatever ya call 'em. Three years' worth. At least I think it's three years. They don't make a lotta sense to me."

"Cuffs?" Kirsten yelled. "Can you hear me."

"Jesus, you don't have to holler. I hear you."

"Hold on to those books." Kirsten struggled to drop down to a conversational tone, but she never quite trusted speakerphones to pick up her voice. "I want to see them before anyone else can—"

"Little late for that," Cuffs answered.

"What are you talking about?"

"Hoffmeier's been after me, too. Said if I found any records he wanted them. Or he'd have my ass. Didn't want no copies made, he said. Jeez, you'd think I was some goddamn kike, the way he . . . Anyway, I don't need trouble with Herr Hoffmeier, so he left here five minutes ago—with the goddamn ledgers."

Kirsten had to swallow hard before she could get an answer out, and Dugan got in ahead of her. "Cuffs?" he said.

"Oh . . . you back on the line?"

"Yeah," Dugan said. "Did you . . . *do* anything before you gave the records to Hoffmeier?"

"Do anything? Hell yes. Copied every fucking page. I figure *you* ain't gonna tell him, right? Like I said, I don't need trouble with Hoffmeier. But fuck that Nazi prick if he thinks I'm gonna follow his orders."

"Is there a fax machine there?" Dugan asked.

"Not here, but I checked with that beauty parlor. They got one and I . . . uh . . . talked the guy into letting us use it. Freddy'll send the stuff to you while I watch the—" There was a pause. "Gotta hang up. One of them freakin' fags has got his hands in his pants up in the front aisle." The line went dead.

"So," Kirsten said, "I guess it's not only people of color that Cuffs despises."

"The list is endless. But his is the consistency of a pure heart. For example, he calls the Aryan Nation people a pack of frustrated punks who play with guns because they can't score with their girlfriends." He stopped, then added, "Actually, I cleaned that up a little."

By three o'clock, Larry Candle hadn't been called by anyone about endorsing a check, and Dugan's CPA had a copy of Anton Bulasik's ledgers. It hadn't taken the accountant long to call back and say there was something fishy about the books.

"Call Bruce Hardison," Kirsten suggested, "and tell him you still don't have any records to deliver to WARP."

Dugan got Hardison on the line and put him on the speaker-phone.

"About those records for Cousin Freddy's," Dugan said. "I wonder—"

"You didn't *find* any, did you?"

"Uh . . . no, not yet. But you knew that already, right?"

"I only know what Larry Candle told me, that Anton said he couldn't find any records. I told Candle that was hard to believe. But, who knows? Maybe Anton lost them deliberately. Maybe they show something he didn't want anyone to know."

"You mean, like maybe Cousin Freddy's *was* paying off the Mob, or—"

"Not unheard of, you know." There was a silence, during which Kirsten opened her mouth, then decided to stay out of the conversation. "Anyway," Hardison continued, "how about you? Have you received any . . . messages the last few days?"

"What are you talking about?"

"I received a note Monday, mailed to my home. 'Pornography is terrorism,' it said, 'and we won't be victims anymore.'"

"Jesus."

"Then another one, yesterday. The new one says, 'Join up with terrorists; become a victim.' Needless to say, I've given them to the police." A buzz sounded through the speakerphone, followed by Hardison's voice again: "I have a call coming in. Let me know if you get any similar messages."

"Yeah, sure," Dugan said, but the line was already dead.

Kirsten watched him put the receiver down. He looked a little worried—even a little afraid. But mostly he looked puzzled.

She didn't blame him a bit. Why did Anton tell both her and Dugan that he never talked to Larry, when Hardison said he learned from Larry that Anton claimed he couldn't find any records?

FORTY

N ot everything's here, of course, and I haven't had much time.
But come around and take a look at this."

Dugan gladly circled the broad, white-topped table to the
side where his accountant had laid out copies of Cousin Freddy's
records. The accountant's name was Lesley Fernholz. Her office
was on Sheffield, a few blocks north of Wrigley Field, and had the
feeling more of an artist's studio than an office. It was a corner suite
on the second floor, full of colorful prints and fresh flowers—and
the permanent scent of fresh-roasted flavor-of-the-day drifting up
from the coffee shop on the first floor.

Lesley Fernholz was the only woman Dugan had ever been close
enough to talk to who he thought was as lovely as Kirsten. She was
also solidly married, with three kids and a husband who was just
as smart, good-looking, and sweet-natured as she was—and who
was just then sitting with another client about thirty feet away, in
the adjoining office.

Still, Dugan didn't mind moving around to her side of the table.
He stared down obediently at the materials laid out in front of
him, then looked at Lesley and shrugged.

"I see," he said.

"No, you don't."

"Yes, I do. I see faxed copies of ledger pages and invoices and tax
returns and whatever, plus what looks like some spread sheets you

did. I see the top of the table, too, and that tells me just about as much as the documents. Why don't you just give me your preliminary impression? And keep it simple. 'Ledger' and 'invoice' are about as sophisticated as my accounting lexicon gets."

"Don't worry. I've done your books and prepared your returns long enough to know that." She rearranged some of the papers on the table in front of her. "The system is very primitive. Not set up by an accountant. All done by hand, not computerized. There are fairly complete records of costs of inventory, expenses, and overhead, not as much on gross sales. There are also copies of tax returns. I could go into things in more detail, but—"

"Thank you."

"I'm no expert on the pornography business—thank God—but Cousin Freddy's is essentially a bookstore, and even assuming a very high retail markup, it sure looks to me like the reported income from sales is too high in comparison with the purchase of inventory."

"Which means?"

"Which *may* mean they've been laundering money through the business. As I said, a preliminary observation. A business adds cash from an unknown—generally illegal—source, and then reports it as though it were earned."

"So, because the business pays taxes on it, it looks like legitimate money."

"Right. The business pays sales taxes. Depending on the setup, there might be no income tax, because there's no profit. Anyway, depending on how sophisticated the setup is, it can be relatively easy or difficult to uncover. This one is not very sophisticated."

"So someone at Cousin Freddy's had income that wasn't from selling dirty books."

"The prevailing wisdom has it that Syndicate people own all the porno stores. I don't know about that. They certainly have their hands on lots of money that needs washing. But a business could also launder money that comes from an outsider, a third party. Again, it would be money obtained illegally."

"But why would . . . ? Let's say it's stolen money. Why wouldn't the thief just keep it?"

"I thought lawyers were up on all this stuff," Lesley said.

"Not this lawyer. I prosecuted armed robbers and burglars for a while, but most of those guys could barely read their plea agreements. Now it's strictly personal injury."

"Anyway, people who are discovered to have large amounts of cash or—maybe more often—lifestyles that cost far more than what they've been reporting as income, can run into big problems. First, the IRS figures they're not paying all their taxes. Then, various law enforcement agencies tend to wonder just where all that nonreported income comes from."

"So the business reports the money as income, then returns it to whoever it came from."

"After deducting . . . I don't know . . . maybe twenty percent—enough to cover sales tax on it, plus something for their trouble."

"This third party contributes, say, ten thousand and gets back maybe eight thousand."

"Then he pays income tax on that, and . . . " Lesley droned on, with more talk about money laundering than Dugan was interested in. What he really wanted to know was where the Cousin Freddy's money went after it was laundered. So far, Lesley had no idea. "Maybe if we found someone who knows the pornography business—and will admit it . . . "

Meanwhile, Dugan's mind kept wandering off to wonder what all this had to do with the *terrorism* of pornography. He wondered, too, whether there were any *independent* adult bookstores. Because, try as he might, he just couldn't see Fredrica Kalter as part of the Outfit.

FORTY-ONE

After her lunch with Dugan, Kirsten waited until midafternoon to break into the offices of Morelli & Fincher. Of course, as she'd told Dugan a few nights ago outside Double-M Leasing, it wasn't exactly a *break-in* if you had the keys. Then again, if you'd stolen them from someone's purse . . .

She tried not to think about all that as she impatiently jangled Cynthia's ring of keys on the sluggish elevator ride up to the fifth floor. There were more immediately worrisome considerations, after all. Such as, what if she walked in on someone when she unlocked the door? Cynthia had said the office was definitely closed until Monday, and when Kirsten had called the law firm's number, the message on the answering machine said the same thing. Cynthia was in Buffalo. But was Debra Morelli really in Miami? Somehow, that seemed unlikely.

She walked down the empty corridor to 504, and obeying the sign this time, pressed the button. She heard the buzzer from inside, but no one came to the door. Trying several keys until she got it right, she stepped into the waiting room. The door from there into the office area was standing open, but she decided to press the second button, too. Same buzzer. Same lack of response. Locking the hallway door behind her, she went inside and took a quick tour through the entire suite. No one was there.

She'd have felt safer searching through the offices at one A.M., but couldn't figure out how she'd get inside the building at night. Besides, the feeling of safety might have been an illusion. According to the statistics, most successful burglaries take place during broad daylight. Not that this was a burglary, mind you. Just a look around. A search for an answer to whether WARP, or Morelli & Fincher, was tied to the warnings to porno stores, or to the killings at Cousin Freddy's, or—what seemed most urgent right now—the disappearance of Rita Ranchero.

At night, she'd have had to turn the lights on, or use a flashlight. But now there was plenty of sunlight filtering in through huge, dirt-streaked casement windows that faced across empty space to the building's nearest neighbor to the south, maybe half a block away. She looked down from one of the windows onto a vacant lot. Dark shadows stretched across the brick-strewn ground, broken by wide, bright bands of sunlight that sparkled with thousands of bits of broken glass, announcing better days ahead with the seemingly haphazard, but inexorable, advance of real estate developers through the South Loop.

Beyond the secretaries' room there were three offices, all opening along one side of the hall where she'd first seen Cynthia. At the far end of the hall was a large room with a scarred but stately conference table surrounded by chairs. The wall opposite the entrance to the conference room was mostly lined with shelves that held a rather meager law library. Heavy drapes were drawn closed across the windows that took up most of the wall to the left. To the right was a door with a frosted glass panel. It opened onto the same outer corridor as did the entrance to the suite. It was locked from the inside with a turn bolt. She opened it and there was no key slot on the outside. In the wall with all the shelves there was another door, this one made of a heavy-looking, dark-stained wood. It was also locked. None of Cynthia's keys fit this door, and Kirsten guessed that it opened into an adjoining suite.

The first of the three offices, closest to the front of the suite, appeared to be used primarily for storage. The framed licenses on the wall of the second office identified it as Cynthia's. The third, larger than the other two, was Debra Morelli's office. The rooms on the other side of the hall had no windows. There was a small room with a copy machine, then a storeroom with a counter and a coffeemaker, and finally a tiny bathroom.

She slipped on a pair of thin cotton gloves and chose—for want of any better plan—one end of the large secretaries' area to begin her sweep. Every room in the suite was as overfull, yet as conscientiously neat and organized, as Kirsten remembered from her previous visit. She worked methodically, but as quickly as possible, replacing everything as she found it. She had always been very good at this, no matter how jittery she felt. She went through every drawer of every file cabinet, every desk, every table; not reading each individual piece of paper, but at least glancing into every manila folder.

The phone rang three times during her search—each time with a rasping buzz that stopped her breath and froze the blood in her veins. The machine answered each call after four rings, and each caller hung up without leaving a message. She was afraid she'd lose track of time, so she kept checking her watch. The longer she was there, the tighter her nerves seemed stretched. Once, while she was going through the desk in Debra's office, she thought she heard a noise, like a soft thud, maybe from the direction of the conference room. But when she ran to check, she heard nothing. She couldn't see anyone through the frosted glass of the door to the hall. She even opened the door, but there was no one there.

When she finally finished, her joints and muscles ached like the second morning after an unaccustomed workout. All she'd learned was that—at least as far as a two-hour search could turn up— Morelli & Fincher had absolutely nothing to hide. There were no locked drawers, no safes. In the office used for storage there were materials related to WARP—mailing lists and cartons of brochures explaining why pornography is itself the equivalent of rape. Otherwise, she found nothing at all that related to anything but the firm's clients and their cases.

She leaned against the doorway and stared into Cynthia's empty office, frustrated, her feelings frantically contradicting each other. On the one hand she was relieved because she didn't want to find out that Cynthia was somehow involved. On the other hand, she was bitterly disappointed. Rita Ranchero didn't have long to live and she had hoped to find some ans—

She stiffened. She might have heard something again, maybe that same thumping sound she'd noticed earlier. Or maybe she didn't hear anything at all. She walked back to the conference room and stood by the door to the corridor. With her right hand deep in her purse and wrapped around the Colt .380, she unlocked the door and looked out. No one was there. She closed the door again. She walked over and stood near the door she couldn't unlock. Nothing. The room was absolutely silent.

When you find yourself hearing imaginary noises it's time to move on. She headed back down the hall, past the lawyers' offices and into the secretaries' area. As she started toward the door to the waiting room, the damn phone rang again not three feet away from her, that same ungodly rasping buzz. The sound of it almost knocked her down.

She looked at her watch. This was the fourth call since she'd been in the suite, and suddenly, for some unknown reason, she noticed that the four calls had been evenly spaced, almost exactly a half hour apart. She stared down at the phone as it buzzed a second time. It seemed an odd coincidence. Or maybe the caller was checking to see if someone was there—or had returned. The phone sounded a third time. The urge to pick it up was almost overpowering—but clearly foolish. What good could that do? The phone screamed at her a fourth time.

It made no sense to answer it. But something—intuition—told her it might be important to know who was calling. Should she take the risk and try to find out . . . or should she play it safe?

"Morelli and Fincher," she said, putting an expectant lilt in her tone. "May I help you?"

"What? Who is—" But that's all he said. Then there was a hiss that may have been a breath inhaled, and then there was a click that was certainly the end of the call.

She hung up, too. Intuition or not, sometimes taking a risk can be a big mistake.

She left quickly then, locking the door behind her. Turning left, she hurried down the empty corridor, nearly running by the time she got to the elevators, just past the door to Morelli & Fincher's conference room. She pushed the *Down* button and listened as the creaking elevator came up the shaft.

Rita was dead.

Or as good as dead, anyway. She just didn't know how long she could hang in there. She could feel her mind going crazy, thinking all kinds of weird things, especially whenever she started to fall asleep. And then her dreams were all about being dead, or lying in a coffin with people standing around talking and ignoring her like she was dead. It seemed like she was sleeping a lot and sometimes she couldn't really tell if she was awake or asleep.

She wanted to cry now almost all the time, too, but when they left they always stuffed a rag into her mouth and then put tape over it. So she could only breathe out of her nose, and if she cried her nose got stuffed up and she thought she would suffocate. So she made herself *not* cry.

She could do that, and that proved she wasn't crazy. Not yet.

She would only let herself cry when the Evil Twins were around and took the tape off her mouth. Not just because she could breathe through her mouth then, but also because it kept them thinking she was a helpless baby and they didn't have to worry too much about her doing anything to try to get away.

Otherwise, she wouldn't let herself cry, and she wouldn't let herself go crazy either, dammit. If she did, if she lost it entirely, she'd never get away from them alive. She figured God wouldn't be mad no matter how much she hated them. And she'd made up a new name for them—the Evil Twins. That might have been from some movie from when she was a kid, too. Seemed like it was a science fiction flick but she couldn't remember the name.

She wondered if they ever thought about how keeping her tied up and gagged so much might make her go really crazy. Then she wouldn't be able to sign her name to their precious check and they'd have to forge her name anyway and they'd get caught and go to jail . . . or maybe even get the electric chair. She'd be dead by then, of course. She hoped when they killed her, God would put her someplace where she could watch the government fry the Evil Twins. After that, she didn't care.

She lay on the floor now, wide awake in the dark. They had her tied up and zipped into a sleeping bag that just had room for her face to stick out. The sleeping bag was tied real tight to some pipes in a way that kept her back pressed up hard against the baseboard of the wall. She couldn't move hardly at all, but she'd given up a long time ago worrying about how her muscles kept aching and cramping up.

The way they had her tied she could see the door and the little bit of light that creeped in underneath it. The room wasn't much more than a big closet. It was empty, except for her and the bag with her clothes in it. She couldn't see it now, but it was a plastic shopping bag that said *Marshall Field's,* mostly green and kinda cream-colored, with a drawstring. Very classy. She didn't remember ever shopping at Marshall Field's and now she'd probably never get a chance to. But she loved that plastic bag. Partly because everything she owned in the world was stuffed down in there. But mostly because hidden with all her dirty clothes was her only hope—the Crystal Dagger.

She knew it was kinda stupid, making a big deal about a piece of broken glass wrapped up in a *People* magazine. But she kept thinking that was what God had given her to get away. And that was helping to keep her from going crazy. It was a *miracle* that they hadn't found it. Maybe her mother was up there in heaven and was praying to Jesus or Mary or somebody. Anyway, she still had the Crystal Dagger, and every time the Evil Twins came back, or one of them alone, she thought: *Get ready, 'cause this might be the time.*

A couple of hours ago she heard the elevator come up and stop, and it hardly ever stopped there unless it was one of them. She heard them walking around, or one of them anyway. But they didn't unlock the door. Whoever it was just kept making noises but only came to the door once and rattled it but that was all.

Then she knew it wasn't one of the Evil Twins and it must be a cleaning lady or someone. So she tried to make some noise. But she was wrapped up and tied so tight she couldn't do anything. She almost cried then, but stopped herself.

The person didn't go away for a long time and Rita got almost hysterical trying to move and make some noise. A few times she was able to bang her butt against the wall. It didn't make very much noise. Twice, someone came close to the door and she thought they came to see what the noise was. But that wasn't it. Nothing happened.

The phone rang a few times, but the person didn't answer it— except maybe the last time, she wasn't sure. Then after that she thought she heard the front door close. And then it got quiet again. And then she couldn't help it anymore. She just cried and cried. It didn't matter. She was dead.

The elevator cage groaned its way up to the fifth floor, while Kirsten stood there rocking from one foot to the other, glancing nervously back toward where she'd come from.

Then, just as the elevator stopped, something struck her. She stared at the door as it slid open, then looked around again. There were maybe eight or ten feet of blank wall between the elevator shaft and the door that opened into the Morelli & Fincher conference room. So there could only be that much space beyond the locked door in the conference room wall with all the shelves. It couldn't open into an adjoining suite of offices, because the next suite started on the other side of the bank of elevators.

So what was behind that door, the one to which Cynthia's ring held no key? Was it something that might make muffled, thumping noises every so often? She could call the police. Uh-huh. And explain how she'd been doing an illegal search of this law office? And thought she might have heard a noise and that it might be a woman named Rita Ranchero who was being held captive. . . .

Or she could go somewhere and give herself a chance to think about what to do. Maybe call Dugan?

There were a lot of reasons why she shouldn't go back right now to find out what was behind the door. The first was that she had no key, and she'd scarcely looked at the lock but she didn't know if she'd be able to open it. If not, she wasn't sure she could blow it open like that flimsy door at Double-M, even if she were willing to fire a gun late in the afternoon on what *seemed* to be an almost vacant floor of an office building at the south end of the Loop. Which she wasn't.

Another reason was that she probably wouldn't find anything important behind the door if she did succeed in opening it. Besides, if there *were* something important there, she might be better off not finding out.

A third reason—or was it a fourth?—was that a few moments ago she had picked up the phone and announced the presence of a woman in the supposedly closed offices of Morelli & Fincher. By her voice she may even have identified who the woman was. And even if the man hadn't recognized her voice, she certainly recognized his.

By the time she'd reviewed all the reasons why she shouldn't go back into the Morelli & Fincher suite, Kirsten was already inside and headed down the hall, past the lawyers' offices, toward the conference room.

FORTY-TWO

Before he left the accountant's office, Dugan called Molly for his messages. Still no word from Kirsten. He returned the only other call he had any interest in.

"Hi there!" It was the answering machine. "Maybe you've been having trouble reaching—"

"Pick up, Larry. It's Dugan."

There were two clicks. Then, "Hey, pal, I thought you guys were gonna keep checkin' in with me."

"I forgot. You hear from anyone?"

"Hell yes. I got the call Kirsten told me I'd get."

"Did you pick up?"

"Are you kidding? Anyway, this guy comes on. Says he wants to talk to me right away about Rita Ranchero. Doesn't leave a number. Doesn't even leave a name, for chrissake. Says he'll call back. Scared the shit outta me. Kind of a creepy voice, like a fucking gangster. If it ain't the same guy was with Lynne Bulasik, then I'm the goddamn pope."

"You're at home, right?"

"Yeah. The office is closed and my calls are all switched here."

Half an hour later, Dugan was sitting at Larry Candle's card table, staring out at the lake. Wishing Kirsten were there. Wishing he knew she was all right, at least.

"Great view, huh?" Larry said. "Y'know, sometimes I sit here and look out and wish me and my ex-wife could—"

"C'mon, Larry. Knock it off."

Dugan called and checked their machine again. No messages.

"Y'know? I been thinking," Larry said, his third try at starting a conversation in five minutes. "When I get my friggin' ticket back, maybe—"

"You mean *if*. Besides, I told you I don't feel like talking. Okay?"

"Sure. Fine. But I just—"

The phone rang. Larry reached out, but Dugan clamped his hand over the receiver and let the machine answer. After the tone at the end of Larry's message, there was silence. Finally, a man said, "I'm the one who called earlier, on behalf of Rita Ranchero. I want to talk to you." When he paused, they heard distant laughter, like he was calling from a bar or a restaurant. "Mr. Candle, I have the feeling you're listening. Pick up the phone."

Lifting the receiver, Dugan said, "Larry Candle here."

"Why don't you answer your phone when you're there?" Larry was right about the man's voice. The sarcastic, compelling tone sent a little shiver through Dugan, too.

"Hey, just comin' in the door while it was ringing," Dugan said. "Course, you gotta tell me who you are, pal, but I'll be glad to help Rita any way I can." Dugan was trying to sound helpful and sincere, and trying to imitate Larry at the same time. "Anything for a client, I always say, pal."

"I'm a friend of Miss Ranchero's. She received her check from the insurance company and it requires your guaranteed endorsement." The threat in the man's voice was gone. Apparently, he could turn it on and off at will. "She . . . leaving on a trip and wants you to sign the check immediately. I'll pick you up now and take you to the AmFed Bank for the guarantee of your signature. What's your address?"

"Jeez, pal, I still didn't catch your name," Dugan said.

"I . . . Anderson. John Anderson."

"Sorry, Mr. Anderson. Can't make it today."

"But—"

"Sorry. But the cops are due here any minute. Had a guy take a shot at me not long ago and they want me to look at photographs. Maybe tomorrow? Say . . . ten o'clock? I'll meet you at AmFed."

"I don't—"

"That's settled, then. Thing is," Dugan added, "you'll have to have Miss Ranchero with you. No offense, pal, but she *is* my client, and I wanna be sure—"

"She can't be there, Mr. Candle, and she's not your client any more. I . . . ah . . . I hope you're not going to cause a problem about this." The menacing tone was in full force again. This was a man used to having his own way.

"Jeez, pal, like I said, no offense," Dugan said. "I'd sure like to help Rita. But I already got problems up the wazoo with the friggin' Disciplinary Commission yanking my ticket. Maybe she's not my client anymore, but the rules say I gotta protect her interests. I mean, what if I sign and it turns out you're bullshitting me? I'd *never* get my friggin' license back. So, if she's there, I sign. If not? I don't."

There was no response.

"Hey, pal," Dugan said, "you still on the line, or what? 'Cause I think the cops are out front already."

"She'll be there, Mr. Candle. And you'd better be, too. Ten o'clock." He hung up.

"Shit," Larry said, heading for the kitchen, "I need a drink."

"Me, too," Dugan said. "Bring out the friggin' bottle . . . pal."

FORTY-THREE

A s it turned out, the door in the conference room had a very old lock that Kirsten thought she could pick. She crouched on one knee in front of the door. As she worked at the lock, the room gradually darkened, sunlight not leakingin around the drapes as before. Suddenly she stopped, and momentarily pressed her ear close against the wood. Yes. She heard it again, the *thump* from beyond the door, and she knew now that she *would* use the gun if she couldn't manage the lock in just a few minutes—or even call the cops, if it came to that.

But it didn't.

A minute later she stepped into a small, dark room, maybe eight feet square. It was an electrical closet, housing two huge, gray circuit-breaker boxes, with heavy veins of conduit of various thicknesses snaking out from the bottoms and the tops of both boxes, running up and down along the walls, disappearing into the ceiling and the floor.

Beneath one of the boxes was what first seemed in the dark to be some large caterpillar-like creature, tied tightly up against the wall to several of the thickest conduit pipes. Now the creature started making very soft, unintelligible humming sounds, and it writhed and twisted as though trying to break free of its bonds.

Kirsten found a switch on the wall just inside the door, and in the dim light of a bare, low-watt bulb in the ceiling, she saw that the captive creature was a human being, zipped into a dark-colored sleeping bag. It was a tapered bag, what her outdoorsman brother once told her was a "mummy bag," designed for cold weather use, narrow at the feet and widening to accommodate the shoulders at the top. A built-in hood covered the head and was tied tight around the person's face. Silver-gray duct tape ran across the mouth and the chin and was wrapped all the way around the hood that shrouded the woman's head. Kirsten was sure it was a woman after she crouched down for a closer look, even though only her nose and eyes were visible.

Those eyes, glistening with tears, shone simultaneously with the madness of terror and the possibility of hope. All at once she started to sniffle uncontrollably, then sneezed violently, time after time, expelling thick gobs of mucus from her nose. Kirsten stood there staring as though frozen in place, then suddenly realized the woman was having trouble breathing, and must be choking on fluid draining down the back of her throat.

Dropping to her knees, Kirsten tore at the tape, working clumsily, trying not to bang the woman's head on the floor. She unwrapped layer after layer of tape until finally the lower half of her face appeared and Kirsten could see the circle of her mouth—forced wide open—and her red-blotched, puffed-out cheeks.

At least the woman wasn't crying anymore. Kirsten gently tugged on the washcloth that had been crammed into her mouth. When she had it out the woman moved her jaw up and down and Kirsten knew she was trying to say *thank you,* but couldn't get it out. She coughed, and vomited a small amount of thin, brownish liquid.

"Don't say anything, honey," Kirsten whispered, loosening the hood from around her face. "Just relax until I can get you free." The woman began again to sob—softly now, almost gently.

The ropes were tied with numerous tight, amateurish knots, and it took several minutes and as many broken fingernails to get them loosened. Finally, with the woman lying on her back, Kirsten unzipped the mummy bag and lifted her to a sitting position against the wall.

"Can you talk?" Kirsten asked. "Are you Rita?"

"Yes. Oh yes." And then the sobs started all over again, as Kirsten helped her to her feet.

She was young and slim—a dancer's figure, Kirsten thought. Her feet were bare, but she was wearing bleached blue jeans and a dirty white sweatshirt that said *York Beach, Maine* in red letters that encircled a smiling lobster holding a knife and fork in its claws. The sweatshirt—and the jeans, too—were soaked in sweat. Her hair was damp and straight and a reddish-blond, except closer to the roots where it was black.

"Heard the elevator," Rita managed. "Thought you went a—" Her voice broke at the end and she began to cry again.

Kirsten took the woman in her arms and held her. "It's okay now," she whispered. "You're okay." As the shaking slowly subsided, Kirsten pushed herself away, and holding Rita by the shoulders, she wrinkled up her nose at her and smiled. "At least, you will be okay . . . as soon as you take a shower."

"Thank you so much. Oh my God, thank you," Rita said. "Oh my God, oh my God, oh my God . . . "

Rita kept repeating the phrase until Kirsten thought she was getting hysterical and wondered if face-slapping worked in real life like it did in the movies. Then she saw that Rita wasn't looking at her at all, but past her, over her shoulder and toward the door to the conference room behind her.

"Oh my God," Rita said, one last time.

Kirsten turned slowly around. Beyond the open doorway the conference room would have been completely dark, but for the dim light coming from the electrical closet. Out there, motionless in the shadows and staring in at them, was the man with the pony-tail. Dangling from his left hand by its shoulder strap was Kirsten's purse. Pointed at them from his right hand was Kirsten's pistol.

"I took the stairs," he said. His smile was sly, cold. "Poor babies."

That same sense of . . . what? . . . panic?—swept over Kirsten as when she'd let herself be ushered like a child out of the Cubic Globe Gallery.

But then she heard Rita's quiet crying behind her. She remembered the bundle she'd found on the floor—struggling silently, helplessly, against the ropes wrapped around her. A caterpillar trapped by a spider, bound up and stowed away in the dark for future use. Yet Rita hadn't given up, had somehow made enough noise to alert Kirsten to her being there.

And Kirsten wasn't giving up, either.

She stepped forward, straight toward the man, stretching out her hand. She stopped in the open doorway. "I'll take my purse," she said, her voice firm and commanding, "and my gun."

She was sure he stiffened, maybe even flinched just slightly. But then he raised the barrel of the gun a few degrees. "What you'll take, you fucking cunt, is a bullet in that pretty face."

She gasped, deciding to tell him what he wanted to hear: that she was whipped. Shaking visibly, she steadied herself with her left hand on the door frame beside her. She let her knees buckle, and as she began to sag limply toward the floor, she moved her hand a little farther to the left—and flipped down the wall switch.

In the nearly total darkness Kirsten screamed, shrieked mindlessly—the word that came was *Rita*—and dove forward at the ponytailed man, low to the floor, in a rolling block. Her right shoulder caught him in the knees, and cut his legs from under him. He fell heavily forward over her and she heard something hard—his forehead? chin?—strike the bare oak floor with a sickening sharp crack.

Her momentum had carried her under the edge of the conference table, and tangled in his legs, she struggled to get herself free of him in the darkness. He kept kicking at her—thrashing about with strong, hard kicks. *How the hell could he still be conscious after taking that hit?*

A vicious kick that would have knocked her cold if it had been a direct hit glanced off the side of her head, the rough sole of his shoe scraping across her ear. His other foot, though, caught her square in the abdomen and drove all the breath out of her. Gasping for air, she rolled farther under the table, crashing against the legs of a chair on the other side. The chair went down and she grasped the edge of the table and pulled herself up to her feet.

The man was facing her, his arms stretched out toward her across the table. Her eyes were adjusting to the dark. She saw blood streaming down over one of his eyes, and she thought he looked groggy, probably not thinking clearly. But most important—his hands were empty.

"Rita!" Kirsten yelled. "Turn on the light! Find the gun!"

As soon as she said it, though, she regretted it, because it reminded the Ponytail, too. He turned away from Kirsten. The dim light in the closet went on and Rita was in the doorway, clutching a plastic shopping bag to her chest with one arm. The Ponytail had his back to Kirsten now, facing Rita. Both of them stood still, heads down and moving aimlessly from side to side, searching for the gun on the floor somewhere.

Meanwhile, Kirsten was looking for something, too, anything she could use as a weapon. Books and papers and manila folders— all useless—lay around in abundance. But sitting on a chair near the conference table was a huge, black, square-cornered briefcase, the kind salespersons carry their samples in—and the kind Dugan used back when he tried cases and had to lug huge files to court. The briefcase was closed. She grabbed it and found that it was full. It weighed twenty pounds, easy.

All this was a matter of seconds, and the Ponytail still had his back to her. Kirsten climbed up on the conference table, lugging the briefcase up with her, holding it by the handle with two hands. The Ponytail must have heard her, because he started to turn around. She switched to a one-hand grip on the briefcase, and swung it in a wide arc with her right hand, starting a little behind her. The Ponytail was a tall man, and she was standing on the table. Her circular trajectory was perfect. As he turned to face her, the flat end of the briefcase caught him square on the left side of his head. He staggered to his right, then stood for what seemed a long time, with his arms hanging limply at his sides and a vacant look on his face. But finally his knees gave way and he crumpled to the floor.

"He's . . . breathing isn't he?" Rita asked.

"Yes, and it probably won't be long before he's up and running again."

"He's one of the Evil Twins. I call him the Really Weird One."

"Oh?"

"Yeah. You don't want to meet the other one either, the Silent—"

"Let's talk about all that later. We have to get out of here."

They dragged the Ponytail into the electrical closet, where Kirsten retrieved the Colt .380 and put it in her purse. They couldn't relock the closet door without a key, but they closed it and managed to maneuver the conference table until one end was jammed against the door and the other end against a couple of chairs that were wedged against the wall opposite the door.

Out in the hall, waiting for the elevator that they could hear was on its way. Rita said, "He's lucky it was you who found the gun, not me. I might have shot him. He's a bad man," Rita's voice quavered, "and he's gonna get outta there, you know."

"He'll get out, but by then we'll be long gone." The elevator groaned to a stop. As the doors slid open, Kirsten turned to Rita and swept her hand toward the elevator. "After you, my dear."

But Rita didn't move. She just stared ahead of her into the elevator.

Kirsten turned back and looked right into the eyes of a woman on the elevator, a large woman, who was clearly as startled as she was. "Well," Kirsten managed to say, "Debra Morelli. I suppose—"

"That's her," Rita said, "the Silent Partner."

FORTY-FOUR

It was well past six o'clock and Kirsten still hadn't called. They'd agreed he'd go to Larry Candle's place if Larry got a message about signing the check. But she hadn't called, hadn't left any messages anywhere. Larry had Chinese food brought in, which Dugan paid for because Larry was "a little short," and he'd finally gotten Larry to stop trying to make inane conversation, especially about his outlandish hopes and dreams for after he got his law license back.

But surprisingly, it was Dugan who put away the bottle of Scotch—after only a couple of shots apiece.

"Jesus," Larry said, "whaddaya wanna do, drink yourself blotto? I thought you guys were gonna figure out a way to get me outta this mess."

"Yeah? What about—" But he stopped. "I don't want to talk about it . . . or anything else."

"Fine. I'll just keep my mouth shut." Larry sounded genuinely hurt. "It's dark out now, anyway." Larry dragged his folding chair from the table, switching off the dining room light on his way out to the living room, and across to the telescope on its tripod by the wall of windows. "And a *very* clear night it is," he added, with obvious satisfaction.

"Jesus," was all Dugan said. He turned his back to the open living room doorway and thought of all the lights going on in all the

210

unsuspecting windows up and down the curve of Lake Shore Drive. Somewhere in one of those apartments, someone would be—

"Wow, is that great, or what?" Larry called. "Hey, turn off the kitchen light, too, would you. It's reaching in here and reflecting off the glass."

"You know, Larry," Dugan said, standing up to switch off the light, "you can get in trouble for—"

"Whooee! You oughta see this. You don't get to see this very often. Not this early, anyway. Come and take a look."

"I don't think so," Dugan said, but he headed for the living room despite himself. "I was saying, you can get in trouble for that kind of activity."

"What the heck you talking about?" Larry sounded surprised.

"I'm talking about—" Dugan stopped, himself surprised to see Larry's telescope fixed firmly on the clear, star-filled sky above Lake Michigan.

"Look through here, pal," Larry said. "I didn't think you ever saw Mars that close to Venus, not this time of the year. Except, maybe it's not." Larry stood up. "I'll go get my book."

"Uh . . . no thanks." Dugan stared out the window, down at the streams of traffic flowing in both directions on the Drive. Larry padded out of the room in his stocking feet and came back carrying an oversized book in two hands. He held the cover out toward Dugan. *Diving into the Stars: A Guide for the Amateur Astronomer.*

"This is a great book. My daughter Felicia—she's nine years old and she's just as cute as she is smart. I don't get to see her much now, and I . . . anyway, Felicia gave it to me for my birthday. Here, you see?" Larry started, "There's—"

"Forget it. I'm going out for a while."

"Yeah, but . . ." Larry, obviously disappointed, closed the book and carefully laid it on the seat of the plastic folding chair by the telescope. "All right. I'll come with you."

"No. You stay here, in case Kirsten calls."

"What'll I tell her?"

"That I went to see what's taking her so long. Ask her where she is. I'll keep calling in to check."

"Sure," Larry said, sounding worried, "like you kept calling in before."

But Dugan was halfway out the door by that time and didn't have to come up with an answer. Somehow it was simpler when Larry Candle was just this round little guy that he—like everyone else—thought of only as one more embarrassment on the face of a legal profession with more than its share of blotches. Then you find out he can't get over his ex-wife. And he's got a *hobby*, for God's sake, and a birthday . . . and a daughter he wishes he could see more often.

Dugan wondered what it would be like to have a daughter.

Down in the lobby, as though put there to reinforce his imaginings, two young girls—maybe eight, nine years old—were sitting cross-legged on a sofa playing *Scissors-Paper-Rock*. "Scissors cuts paper . . . paper covers rock . . . rock breaks scissors," they chanted, thrusting fists or flat hands or two fingers at each other, then giggling hysterically.

"Waiting for Grampa," the doorman said. He smiled. "Don't get many kids in here."

Dugan went out and hailed a cab.

Fifteen minutes later a man in a well-worn security guard's uniform, at least two sizes too large for his little frame, unlocked the sidewalk entrance and let Dugan into the lobby of the building. But he wasn't about to let him go any farther.

"This late, sir, you can't go up unless you got an ID, or one of the tenants leaves special word." The guard had to be as old as the ancient elevators he insisted were off limits.

"But my wife's up there," Dugan said, giving his own name and Kirsten's. "I need to find out how much longer she'll be."

"Don't know you nor your wife, sir." The guard peered up at Dugan. "Although you *do* look sorta familiar." He blinked, then shook his head. "Anyway, your wife isn't up there."

"If you don't know her, how do you know that?"

" 'Cause there isn't *nobody* up there. I know all the tenants. I been here thirty years, started part-time, moonlightin' when I was a copper." His guard's uniform probably fit when it was new. "I knew all the tenants, even back when the building was full up, and I still do. Anyway, everyone's gone for the day."

"Just let me check out Morelli and Fincher, that's where she might be."

"She might be, but she isn't. No one's up there. I told you that."

Dugan could easily have picked the guard up and hung him from one of the ornate old coat hooks on the wall behind his lobby desk. But he had to admire the man's determination. So he took out a bill of a much larger denomination than he thought should be necessary and thrust it forward. *Rock breaks scissors, scissors cuts paper . . .* paper—green paper—covers determination.

But not this time. The guard refused the money.

"I don't get it," Dugan said. "Whatever became of the old values we all used to share?" He stuffed the bill back into his wallet.

"Wait," the guard said. "Lemme see that again."

"It hasn't gotten any larger."

"No, not the money. That card in your wallet, is that a lawyer's ID?"

"Yeah, but it's out of date." Dugan showed him the card.

"How come you didn't tell me who you were? *Now* I know why you look familiar. I mean he had maybe seventy pounds on you, but I knew your old man pretty well, for chrissake. Used to send him accident cases. He took care of me good, your old man did. Shoot, when I was in the old Traffic Division, driving a squad on the expressways, I used to—"

"So you're gonna let me go up, right?"

"Well, I guess it won't hurt nothin'."

The guard went with him up to the fifth floor. And, just as he said it would be, Morelli & Fincher was as dark as a tomb and locked up tight, both doors.

"They're not coming back until Monday, right?" Dugan asked.

"Who?"

"Morelli and Fincher. I thought their office was closed until Monday."

"I didn't hear that." He shook his head in confusion. "But if that's so, what would your wife be doing here?"

"Well . . . uh . . . "

"Anyway, I saw 'em today, or one of 'em anyway. The big one. Morelli."

"Oh?"

"Sure. They left maybe a half hour before you got here. Morelli and a couple of clients and that man they say is a paralegal. Can't believe—"

"The clients," Dugan cut in, "were they women?"

"*All* their clients are women. One of 'em looked kinda wasted, like their usual battered-woman–type client. Started to say, I can't believe two so-called feminist attorneys hire themselves a male paralegal. Especially one looks like a goddam hit—"

"The other one. What about the other one?"

"They only got one paralegal, far as I—"

"The other *woman*, for God's sake." The adrenaline was running and Dugan was afraid he might grab the man and start shaking him. "What did she look like?"

"I dunno. I mean . . . tall, dark hair. Didn't really see her face. I was working on that damn report I gotta turn in every day, and they all kinda hustled on out. She had on a long leather coat. Like a lightweight-type coat, but leather, you know?"

"Yeah," Dugan said. "I know." He took a deep breath, trying to slow down his heartbeat. "How about the man? He . . . he doesn't have a ponytail does he?"

"You got it." The guard looked surprised. "Big, mean-looking fucker."

"You gotta let me in here," Dugan said, grabbing the doorknob and shaking it.

But the man turned away from him. "Forget it. Let's go."

"Wait." Dugan grabbed the guard by the shoulder, then let go immediately as the man spun around angrily. "Sorry," Dugan said. "But look . . . you must have a key. You can come in with me. I just wanna look around. That was my wife, the one with the leather coat. I think they've . . . taken her somewhere."

The guard stared at him. "You really ain't shittin' me, are you." A statement, not a question. He took out his keys and as he selected one he added, "Maybe I shoulda seen something suspicious. But I recognized the Morelli woman, and the guy. So . . . We oughta call 911."

"Yeah," Dugan said, "and wait around for the beat car to arrive. I give a statement and then they tell me there's not much they can do. Think about it, it's only because you knew my old man that *you* think I might not be crazy. And you're really not so certain about that yourself."

"You got that right." The guard smiled. "Hell, it's been a boring week. Let's take a look around." He unlocked the door. "We get caught . . . *you* make up the story."

They hurried through the suite, hitting light switches on the way. No one was there. In the conference room the furniture was oddly placed and there were papers and books strewn around. It was obvious something unusual had gone on, but not at all clear what it was. The door to an electrical closet was open. It was the guard who noticed the sleeping bag rolled up in the corner. Dugan shook it out and several balls of wadded-up duct tape fell out onto the floor. He dropped the bag and went back into the conference room.

The guard rolled up the sleeping bag with the duct tape inside and replaced it in the corner. Back in the conference room, he said, "It all seems kinda funny, for sure. But it don't prove anything."

Dugan didn't answer. He circled the room, forcing himself to take his time, looking for some sign of Kirsten. A few feet to the right of the closet door stood a blue plastic wastebasket. It was three feet tall, had a recycling logo on its side, and was matched by a half dozen others in Dugan's own suite and who knows how many thousand more in the Loop alone. A sign taped to the wall above the container said: FOR NON-CONFIDENTIAL DOCUMENTS ONLY. Dugan stared down, then reached deep into the container and pulled out a leather purse with a shoulder strap.

He opened the purse and removed Kirsten's billfold. "Here," he said, handing it to the guard. "There's all kinds of snapshots and cards that'll prove it's my wife's purse."

While the man looked through the fat billfold, Dugan satisfied himself that if anything else in the room had something to say about Kirsten he wasn't going to find it in the time he had.

"I guess you're right," the guard said. "Still doesn't prove anything illegal happened. So, now what do we do?"

"We turn out the lights, lock the door, and get the hell outta here."

Back down in the lobby, Dugan said, "I can't tell you what to do, but neither one of us has much of anything helpful to say to the police, as far as I'm concerned."

"Jeez, I just don't—"

"Anyway, I'm leaving. And whatever you decide to do, you're entitled to this." He held out the bill he'd offered earlier.

The guard took the money and looked up at Dugan. "You're a lot like your old man." He paused. "But, goddamn . . . I sure hope you know what you're doing."

Dugan went out the door and walked slowly along the deserted sidewalk, Kirsten's bag hanging from his shoulder, banging heavily against his side. When he got to the Grand Am, he tossed the purse onto the passenger seat and sat behind the wheel for a while, staring out through the windshield. He wasn't about to sit around in some police station half the night. There were only two places he could think of to look for Kirsten, and he might as well try the closer one first.

He started the engine. But before he drove away he picked up Kirsten's purse and set it in his lap. He opened it. Her billfold lay on top of all the other accumulated stuff of her daily life. He pushed the billfold to the side and stared down at the next item.

A blue-steel Colt .380 semiautomatic pistol.

FORTY-FIVE

J eez, I'm real sorry I got you into this mess."

"It wasn't you," Kirsten said. "It was Larry Candle. You made that complaint and he hired me and then didn't tell me everything. And I . . . I guess I got myself into it, too."

She and Rita were whispering, although it seemed unlikely they'd be heard. They were handcuffed to an iron bed, locked in the bedroom of the apartment over what used to be the Cubic Globe Gallery. They could hear the television going in the living room.

Rita had collapsed into Kirsten's arms at the elevator, and Debra pulled a gun and ordered them back into the office suite. They'd found the Ponytail on the floor of the electrical closet, still groggy. Debra had made him get up and then hustled them all out, and in the darkness and confusion no one noticed Kirsten drop her purse in the wastebasket. Dugan knew she'd planned to go there, so . . .

"Anyway, Rita," Kirsten said, "if we're gonna get *out* of the mess, first you have to tell me what's been going on."

"Yeah, well . . . I guess I started the part that got you in it when I got so pissed off at Larry for losing my money in those stupid stocks . . . which was wrong, because I told him that day that he might as well give it a try."

"You mean you really gave Larry your permission?"

"Yeah. I thought I had lotsa money . . . so why not let him try it? That was just after Lynne introduced me to Carlo—that's the

Really Weird One's real name—and before I gave *him* all my money. I had met Lynne at this really bizarre party a long time ago, not too long after my husband got killed. I was looking for a lawyer, and she's the one gave me Larry's name. Said he'd done a good job for her father. I used to run into her after that once in a while, and one time me and her got talking and stupid me tells her about the settlement from my husband's death. She said she knew this guy Carlo, whose uncle was a big shot with the Outfit, but Carlo wanted to get away from all that, and needed money to get started in something legitimate. So I talked to Carlo, and he said him and me'd put our money together and open this high-class art gallery. I mean, it sounds pretty stupid now, gettin' mixed up with someone who's connected. But at the time . . . y'know? Plus Carlo . . . I kinda liked him at first."

"But how did Lynne know Carlo? Were they . . . going together or something?"

"Oh no. Lynne's . . . you know . . . a dyke. I found out later she knew Carlo from when his uncle had sent him to her father's dirty bookstore. Carlo's uncle was shaking them down, or trying to buy into the store or something. Anyway, Lynne's old man was objecting and Lynne . . . I don't know if she was gonna double-cross her own father or was trying to help, or what. Anyway, she got hooked up with Carlo and she told him about me."

"What'd Larry have to do with all this?"

"Larry? Nothing. Carlo and Lynne just happened to be there that day when I told Larry he could use the money. I think Carlo scared the crap outta Larry just by sitting there." She paused. "Carlo scares people."

"So what happened with you and Carlo?"

"Well, him and me opened up this Cubic Globe. He ran it, but it wasn't much of a store, really. No one hardly ever came in or bought anything, and I bet most of the stuff was stolen property, anyway. Carlo kept asking for more money—for the store, he said. Pretty soon, most of the first part of my settlement was gone. Then he said he's gonna need the second part when it comes in and I said—"

"Wait. Did he say why?"

"Finally he did. Turns out he had got into some bad trouble by buying boxes and boxes of really nasty dirty magazines and books—the kind, like, with little kids and even some with animals?—which later he found out he couldn't find no one to buy. He couldn't return the stuff and he couldn't finish paying for it, and the sellers were after him. He hadda keep it hidden all the time, too—from the cops, from his uncle, everyone. So he comes up with this plan to use *my* money to make a real *lot* of money to pay for those books and magazines and then to send 'em to someplace in Mexico or South America where someone was gonna buy 'em. I told him he was crazy if—"

"But what was the plan?"

"He made this deal to buy some dope—heroin, I think—without telling his uncle. Then he's gonna sell it through somebody else to his uncle's people. It's a really stupid idea. Plus, it scared me. I told him no—absolutely, positively no more money."

"And that's when he locked you up?"

"Uh-uh. At first he just got real mad. Lynne told me I better do what he said, and we all kept arguing. Then one day Debra shows up and I knew she was a wacko the first day I met her. Then Lynne tells me Debra's Carlo's sister, and—"

"That explains it."

"Explains what?"

"Why I kept thinking I'd seen Debra before. She looks so much like Carlo."

"Yeah. Well, it was sometime after she came along that Carlo locked me up, but I didn't know she was helping him. After a while, I didn't hear anything more about Lynne. Seems like she's outta the picture or something."

"She's out of the picture all right. She's dead. Someone broke her neck."

"Jesus." Rita shuddered. "Well, she shouldn't never have got hooked up with the Really . . . I mean, with Carlo. Just like me."

"And Debra?"

"I named her the Silent Partner 'cause I knew someone was

helping Carlo, but at first I never saw anyone. She's really creepy, and as mean as Carlo. Sometimes I think even Carlo's kinda afraid of her. Plus, sometimes I swear her and Carlo act like . . . like they're . . . y'know . . . fucking each other. Jesus, doesn't that make you sick? Brother and sister? That isn't right."

"And the drug deal? When's that supposed to happen?"

"I don't know. All I know is, Carlo and Debra are gettin' real antsy. I think they're both scared they're gonna get caught. And they *will,* too. Maybe not by the cops. But you don't mess with people like Carlo's uncle and get away with it. It's pitiful. Sometimes I almost feel sorry for Carlo. Then I remember what a piece of garbage he is. He musta killed Lynne."

"Except he wasn't there. I saw the guys that killed Lynne."

"Yeah? Well, guys like Carlo don't have to be there. He coulda sent somebody."

FORTY-SIX

Headed west, Dugan slowed down and stared at the sign in the window on Diversey where the Cubic Globe used to be. The word SOLD, in big block letters, was plastered diagonally across the old FOR SALE sign. So they weren't there.

He drove right on by, toward the Kennedy Expressway. Even though it seemed unlikely they'd go all the way up to Lake Forest that night, he knew of only two places to try, and the first one was sold already. Not just *Under Contract,* but SOLD. You could tell the neighborhood was up and coming just by driving through. Must be a very hot market. But still . . .

There was a public phone at the Shell station on the next corner. All the real estate brokers he knew stayed open until at least nine o'clock, especially when the market was hot.

This one was no exception. "That *is* a great location, sir," the woman said. "Unfortunately, as of today it's off the market."

"I saw that. Sold awfully fast, didn't it?"

"Oh no, it's not sold. The owner just took it off the market—at least for the time being. I don't know why."

"But there's a sign there that says sold."

"If there is, it's because they don't want people calling about it. I'm sure it hasn't been sold." She paused. "Of course, once in a while people try to pull a fast one and sell things on their own. But we have a contract. We always get our commission. Anyway, there are other properties I can show—"

"No thanks." He hung up and dialed another number.

After a series of transfers from one extension to the other, Hoffmeier finally came on the line. "So? What's up?" He was his usual aggressive self.

"Just wondered if there's been any . . . progress."

"Nothing to speak of. We're working on it. So . . . is that it?"

"Well, I'm worried about my wife."

"Oh?"

"Yes, I . . . Who would I call if I think she's been . . . well . . . kid-napped?" He told Hoffmeier about Kirsten going to Morelli & Fincher and how she was supposed to call in, but didn't, and—

"Look, uh, I can understand your concern, and . . . " Hoffmeier's voice fell easily into the bored drone of all public servants when they're dealing with citizens who just don't understand a very mun-dane set of circumstances. ". . . missing persons unit," Hoffmeier was saying. "But if I was you I'd wait at least until morning. Situ-ations like this, the people usually—"

"Hold on. The people you're talking about haven't witnessed a Mob-style killing."

"*Mob*-style? Those are your words, not mine." The aggression returned. "And even if that's what it was, which I'm not saying, you two didn't really witness any killing. All you saw was a couple of men at the scene. Men you can't identify. Or . . . you *say* you can't." He paused. "Unless maybe one of you has changed your mind and thinks you might be able—"

"No, no. It's just— But then she was attacked on the street and beaten."

"Unfortunately, that sort of thing happens all the time."

"Just a coincidence, then?"

"Coincidences happen all the time, too. Like, when you coinci-dentally ran into another dead body at the same location as the first one. And coincidentally it was all over that time, too, and you didn't see anything that could help the police department solve the crime." Another pause. "Unless maybe you've changed your mind and—"

"No."

"And I'm sure your wife hasn't involved herself somehow in the Cousin Freddy's investigation on her own, because that would be dangerous . . . and probably illegal." He paused. "So you see? You can go to the nearest district station and make a report, if you're really convinced she's . . . met with foul play." Dugan shuddered at the triteness of the phrase. "The case'll be assigned to an investigator, like every other case. But as a lawyer you understand that the police can't go around breaking into private offices or places of business just—"

Dugan went back and sat in the Grand Am for a minute, trying to think. He probably shouldn't have slammed the phone down. After all, he'd gotten just about the response from Hoffmeier he'd expected, even though he'd thought the call was worth a try.

The Ponytail had promised to meet Larry—with Rita—at the AmFed Bank at ten the next morning. So Rita must still be alive, and had to be the other woman the guard saw leaving with Debra Morelli. Dugan could wait at the bank in the morning and follow the Ponytail when he left. But by then, what might have happened to Kirsten? What might be happening to her right now?

He drove back east past the Cubic Globe, parked a block away, and walked through the alley behind the building. The gate in the chain-link fence was locked. The two windows on the second-floor porch were dark.

Back in front, Diversey Avenue was brightly lit and traffic was still fairly heavy, although there were few pedestrians. The storefront was dark and empty, the entrance locked. Dugan knew what had to be done, and didn't look forward to it. For starters, he pressed the button beside the entrance door, three short rings in rapid succession.

He couldn't hear any ringing from inside, and he didn't expect anyone to come and open the door. No one did. He turned away from the building and walked out to the curb, keeping his back to the painted windows on the second floor, wondering if someone up there was watching him.

A police car drove by, headed west, and he thought for an instant of running into the street, yelling that he'd seen his wife pulled into the building just seconds ago. But even if they believed him and forced their way inside . . . what if Kirsten wasn't there? Then he'd be arrested himself and detained at least the rest of the night, and maybe longer. A taxi drove by and he waved it down and got in. Two blocks away, he paid the surprised driver and got back out.

"All right, what the hell is it *now*?" Debra stood in the bedroom doorway, bouncing her keys up and down in her palm. She was looking straight at Kirsten, even though she must have known it hadn't been Kirsten who called her.

Kirsten stared back at her, saying nothing, wanting to show she wasn't intimidated.

"It's me," Rita said. "I gotta go to the bathroom."

"You already went a little while ago."

"I'm sorry, really. I didn't wanna bother you. But last time I just peed. Now I gotta . . . well, you know . . . go number two." She almost whispered the words, then added in a childlike tone, "I gotta go real bad."

"This," Debra said, unlocking the handcuffs that shackled Rita to the bed, "is the last time I'm—"

The doorbell rang—three short, quick rings. Debra waited, standing perfectly still and silent. But there were no more rings, and she hauled Rita to her feet and recuffed her hands in front of her.

"Um . . . Debra?" Rita asked, looking up at the much taller woman. "I said I gotta do number two. How am I gonna—"

"That's your problem," Debra said, and dragged Rita out of the bedroom.

Kirsten wondered whether weeks of captivity might break her spirit, too, as it seemed to have broken Rita's. She seemed shy and childish—terrified to the point of being tongue-tied—whenever Debra or Carlo were around. On the other hand, alone with Kirsten, she seemed stronger. Although insisting that both of them were going to die, she still hinted at some secret she was holding onto, something Carlo and Debra didn't know about.

Whether or not that was true, Kirsten had her own secret now to hold onto. Those three short rings. Those were Dugan's rings—the way he always announced that he was home and on his way up to their apartment.

Back at the rear of the Cubic Globe, the parking area behind the building was still empty. Dugan hauled himself up and over the chain-link fence, making no attempt to be quiet about it. No one challenged him. The ground-floor door was locked. There were three windows, each of them covered with a heavy metal grate.

Moving quietly now, he climbed the stairs to the second floor and tried that door. It was locked, too. Farther east along the porch were the two windows. The room behind the curtains was dark. There was no burglar alarm tape on the end window, and the glazing compound was fresh. Dugan turned back to the locked, windowless door and leaned against it, pressing his ear to the wood.

He wanted to pound on the door then, but didn't. It was still true that they could have taken Kirsten anywhere. But this had seemed the most likely place. And now, the faint sound of a radio or a television, barely audible through the door, told him at least someone was in there and—

The sudden roar of a car, racing down the alley from the east, made Dugan drop down instinctively, below the porch railing. But the car was an old Chevy and it went right on by, leaving a trail of rock music streaming behind as it passed. He heard the squealing of its tires as it turned onto the street from the alley and was gone.

Dugan stayed in a crouch and looked down through the wooden slats of the railing. The rear of the building faced south. The porch steps from ground level angled upward first to the west, then reversed themselves at a turnaround halfway up and continued on so that someone stepping up onto the second floor level was facing east, with the locked door just a few feet ahead on the left, and then the two windows beyond the door. In the other direction, the platform of the open porch extended about ten feet west from where the stairs came up.

Sodium-vapor alley lights bathed the rear of the building in a soft orange glow. But by staying low and close against the brick wall, Dugan would be out of sight to everyone nearby on the ground or coming up the steps, and would be behind them when they arrived at the second floor.

He sat down, drew his knees up toward his chest, and settled his back into a comfortable position against the wall. That's when he first discovered that his shirt was soaked with cold perspiration. Ten minutes later, he'd learned that no position stayed comfortable for long, no matter how much he shifted and wriggled around. If someone was going to come, he hoped it wouldn't be long.

FORTY-SEVEN

He'd been afraid he might fall asleep, but an hour later Dugan was still awake, lying flat on his back, shivering, watching the cloud of each exhalation vanish quickly above him in the cold, dry air. The traffic noises drifting around and over the building from Diversey Avenue diminished as time passed. On rare occasions, cars drove by in the alley. But none of them stopped. He closed his eyes and thought about Kirsten's brother's slides of his New Zealand trek. It was spring now in New Zealand. . . .

A sudden sound caught him unaware and his head jerked upward, contracting his neck muscles painfully. It was the metal gate banging softly against the fence. He'd missed the approach of the car, but heard the motor now, idling in the alley. He stayed on his back, not moving except to stretch his aching legs and arms, neck and shoulders. A car door closed softly. He rolled onto his left side and peered through the porch slats as the car—a dark, late-model Mercedes—came through the open gate and pulled close up to the building, until he could see nothing but the trunk. The engine stopped. The car door opened, then closed again. Dugan waited, but there was no opening of a second door.

By then he was on his hands and knees, his head still below the top of the porch railing. He wanted to retreat back to the brick wall, out of sight from the ground, but he had to know who it was in the Mercedes. A man appeared below, headed back toward the open gate. He wore baggy light-colored pants and a dark sport coat, and moved swiftly—not as though in a hurry, but as though that's how he always moved. His long hair was pulled back in a ponytail. He seemed ordinary enough, maybe taller than most, with broad shoulders.

The man swung the gate closed and by the time he had snapped the padlock shut Dugan was crouched back against the wall, his left hand steadying himself against the bricks. Kirsten's Colt .380 was in his right hand and locked—a round in the chamber, the hammer cocked, and the safety set. Now, as the Ponytail came up the steps, Dugan released the safety and waited, absolutely still and silent.

There had been plenty of time to consider how to handle this, and he'd decided to come at the man from behind before he un-locked the door, let him feel the gun in his back. Then Dugan would take his keys and go inside, leaving the Ponytail locked out. He didn't spend much time on what he'd do if the man resisted. He'd never shot a living being in his life.

Suddenly the man burst up into view, his back to Dugan, and was at the door almost as soon as he appeared. He was unlocking the door before Dugan could even get near him. He had the door open and had just switched on the light when he must have heard—or felt—Dugan behind him. He stiffened visibly. At that moment Dugan, bending low, hit him just above the small of his back with his left shoulder and drove him ahead into the room.

The Ponytail flew forward, arms flailing. But there wasn't far to go in the small kitchen, and he crashed face-first into the front of the refrigerator opposite the door and dropped to the floor. Dugan stood just inside the door. His long-ago training at the police acad-emy had taken over almost unconsciously, and he held the gun steady and motionless in his right hand, extended far out ahead of his body.

Keeping his face toward the Ponytail as the man climbed to his feet and turned around, Dugan reached behind himself with his left hand and, without really thinking about it, closed the door. Maybe it was because you always close the door when you come inside, or maybe because cold air was pouring in through this particular open door. But when he heard the almost simultaneous clicks of two spring locks, it was an action he regretted at once. The idea had been to put the Ponytail outside.

Dugan struggled to open the door again, his left hand fumbling around behind his back without success. Meanwhile the man in front of him stood motionless, hands hanging at his sides, and stared at Dugan. The left side of his face was terribly bruised and swollen, but he showed no fear, no anger, no surprise. If there was anything at all in his eyes, it was patience—the cold, dry patience of a predator who could easily wait for hours . . . until the prey made that one inevitable careless move.

"Put your hands on your head," Dugan said.

Maybe the man smiled, just slightly, but he did as he was told.

"Where is—" Dugan stopped. He gave up trying to open the door. He couldn't do it without looking, and he wouldn't turn away from the Ponytail. "Where are they?" he corrected himself.

"There is no one else. I live here alone." He spoke with a flat, dull voice, as though the words ought to be said even if no one would believe him in the face of the circumstances. The kitchen was absolutely bare—the counters, the sink, the stove. Even the air was empty. No cooking odors, nothing of anyone living there, beyond perhaps the faintest trace of an ammonia-based cleaner. If there had been a radio or television on earlier, there was no such sound now.

"On your knees, then," Dugan said.

The man didn't move. Maybe if he had said something, anything at all that showed he was a human being, Dugan would have felt differently. As it was, his feelings moved beyond fear to anger. And to something else, too—something uncomfortably close to hatred.

"You mean as little to me as I do to you," Dugan said. "Leave your hands on your head and drop down to your knees. If you don't, I'll shoot you. Believe me."

Dugan himself was convinced now that he *would* shoot the man, at least in the legs. The Ponytail showed that he believed, too, and dropped down to one knee, then two.

"Walk on your knees down that hallway."

The man moved awkwardly through the open kitchen doorway and down the hall, his knees banging against the hardwood floor. Dugan walked behind him, and noticed how the man's long, muscular fingers were laced loosely together above his ponytail, the tips of his thumbs disappearing beneath it. The only light came from the kitchen behind them.

The hall ended with a turn into a foyer at what had to be the apartment's front entrance. Opposite the front door and to Dugan's right, there was another closed door. Dugan tried it and found it locked. Ahead of him the Ponytail was clumping forward toward an open, wider doorway that led into total darkness.

"Stop," Dugan said.

Right at the doorway to the darkened room, the Ponytail stopped. "I'm on my knees," he said—surprisingly, as though Dugan didn't already know that.

"I can see that, Carlo." It was a familiar-sounding woman's voice, coming out of the darkness. "But soon you'll be up on your feet," she added.

"No, I don't think so," Dugan said, stepping to his left and out of sight from inside the room, but jamming the barrel of the Colt hard into the flesh of the Ponytail's neck, two inches beneath and behind his left ear.

The man didn't move. Dugan wondered whether he was even breathing.

"For now, Carlo," the woman said, "don't move . . . not until I convince Mr. Wonderful here that he ought to stick to playing nickel-and-dime with his chickenshit insurance adjusters—and put away the pistol."

"I don't convince easily," Dugan said.

"My, my. Aren't we the big strong man, though? Frankly, I doubt you've got the balls to pull the trigger, even under other circumstances. But I like to keep an open mind . . . and I suggest you do so, too." Her voice was strained somehow, as though she were exerting herself as she spoke. "Now," she said, "the wall switch is to

Carlo's left. When I say so, he'll lift his right hand slowly from his head, reach across and up a little, and turn on the light. Then . . . *you* decide how convincing I am." She paused. "Okay, Carlo. But . . . move very slowly."

The Ponytail was Carlo now, and Dugan let Carlo switch on the light. And then whether he should shoot Carlo was a question no longer even up for consideration.

The Debra Morelli on the sofa was the same tall, full-figured woman all right, but still scarcely resembled the one Dugan remembered from the courtroom. This one wore stonewashed blue jeans and a pale blue T-shirt. Her bare feet and ankles were nicely tanned, and she sat facing them, with her knees spread wide.

Between those knees, sitting on the floor with her back against the sofa, was Kirsten. Her own left leg was extended, but her right leg was bent sharply at the knee, the ankle handcuffed to her right wrist. One of Debra's hands was cupped under Kirsten's chin, pulling her head back and up so tightly that Dugan could see the stretched tendons of her neck. With her other hand, Debra held the point of an ordinary-looking ballpoint pen pressed into the side of Kirsten's windpipe.

Carlo was standing now. He turned around and Dugan laid the gun carefully onto his outstretched palm. Carlo dropped it casually into the pocket of his sport coat. Then, without a word or a change of the blank expression on his face, he slapped Dugan on the side of his head. The blow nearly lifted Dugan off his feet, sending him across the foyer and against the locked door.

Struggling to maintain his balance, Dugan turned as Carlo came at him. He wanted to charge back, drive into Carlo, slam the man's head against the wall. But he was afraid for Kirsten, and with his own head spinning wildly, he wanted also to slump to the floor and not be hit again. What he did was stand there feeling stupid, both hands down at his sides, looking past Carlo toward Kirsten on the floor by the sofa. Neither she nor Debra Morelli had moved.

Carlo slapped him again, just as hard, this blow on the other side. Pain screamed and swirled like a tornado trapped within his head, pounding his eardrums from inside. The pain was a roaring whirlwind, bellowing, raging to escape the confines of his skull and fill the room, the universe.

He waited for the next blow, forcing his eyes open even though tears blurred his vision. Through the rushing wind he heard Debra's voice. ". . . enough, Carlo," she was saying. "You're embarassed, I know. But it wasn't your fault." She had left Kirsten on the floor and was standing now beside Carlo. She was almost as tall as he was. Her voice was soothing, yet had a husky, seductive sound. "I understand, Carlo."

Dugan blinked and stared at her through the tears of pain that filled his eyes.

She held one hand resting gently on Carlo's wrist to calm him, but her own face was flushed and thin beads of perspiration glistened just above her upper lip. It was becoming increasingly obvious that there was no bra beneath her T-shirt.

Carlo jerked his arm away from Debra. "Leave me alone," he said. He took the gun from his jacket pocket and turned away.

Dugan looked past the two of them at Kirsten, still on the floor against the sofa. Her feet were bare also, and she was wearing the dark green wool slacks he gave her last Christmas, and the tan tailored blouse she'd gotten on sale at Bloomingdale's. She looked back at him, and then, with the tiniest hint of a wink that rekindled his hopes, she slumped and dropped her chin to her chest.

"What's wrong with her?" Dugan cried. He ran over, and crouching beside Kirsten, looked back at Debra and Carlo. "She's fainted or something."

"Nothing's wrong with her—not yet, anyway," Carlo said. He nodded toward Debra. "Make sure this dumb fucker's got no other gun."

Debra stood him up and searched him clumsily, then sat him back down beside Kirsten. "Now," she said, "we got another one to figure out what to do with."

"Shut up so I can think," Carlo said. "And go put on a sweater or something. This isn't a fucking whorehouse, for chrissake."

Debra recoiled as though he'd slapped her, but her eyes blazed even more brightly than before.

"Hold on," Carlo said, and tried the door in the foyer. "Why's the bathroom door locked?"

"It's the crybaby," Debra said. "She had to go to the bathroom. You took my gun with you and I didn't like moving her back and forth without it, so I just locked her in and let her stay there. By now she's curled up in the tub, crying and sucking her thumb."

FORTY-EIGHT

S o whadda you just standing there for?" Carlo said. "Uncuff the bitch's foot, so she can walk."

Debra stood absolutely still. "I didn't say anything a minute ago, Carlo, because I know you're upset. But now . . . " her voice suddenly hard and cold, she continued, "now you listen. You don't *order* me to do anything. Not now. Not ever. Do you hear me?"

"Yeah. All right. I'm . . . I'm sorry, okay?" Dugan watched, amazed at how quickly Carlo backed down before her wrath. "But right now," Carlo continued, "we gotta lock 'em all in the bedroom. I need time to think."

"We only have two sets of cuffs."

"Okay. Then we'll cuff these two to the bed and find something to tie up the crybaby with."

As Debra started their way, Dugan calculated how long it would take him to get across the room to Carlo, and how many times he'd be shot before he got there.

Carlo stared right back at him, but kept the gun pointed obviously at Kirsten. "You get any courageous ideas, friend, and I blow the fucking cunt away." He paused. "Hurry up, Debra. Christ, you're so goddamn—"

"Carlo!" Debra snapped. She swung around to face him. Her tone was strong, authoritarian. Maybe even *maternal*. "I *told* you—"

"All right, all right." Carlo backed down yet again. "I'm sorry, but—"

"Hey!" It was Kirsten, speaking up for the first time, making Dugan jump a little. "Is it me?" she asked. "Or is there something *wrong* with this picture?"

"*Wrong?*" Dugan said. "These two are just about the most—"

"Shut up," Debra said. "Both of you." By then she was kneeling, unlocking the cuffs from Kirsten's ankle and wrist.

"No, really," Kirsten continued, stretching her newly freed right leg in front of her, "wasn't it Buckminster Fuller's comparative studies of converging incest and sibling rival—"

"That's enough, bitch." It was Carlo this time. "Up on your feet."

Dugan stood and helped Kirsten up. Once standing, she immediately started bouncing up and down on the balls of her feet. "My foot's asleep," she explained. "Oooh. Awful."

Still never taking his eyes off Dugan, Carlo nodded toward Debra. "Bring the apartment keys."

"Oww, it hurts," Kirsten whined.

"Stop jumping around," Carlo said.

Kirsten kept bouncing, like a boxer skipping rope without a rope. "I can't. It's my whole leg now."

Debra snatched up a set of keys from a table by the sofa. Then, as she crossed in front of them, Kirsten suddenly screamed and dove at her. She slammed into Debra's side, but never stopped screaming and never stopped moving. Wrapping the larger woman in her arms, she drove her the remaining few feet across the room, straight toward Carlo in the doorway.

By then Dugan was moving, too, bellowing, roaring continuously like a maniac. All four of them ended up in the foyer, crashing to the floor in a confused jumble of thrashing bodies, screams, and angry shouts.

Everything stopped when the explosion came—a blast so close to Dugan's ear that he felt it as much as heard it. There was a sudden stillness, followed by the softest of groans, barely audible over the ringing in his ears.

Then more thrashing around, but more deliberate now, as the bodies struggled to untangle from each other. Simultaneous waves of fear, rage, and hopeless panic swept through Dugan's body. Maybe it was one whole second, maybe less than that, but it seemed forever that he couldn't get himself free. And he had to get free. He needed to find out.

Who had groaned? Who had been shot?

Three of them made it to their feet. They stood together and stared down at the fourth. It was Carlo. He was sitting with his right leg tucked under him, his back against the front door of the apartment. Both his hands were pressed to his left thigh, where a dark stain was spreading across his pale tan chinos. There was blood oozing up between his fingers—a great deal of blood, and it didn't seem to be slowing down even though his hands were pressing hard against his leg.

Carlo wasn't looking at the wound. He was looking frantically around him, and he was screaming.

Dugan stood there staring down at Carlo and listening to him scream. How long it took he didn't know, but finally he realized that Kirsten was screaming, too. He turned and saw her struggling to get free of Debra, who had one arm wrapped around her neck. Kirsten was screaming the very same thing Carlo was.

"The gun! The gun! The gun!"

Dugan looked around him, and finally saw the gun on the floor up against the bathroom door. But he was too late. Debra had seen it, too, and she threw Kirsten into Dugan, sending him reeling backwards. By the time he regained his balance, Debra had the gun. Dugan turned and pushed Kirsten all the way across the living room, beyond the sofa to the painted-over windows. Turning around, he still kept his own body between Kirsten and Debra, afraid the woman would be hysterical, afraid she'd shoot without thinking.

But Debra wasn't hysterical at all. She was talking to Carlo, all the while keeping her eyes—and the barrel of the gun—on Dugan and Kirsten, all the while nodding at them as if to say they better stay where they were, far away. "You're going to be all right, Carlo," she said. "Press hard."

If Carlo heard her, there was no sign of it from him. He'd stopped screaming about the gun and was talking incoherently now, muttering and shaking his head from side to side. But he kept his hands pressed to his thigh.

"You'll be all right," Debra repeated. "Press hard, Carlo, right on the wound. That will stop the blood." Her voice was calm and soothing. "I'm getting some towels. You'll be all right."

Dugan marveled at her efficiency. Even as she encouraged Carlo with her voice and kept the gun trained on Kirsten and him, she stooped and retrieved the keys from the floor. Then, with her left hand she managed to unlock the bathroom door and push it open.

"Rita!" she called over her shoulder, not looking into the bathroom. "Rita! Bring some towels out here."

"I can't . . . I'm afraid." The voice from the bathroom was thin, weak—the voice of a frightened child. Whatever little help he'd been hoping for from Rita, Dugan gave up on it.

"Bring out the towels off the racks . . . right now. And if you don't hurry, I'll—"

"Please, don't hurt me," Rita pleaded. "I'm coming. There's only one towel, but I'm bringing it. Whatever you say. Just don't hurt me."

"Hurry up!"

Rita came out of the bathroom, holding her arms out in front of her close together, a thick white bath towel draped over her hands. She stopped and looked at Debra. "My hands . . . they're cuffed," she said, raising her arms a little, "so I can't—"

"Just give me the towel," Debra said, "and then go back in the bathroom and close the door."

"Okay," Rita said. "Just don't hurt me . . . please." She stepped timidly forward, and Debra, managing still to keep the gun in her right hand pointed toward Dugan and Kirsten, snatched the towel from Rita's outstretched arms.

And then Dugan saw it . . . something clenched in Rita's two fists, something blocked from Debra's vision by the towel in her own hand, even if she'd been looking at Rita. Kirsten must have seen it, too, because he felt her stiffen against his side. Maybe Debra caught Kirsten's reaction, too, because she swung around toward Rita.

But even as Debra turned, Rita's hands, cuffed together, were sweeping up and to her left. Debra stood wide-eyed and frozen for an instant. What Rita held was a piece of broken glass, glass that flashed reflected light as she reversed her swing and swept her cuffed hands together, slashing through the air toward Debra's throat. Finally, the larger woman moved, ducking to the side and away—but not quite fast enough.

The shard of glass raked the side of Debra's neck, starting below her ear and ripping open the skin all the way to her chin. She fell back, eyes wide and empty, and blood—dark, almost black blood—poured down over her T-shirt.

By then Kirsten was across the room, Dugan behind her. Kirsten grabbed Rita and shoved her into the bathroom. Dugan pushed Kirsten in behind Rita and pulled the door closed.

He turned—half expecting to see Debra slumping to the floor, half expecting to absorb a bullet. Instead, Debra was simply standing there, absolutely motionless, pressing the white towel to her neck, looking down at Carlo on the floor. Strange, guttural sounds came from deep in her throat, moans Dugan knew had nothing to do with the savage gash Rita had opened in her neck.

The moans were for her brother.

Carlo's head was slumped forward, his chin resting on his chest. His hands had slipped off his thigh and lay limply against the wooden floor.

"He's dead." Debra's voice was dull, flat. She turned and raised the gun toward Dugan as he backed away. "Carlo's dead."

"Give it up," Dugan said. "It's over."

Debra stared at him. The gun in her hand was shaking, quite visibly.

The bathroom door opened and Kirsten stepped into the doorway. Debra turned her head—and the gun—that way. "He's right,

Debra," Kirsten said. "You haven't killed anyone. No one can prove you were involved in any of the killings."

But by then Debra was stooping to the floor, the towel pressed to her neck with her shoulder. She scooped the keys from the floor one more time. Then, backing away, toward the hallway, she swung the gun barrel back toward Dugan. "Carlo's dead," she said.

Dugan dove to the floor to his right as the shot exploded into the room and the window behind him shattered. Debra was gone then, down the hallway, firing two more shots as she fled.

Dugan started instinctively toward the hall.

"Wait," Kirsten said. "Let her go." Dugan stopped, knowing it made no sense to chase Debra.

Rita was standing beside Kirsten. "I called it my Crystal Dagger," Rita said, as the slam of the back door echoed down the hall. "I hid it again on top of the medicine cabinet when we first got back here. I . . . I would have killed her if I could have." Rita didn't sound like a little girl any longer. "I'd kill her now if I could. I swear to God." She was staring down at her open palms, empty now—but bloody.

"No," Kirsten said. "By this time tomorrow you'll be thinking differently."

"No way," Rita insisted. "If she was here right now, I'd—"

"Anyway," Kirsten interrupted, "now we have to call the police. They'll catch her before she gets far, if she doesn't bleed to death or freeze to death, or . . ."

". . . or kill herself," Dugan said.

"Yes, or kill herself."

FORTY-NINE

I t was eleven o'clock at night, and Rita was in bed in the extra room at Kirsten and Dugan's place. A soft, safe bed for the first time in God knows how long. So much had been happening she was having a hard time remembering it was just last night that she'd taken that slice out of Debra Morelli's throat.

They had spent the rest of the night with the police, and even after they found her settlement check in Carlo's pocket no one thought of calling Larry Candle. All of a sudden it was time to meet him at the bank, so they decided to go there and see if he'd be there. Rita had figured he'd be too scared to show up by himself. She sure would've been.

But Larry was there. They saw him before he saw them. He was walking around in little circles like he had to go to the bathroom or something, and she could tell he was scared to death. When he saw her and Dugan and Kirsten, she thought at first he was gonna cry, he looked so relieved. But he didn't. He just kinda puffed up and acted like he hadn't been scared and told them he knew something musta gone wrong and he knew he'd have to do something to protect her if her and Carlo showed up with the check.

He didn't say what it was he figured he'd do. And she didn't ask.

Anyway, the fact he showed up at all surprised her. He really looked kinda cute—all rumpled up like he hadn't slept in a week.

Sorta like Danny DeVito, but a little more cuddly. She told him she was glad to see him and leaned over and gave him a little kiss on the forehead.

The rest of the day kinda flew by, with more talking to the cops, and lunch, and whatever. By late afternoon, Rita found out that most of them had guessed wrong about a few things the night before. Kirsten had been wrong about Debra being caught before she got far. In fact, Debra had vanished. And there was no sign that she'd bled to death or frozen to death—or killed herself, either.

But Debra had been wrong, too, because Carlo wasn't dead after all, even though he did lose his left leg. So far, he'd been charged with kidnapping and possession of child pornography. But he hadn't spoken one word in public since the paramedics hauled him out of the apartment. The cops figured that even when they got a chance at him, he'd leave all the talking to his uncle's Outfit lawyers.

The two chief investigators—LaMotta and that pale guy with the German name—were working on tying Carlo into the killings at Cousin Freddy's. They said they already heard about Carlo's uncle trying to move in on the business, and Anton not wanting to give in. So far that was still all they had, but their minds were made up it was Carlo—or the Mob, anyway. Kirsten said she wasn't so sure, and Rita thought Kirsten was awfully smart. So who knows?

Anyway, Rita figured Carlo would be lucky if his uncle didn't bust him out of jail and drop his one-legged body into the river.

Plus, Rita discovered pretty quick that she'd been wrong about something, too. Because it turned out she was glad now she hadn't killed Debra. God had given her the Crystal Dagger to get free, and it had worked just perfect without her having to kill anybody. Jesus, she was glad she wasn't gonna go to bed every night the rest of her life thinking Debra was already burning in hell because of her.

So it was a long day and she'd finally went to bed after she kept falling asleep sitting up in a chair. And now she was lying down, and it was quiet and comfortable, and she was free. But what with her mind running from one thing to another she couldn't sleep. Just now she was wondering what she'd do with her settlement money.

She had told Dugan she sure wasn't gonna let that Larry Candle give her any advice. Dugan said maybe there was more to Larry than most people thought, even if he didn't know much about investing money. He did show some backbone by going to the bank.

Funny thing, even if Larry was obviously too short and too fat for her, he *was* a little cuter than she had remembered him. . . .

FIFTY

Two days later, Saturday afternoon, Kirsten was home and answered the phone. She was just setting the receiver down when Dugan came in.

"That was Bruce Hardison," she said. "He called your office but must have just missed you. He heard about what happened, and he wanted to know if you'd still be working on the Cousin Freddy's case. I told him—"

"Guess I ought to withdraw from the case now, really."

"What are you talking about?"

"Well, *A*, you found the witness Larry Candle needed to get him off the hook. *B*, the world would be better off with Cousin Freddy's out of business. And *C*, WARP's lawyer, Cynthia, is now your newfound friend. So why should I stay in the case? Except now . . ." He hesitated, but she knew what was coming next.

"Except now," she said, "you can't abandon Freddy."

"Right. My client. She'll be thrilled to close the store as soon as she can. But if WARP wins the case and they take all her money, who'll pay for her dad's care?"

"That's why you've got Hardison . . . to win."

"I guess. But so far Hardison's strategy is to drag it out forever. Maybe the fact that he's being paid by the hour . . . Anyway, I'm staying in."

"Besides, don't forget why you took over for Larry Candle in the first place. Those two contract killers are still out there, and we—"

"That part's over. The cops are gonna pin those killings on Carlo and the Outfit, and they won't need any testimony from us."

"Only if they can squeeze hard enough to make Carlo cooperate—and that's not likely. Besides, I can't forget Anton's telling you he and I were both wrong about who killed Lynne. Things just don't . . . " She stopped, not able to explain why things didn't quite fit.

"Anyway," Dugan said, "I'll call Hardison back."

"No need. I already told him, of *course* you were staying in. He seemed surprised, but said in that case you should meet with him tomorrow."

"Sunday?"

"Yes. His firm's finally dug its old file for Cousin Freddy's out of storage. He's only had time to skim through it, but he spotted a reference to a 'key employee' insurance policy on Anton Bulasik's life, with benefits payable to Freddy's father."

"That could sure be helpful."

"He'll be out of town all next week and he wants you to come to his office tomorrow morning to go through the file. I'm coming, too. I want to see what's in there before everything's turned over to Hoffmeier."

Sunday morning they took a cab to Hardison's office and were a few minutes late, so Kirsten wasn't surprised to see Hardison already there, pacing the sidewalk along the building's marble and glass facade. The revolving doors were locked, but he slid a plastic keycard in and out of a slot in a metal plate that said "After Hours Entrance," and pushed open a door that said "Handicapped Accessible." The security guard's station, off to their right, was vacant. As they followed Hardison, their footsteps echoed off the marble floor and around the deserted atrium.

The walls were marble, too, smoothly polished and light gray, laced with ivory and green, soaring up three or four stories to meet a ceiling of green-tinted glass that angled downward and back across the huge open area, then dropped straight down to form the front wall of the building's lobby. A cluster of tall, small-leaved willows and aspens, and dozens of shorter potted trees and plants, transformed one corner of the atrium into a miniature forest, with a tiny stream cascading down moss-covered rocks into a pool.

"Like a mausoleum," Kirsten said.

"What?" Hardison seemed lost in thought, but recovered with a smile. "Oh . . . I suppose it is, without the hustle and bustle that goes on during the week. This atrium's proven not to be very fuel-efficient, either. Probably why our rent's going up again." He steered them around a corner to a bank of elevators.

Hardison pressed the heat-activated floor indicator, and the ride up began, silent and swift, in a walnut-paneled elevator that was larger than the reception room at Kirsten's office.

"Fastest elevators in the Loop, they tell us," Hardison said. "What do *you* think?"

She waited for Dugan to answer, but he didn't, so she said, "They can have my vote."

If Hardison wanted to make small talk she wished Dugan would join in, to give her a chance to think. Something had made her curious. Probably not important, but she tried to remember exactly what Dugan had told her more than a week ago.

". . . seldom anyone in the office on Sunday mornings," Hardison was saying. "But there'll be a few coming in later this afternoon, mostly young associates, trying—"

A soft gong announced the thirty-fifth floor, and the elevator doors slid open.

To their left as they stepped out was the entrance to a reception area. Kirsten started that way.

"Follow me," Hardison said, turning right. "The office kitchen is this way. We'll get some coffee." He opened an unmarked door, again using a keycard, and led them out of the lushly carpeted elevator area and down a series of dimly lit corridors with linoleum tile floors. "Mail room, copy machines, and some law clerks' offices are in this area. And the kitchen." He stopped and gestured to his right. "After you."

Kirsten went down a short, narrow hallway that opened into the kitchen, with Dugan right behind her. She blinked at the brightness of the large room. Fluorescent lights reflected off white wallpaper with row after vertical row of tiny clusters of red berries. There were six round, white-topped tables for employees' lunches. To their left loomed a red, white, and blue Pepsi-Cola machine. There was a refrigerator off to the right, and across the room was a counter with a sink, a microwave, and a coffeemaker.

They waited while Hardison made coffee and finally found some mugs in the third cabinet he tried. "Secretaries usually do this," he said, pouring out the coffee. "There should be cream in the refrigerator."

The three of them turned from the counter. And when they did, Kirsten's blood ran cold.

Just inside the door from the hallway stood two men—very large men, wearing ski masks. Both also wore tan coveralls and work shoes, and what looked like skintight leather gloves. The one in the blue mask held an automatic pistol with a silencer, pointed at them.

All five people in the room stood absolutely still for just an instant, with no sound but the humming of the Pepsi machine. Then, when the man with the gun started toward them, Dugan shoved Kirsten to the side and charged, head down. The man with the gun jumped sideways and backwards, crashing into one of the round tables. He swung his arms out to regain his balance, and fired a bullet into the center of the Pepsi machine.

"Fuckin' asshole!" the man said.

The Pepsi machine hummed on, apparently unharmed.

Meanwhile, Dugan's momentum had carried him past the man with the gun, and his head struck the edge of another of the tables. He straightened up, shaking his head and shoulders like one of those groggy bears on public television that's been hit with a tranquilizing dart. But before he was able to get his bearings, the man swung the butt of the gun down, hard, against his head.

Kirsten felt the air go out of her lungs as she watched Dugan sag first to his knees, then fall forward onto his face. She ran over and crouched beside him, hands on his shoulders, wanting to scream, but not able to take in enough air to make a sound.

As though from a great distance, she heard Hardison's pompous voice. "What is this? You can't—"

"Shut up!" This from the man in the red ski mask, who had a gun in his hand now, too, also equipped with a silencer. "Down on the floor, man. On your face!"

It was the voice of a black man, and it dispelled what little doubt Kirsten had about whether these were the two men from Cousin Freddy's—and from the alley near the Blue Sunrise. She knew the black one's name was Andrew. She stared down at Dugan. There was blood on the floor beside where his face was pressed into the tile. She started to turn him over, but suddenly felt his body heave once, then go still.

She raised her head and screamed—no words, just a wail. Both of the masked men moved toward her, their mouths open and yelling at her, but she didn't hear them.

Behind them she saw Hardison, who'd been crouching to lie down on the floor, stand up. He turned and started running toward the door.

The men must have seen something in her eyes, because they both turned around. Hardison was through the door and into the short hallway. The man in the red mask—Andrew—took one step to his right to get a view down the hall, raised his gun, and fired twice.

Bits of wallpaper and plaster flew from where one of the slugs tore a chunk from the edge of the doorway. The other bullet must have continued down the hall.

"Gone," the gunman said. "Motherfucker got away." He took a step toward the door.

"Forget him," the other man said. "Never find him in them god-damn corridors and shit."

"You right," the black man said. "Let's git outta here."

"Wait a minute, asshole. I don't like it. The way these two keep showing up."

"Hell with them, man. We here for the grayhead that got away, not them. Let's go." He dropped his gun in a huge pocket of his coveralls.

"Bullshit. I ain't leaving them alive again, not this time." He raised the automatic, then angled it down toward Dugan, lying on the floor.

"Hold it," Andrew said, and stepped in front of the man. "We—"

"Step aside," the man said. "I don't need a nigger telling me what to do."

Kirsten stared at them, struck dumb, but suddenly Hardison reappeared in the doorway. He had a small chrome-plated revolver in his hand. "No!" he shouted.

The man in the blue mask turned around. And then Hardison shot him, three times, in the chest. Hardison stood there, his eyes wide as the man fell to the floor, as though surprised himself at what he had done, but he finally turned to face the black man, whose hands were empty and raised in front of him. Hardison swung the revolver toward him.

"No!" Kirsten said. "Don't shoot him. He wasn't going to kill Dugan and me now." As she spoke, she wondered if Dugan was even alive.

"But he shot at me. And he still has his gun. See?"

The man had put his hand in the wide pocket in his coveralls, and it did come out again with the automatic, but held between thumb and fingers, at the very end of the pistol grip.

"Put it on the table!" Hardison said.

The man did as he was told. But Hardison didn't relax, and Kirsten believed then that he was going to shoot the unarmed man. The man must have thought the same, because he suddenly dove to the floor, rolling, crashing into Hardison's legs, bringing the lawyer down on top of him. Two more shots came from Hardison's gun, both wild, and the two men wrestled on the floor. The struggle was brief, though, and the masked man wrenched the revolver from Hardison's hand. He stood up and backed away as Hardison, too, got to his feet.

"I'll kill you, too," Hardison said. He was breathing hard, and

248

Kirsten thought he must have gone completely crazy by then, because he moved straight toward the man with the revolver.

The man held the gun pointed at Hardison. "Better stop," he said. But when Hardison kept coming, he pulled the trigger. There was no shot, though, just the fall of the hammer on an empty chamber.

Hardison took another step, then turned abruptly to his left, looking down toward the man he'd shot. Kirsten knew then that he must be going for the man's gun, lying on the floor by his head. But the man called Andrew palmed the revolver and, in one fluid move, stepped forward swinging his right hand in a wide arc that began at his waist and ended when the chrome-plated steel crashed into the side of Hardison's head. The lawyer crumpled to the floor.

By that time Kirsten had moved away from where she'd been kneeling beside Dugan. Andrew turned, then stood and looked at her a long, silent moment. Stared at her. And stared at his own automatic in her hand, pointed at his chest.

FIFTY-ONE

Kirsten spoke first. "Your name is Andrew, and—"

"I told him you musta heard. Him, I mean." Pointing down toward his partner. "Clouder. He said my name . . . in the alley. Stupid."

"You didn't kill Lynne Bulasik, or Anton either."

"Funny thing, if it matters to you or to anyone . . . I never yet killed nobody in my life."

"You'd have killed him," Kirsten said. "Hardison. You pulled the trigger."

"He was coming at me, and I tried to bluff him, the son of a bitch. Turns out he knew as well as I did. This here goddamn five-round Smith 'n' Wesson was empty." He dropped the revolver onto the floor beside Hardison.

"So it was he who did the killing," Kirsten said, pointing down at the man named Clouder, on the floor. "But you were with him. You were there."

"Not when he did the man. I—"

"And Larry Candle? The lawyer? That was you."

"S'posed to just scare him. Same as that time with you, same as this . . . Somethin' ain't right. I mean, Clouder's dead. Why is that? I don't get why . . . " His voice trailed off.

"What about Carlo Morelli?" she asked.

"Morelli?" With the mask, she could only see his eyes. But the surprise in them was genuine. "Never met the man. Heard of him. He's . . . you know . . . connected."

"And are you?"

"You gotta be kiddin'. What? Affirmative action?" The humor in his voice was bitter. "Do a little work for 'em now and then. Or they hook me up with someone, anyone who'll pay."

"And . . . recently? Who'd they hook you up with?"

He didn't answer out loud. He didn't need to. She just kept watching his eyes, and her suspicion turned into certainty.

"No one knows but you?" she asked.

"And Clouder," he said, pointing at the other gunman, sprawled motionless on the floor. "Plus . . . the people that, you know, put us in touch."

"What about my car? How'd you know—"

"The Celica? Shoot, I seen it outside Cousin Freddy's. The people ran the plate right away, but it was gonna take time to find out if you ID'ed us. I guessed what station the sheriff's cops would take you to, and me and Clouder went there. Waited outside, followed you downtown, saw where you parked. I knew you was too far away to get a good look at us, and I finally convinced Clouder. Wasn't for me. Fuckin' Clouder woulda set that thing to blow when you turned the key."

Kirsten believed him—almost wishing she didn't. It was just one more reason to do what her mind, and all her training, kept telling her she shouldn't do, couldn't do.

"But you were there when Lynne was murdered," she said, "so, if they catch you . . . " She stared at the man, her brain whirling with the debate over what she ought to do.

"They catch me," he said, "they fry me. Simple as that."

Simple as that.

She was indebted to this man beyond anything she could pay back. But he was a criminal. She had a responsibility to the public, the common good.

They fry me.

He had protected her, saved her life. Maybe saved Dugan's life, too. But letting him go was a crime, and no one can just make up the rules up as she—

You can't always think your way to the right answer. Sometimes you just have to feel around for it, go with your gut.

The debate was over.

"Go away," she said. "I don't know you. I haven't seen your face. I never—" She shook her head. "Just go away."

When she lowered the gun, he turned and disappeared through the door, not taking time to say thanks. She wouldn't have either. She could hear the squeak of his rubber soles against the tile floor, walking first, then running. There was the close of a far-off door, and then only the steady hum of the Pepsi machine.

There was a telephone on the wall beside the refrigerator. But Kirsten walked back across the room and knelt on the floor. She bent over Dugan, hands on his back.

She could feel him breathing, steady and strong now. He groaned softly and she rolled him over onto his back. Blood was smeared all over his face, and his nose was probably broken, but his eyes opened. He tried to smile and she put her finger to his lips. Just relax. He closed his eyes again.

She still didn't move. She could have checked on the man Hardison shot. Clouder. But she knew in her soul he was dead. And now she knew why.

It was another couple of minutes before Hardison stirred, and a few more before he seemed to begin remembering where he was.

Kirsten waited that long. And then she dialed 911.

She stated her name and location into the phone while she watched Bruce Hardison struggle to his feet. "There's been some shooting," she said. "You'll want to advise Investigators Hoffmeier and LaMotta." She watched Hardison drop down limply into one of the chairs. "Tell them the Cousin Freddy's killers were here. One of them's not going anywhere . . . 'cause he's dead."

Hardison sighed and gave her a little smile, as though of gratitude.

"There's another one. Thinks he's gonna get away. He'll be here, though, when you get here."

Kirsten raised Andrew's automatic and pointed it straight at the bridge of Hardison's nose, directly between his sad gray eyes.

"I guarantee it," she said.

FIFTY-TWO

They never did come up with enough to charge Hardison with the murders at Cousin Freddy's. Eventually, they found plenty of motive, more than enough to satisfy Kirsten. But she already knew, from Andrew himself, that it was Hardison who had hired Clouder and him. She knew Hardison had staged a phony attack on himself, just like he'd set up that phony attack on Larry Candle. She couldn't prove Hardison's shooting of Harry Clouder was anything but the self-defense his lawyers claimed it was. But she was convinced killing his own two hit men had been part of his plan, to eliminate anyone who could implicate him.

The problem was, she couldn't tell Hoffmeier and LaMotta about her conversation with Andrew. That would open up too many questions. The man fled without even taking his weapon, so just how was it he stayed around to talk to her? If he'd answered her questions because she already had his gun—and hers were the only prints found on it—how did she let him get away?

So she told them only as much as she dared to—and it wasn't enough. She explained that Hardison knew she and Dugan had found Lynne's body when their names hadn't been published, how the "warning" to her outside the Blue Sunrise came the very day after Dugan told Hardison she'd never stop looking into Lynne's killing, and that Hardison had somehow known about the attack on her by nine-thirty the following morning in court. She told them how Anton Bulasik had thought the Mob killed Lynne, but changed his mind after talking to Hardison. She told them no professional gunman could possibly have missed Hardison if he'd really been trying to shoot him, and how the same held true of the fake attempt on Larry Candle's life. She reminded them that Hardison's office was on the thirty-sixth floor, as Dugan had told her a week and a half ago. Even if the two men could have found out on their own—impossible—that Hardison would be at his office on a Sunday morning, and somehow got into his building without his help—almost impossible—how could they know he'd stop first for coffee at the kitchen on the thirty-fifth floor?

The two investigators agreed it was at least worth looking for a motive. But even after they found one, they had far from enough evidence for a homicide charge, especially faced with Hardison's high-priced, high-powered defense attorneys.

The motive they found was crystal-clear evidence of Hardison's embezzling large sums of money from clients—and even from his own law firm—over a period of years. Added to that was some so-so evidence that he might have been using Cousin Freddy's to launder the stolen money, and then reporting what wasn't washed away in the process on his tax returns as "attorney's fees" from some unidentified source other than his firm.

They found a secretary who was "pretty sure" she'd overheard part of a phone conversation when Hardison was warning Lynne Bulasik not to get "too greedy for her own good." One of the firm's paralegals might have seen Hardison one day with a couple of men in a coffee shop north of the river, and one of the men was black. But she'd just been walking by outside and couldn't possibly swear to anything.

Kirsten's theory was that there had never been any real "campaign of terror"—by WARP or anyone else—against porno stores, but that the arson of that adult bookstore in Uptown, which the cops were convinced now was torched by its owner, had given Hardison an idea. It was he who mailed the threats, using WARP-type rhetoric, to muddy the waters and to cover up his planned murder of Lynne, who must have threatened to expose him, demanding more for laundering his money.

And Anton? No professional who was serious would have used charcoal-lighter, so the phony arson attempt and the "terrorism" note by Anton's body were to cover up the real motive for his murder. Maybe it was his suspicions about Hardison, or maybe he'd been part of Lynne's shake-down effort. It didn't matter now, though. There wasn't enough hard evidence for the cops to buy Kirsten's theory anyway.

Of course, Kirsten knew all along that Hoffmeier and LaMotta believed there was something she wasn't telling them—and had guessed what it was, too.

"Let's say, just hypothetically," Hoffmeier finally proposed, "that you *could* identify the second gunman—from seeing him first at Cousin Freddy's, then in that alley, then again in the kitchen at Hardison's office—or give us a better description, maybe, or even a name. Say we were able to pick him up. Say he convinces us his partner did the actual killing—Clouder's sheet suggests he did contract work. Then suppose your man fingers Hardison as the one who hired him and Clouder, maybe through an Outfit contact, and we can make that stick. We could probably get the state to cut a deal for your man, maybe manslaughter or something."

"*Probably*, you say?" Kirsten asked.

"Yeah, well, Hoffmeier and me both been around a while," LaMotta put in. "We know people. One hand washes—"

"Doesn't matter," Kirsten said. "He's not *my* man. He had a mask on. He got away. I never—"

"And the fact that he's the same guy who saved you from . . . you know . . . a sexual assault that time in the alley, and probably saved your and your husband's life at the end . . . that's got nothing to do with it, right?"

"I'm afraid so," Kirsten had said.

Hoffmeier and LaMotta weren't happy, but they never raised the issue again.

In the end, Hardison agreed to plead guilty to several counts of felony theft. He was disbarred and Dugan was certain he'd pull a long prison sentence, despite his previously unblemished record.

"Those judges . . . they like to bang lawyers hard," Dugan reminded Kirsten. "They figure it pleases the public."

She thought Dugan was a little paranoid, but didn't say so.

FIFTY-THREE

The Cousin Freddy's suit was finally over, and Dugan had decided they should all get together and celebrate. Part of the idea was to cheer up Freddy. Her father's condition was worse. His latest bout of pneumonia wasn't responding well to antibiotic therapy. She was using the insurance proceeds from Anton's death for the more expensive care he needed, and hoping the money would last.

For old time's sake, Dugan reserved a big table at Palestrina's, except it wasn't called Palestrina's anymore, and didn't serve "Corsican cuisine." It was a Greek restaurant now and the manager, Paolo, called himself Nick, but still seemed like a nice guy to Dugan, as he kept telling Freddy.

The suit had been settled after Dugan convinced the other porno store's insurance company to come up with some cash. The company insisted it not go to WARP, but only to the rape victims—who paid a well-earned fee to Cynthia. Cousin Freddy's was uninsured and paid nothing, but as part of the deal the store was closed.

"But not closed for long," Cynthia Fincher said, after they'd drunk a toast to the finale of Dugan's only non-personal-injury case. "Freddy and Rita and I are going to be partners, and reopen it as a women's issues bookstore. We've already disposed of all the former merchandise."

"How'd you ever get rid of it?" Dugan asked.

"We had this huge going-out-of-business sale," Freddy said. "We had to, because none of the suppliers would take anything back. We were selling that awful stuff for fifty, sixty, seventy percent off."

"You and Kirsten shoulda seen the mob. I mean . . . not the *Mob*, but the crowd that showed up," Rita added. "Poor Cuffs hadda work his butt off. Afterwards, Freddy let him have whatever we didn't sell. Cuffs said he knew a lotta guys who'd take the stuff off his hands. Myself, I kept one of those red-white-and-blue, glow-in-the-dark dildo things—as a souvenir, I mean, not—"

"Not to change the subject or anything," Freddy said, "but besides women's books, we'll carry women's craftwork, mostly handwoven fabrics. We're calling the store 'Warp and Woof, Limited.' Cynthia's doing all our legal work. By the way, doesn't she look *great*?"

Cynthia blushed. "I feel so much better, too, with Debra gone a nd—"

"Let's drink to Cynthia," Rita said, and they did.

"And," Freddy said, "I'm not supposed to tell. But Cuffs said when he sells the stuff he took, he'll put that money back in the store, too. As an investment. Said it won't be the first time he threw away good money on a couple of broads. Deep down, you know, he's really nice." She stopped, as though realizing what she'd just said. "Sort of," she added.

"Where *is* Cuffs, anyway?" Kirsten asked. "And who are the empty chairs for?"

"Cuffs?" Dugan tried to sound nonchalant, but this was the moment he'd been waiting for—his announcement. "Oh, he'll be here. He's picking up the people from my office. Molly's coming. And Peter and Fred. And . . . oh yeah . . . I almost forgot. They're bringing the new associate they hired today."

"What?" Kirsten's eyes widened. "I didn't know they were interviewing again."

"They weren't. I mean . . . they didn't have to. That is . . . they didn't want to, so they went back to someone they already knew."

"Oh?" The arch to Kirsten's eyebrows told Dugan his plan had worked. She was thinking *big boobs*. ". . . hiring criteria," she was saying, "but I'm sure she'll be—"

"We made it!" It was Cuffs, bursting through the restaurant's front door. "Save some of that booze!"

"Sorry we're late," Fred Schustein said, as he and Peter Rienzo hurried across the room behind Cuffs. "Traffic was a goddamn . . . I mean . . . real heavy."

"Well," Dugan said, milking the moment for all it was worth, "and where's the new associate?"

Peter turned back toward the door. "Jeez, I don't know. Must be trapped out on the sidewalk with Molly," he said. "Molly's been going nonstop all the way and she's only up to chapter two of her personal law office training man—"

"Knock it off," Cuffs barked. "They're here. He grabbed a wine bottle off the table and was searching for an empty glass. "Hey Molly! Over here!"

As she hurried across the room, Molly was shaking her head and staring at Dugan with a worried look in her eyes.

But the new associate didn't look worried at all. He bounced his round little body across the room with a happy smile on his face. "Hey hey, everyone!" he called. "Just got the word today! Thanks to Rita's changing her testimony at the Disciplinary Commission, I'm gonna have my ticket back in a few days. Then we'll be ready to roll, hey, Doogie pal?"

"Yeah, Larry," Dugan answered. "Once you get your license back, and . . . " pulling a travel brochure from his jacket pocket, "once Kirsten and I get back from New Zealand. Right, Kirsten?"

Whether she even heard the question, though, he couldn't tell. She just glared at him. "Big boobs I could have lived with," she said, "maybe. But did that little man just say . . . *Doogie pal?*"